Praise for *Dying for Compassion* WITHDRAWN

It is rare indeed to find an author who not only tells a good story but writes with real literary flair. Barbara Golder is such an author. In this latest offering we find the plot twists and twisted characters that one would expect in a good murder mystery but also the fine character development and deep insight into the human condition which separates the truly great mysteries from the run of the mill.

Joseph Pearce, Author of *The Quest for Shakespeare, The Unmasking of Oscar Wilde,* and *Tolkien: Man & Myth*

What I loved about Dying for Compassion was the host of unique characters, who led each other to ways good and not good when their paths crossed. A suave philosophy professor turned assisted-suicide proponent who leads a nurse to murder; an emotionally and morally blunted young woman, who softens through chance meetings in a coffee shop with a forgettable but endearing and insightful Monsignor; a calm Spanish matriarch who brings peace to a priest through cooking and her company. Added to which, the "course of true love never did run smooth" central story, where the author Barbara Golder skillfully dives into the lows of human anguish with ever-present hope and on the last page caused me to....well, read it and you'll find out!

Dr. Annmarie Hosie, RN, PhD, Post-doctoral Research Fellow, Master of Palliative Care in Aged Care

In Dying for Compassion, Barbara Golder has created a different kind of mystery, one that bears on questions of love, loyalty and pain and one that asks: what lives are worth living? In a time when physician assisted suicide is the question of the day, Dr. Jane Wallace's quest to discover who murdered her lover's ex-wife brings unexpected clarity to the issue on several fronts. Read it not just for a great plot and dynamic characters, read it to make yourself think.

E. Wesley Ely, MD, MPH, Pulmonary and Critical Care and Health Services Research
Vanderbilt University and VA-GRECC

ID666919

DYING FOR COMPASSION

Book #2

The Lady Doc Murders

by

Dr. Barbara Golder

FQ Publishing

Pakenham, Ontario

This book is a work of fiction. Characters and incidents are products of the author's imagination. Real events and characters are used fictitiously.

Dying for Compassion (The Lady Doc Murders #2)
copyright 2017 Dr. Barbara Harty Golder

Published by Full Quiver Publishing
PO Box 244
Pakenham, Ontario K0A 2X0
www.fullquiverpublishing.com

ISBN Number: **978-1-987970-06-7**

Printed and bound in the USA
Cover design: Doreen Thistle
Artwork by: James Hrkach
Back cover photography: Stephen Golder

NATIONAL LIBRARY OF CANADA
CATALOGUING IN PUBLICATION

ALL RIGHTS RESERVED

No part of this publication may be reproduced, stored in a retrieval system or transmitted, in any form or by any means — electronic, mechanical, photocopying, recording or otherwise — without prior written permission from the author.

Copyright 2017 by Dr. Barbara Harty Golder
Published by FQ Publishing
A Division of Innate Productions

To the memories of two great physicians: James Daly, who taught me what good death looks like and John Ross, who showed me how to value the least of these in spite of my fears. Thank you.

PROLOGUE
January 9

"Father! We need you now, down at the clinic! There's a man with a gun, threatening staff. Hurry!"

The female voice was measured, but the anxiety in it was enough to propel Father Matt toward his closet to get his jacket and gloves without waiting for any further explanation. He took the stairs two at a time, pausing only to pull on his snow boots before going out into the cold. As he went, he felt to make sure the oil stock he kept in his jacket pocket was still there. He'd not had much occasion to anoint people since coming to Telluride to pastor the good parishioners of St. Pat's, but no one could accuse him of not being prepared. He kept his stock in his jacket pocket and a small bottle of holy oil in his backpack and his Jeep.

One of his professors in seminary had made an impression on him with tales of his life in Northern Ireland during the hottest part of the civil war there. He'd never been without holy oil, had used it often, and Matt was determined to follow in his professor's footsteps. The oil carried God's grace, and God knows, people need it.

He had to slow his steps when he got to the main road. The gritted sidewalks were still thick with ice. He almost wished it were snowing; clear nights were always colder. He regretted not pulling on a cap. Still, his long legs made short work of the blocks to the clinic.

He threw open the door, grateful for the warmth, pulling off his gloves and feeling a trickle of water from his hair as the ice in his curls melted with the shock of the heat of the waiting room.

The receptionist had been waiting for him. "This way." He followed her slim form toward an open door. He heard the voice of one of the deputies coming from the room. "Clint, come on now. Let me have the gun. Don't make this harder than it is." Father Matt stopped and reached a hand to the woman in front of him, pulling her back to his side.

"What's going on?"

"We had a little girl in here, real sick. Dying, I guess. Some kind of awful disease. Her parents knew it would happen sooner or later. Honestly, I don't know why they kept treating her, a gorked-out kid like that. She isn't even awake most of the time these days. Letting her go would be a blessing. Anyway, she came in all dehydrated from a stomach bug. The doctor put her on an IV, and they were making arrangements to transfer her to Grand Junction. Anyway, she died, poor little thing. Her father refuses to let us take her away. He threatened the nurse with a gun. The deputy has been trying to talk some sense into him, but he just won't listen."

"Who called me?" A note of suspicion crept into Father Matt's voice.

"I did." The woman flushed and looked uncomfortable. When Father Matt didn't respond, she added hastily, "I didn't know what else to do. The father is so upset. Priests always know what to do at times like this, don't they?"

No, thought Father Matt, *they don't. At least I don't. Why is it that the first people to call the priest in an emergency are the last ones to come to Mass on Sunday?* He doubted the woman was Catholic. Maybe not even Christian in this town.

When his silence continued, she added, "You aren't mad, are you?"

Father Matt shook his head and shaded the facts just this side of an outright lie, as any good priest would have done in his shoes. No need to add to her anxiety just now, and "mad" had a lot of nuance to it. "No, I just need a moment to think, that's all." He closed his eyes against the light from the room as his lips moved silently in prayer and fear. When he opened his eyes again, he nodded in the direction of the waiting area. "You go back. They don't need any more people at risk than already are."

Skittish at coming up on the back of a policeman, he announced his arrival well in advance. "Father Matt Gregory here. First Responder Chaplain. I was called. Let me in, please." He was glad, at least for the moment, that he'd taken the position as chaplain for the local law enforcement. It gave him a certain form of credibility.

The door opened wider, pushed by one hand of a deputy who held a gun in the other. A second deputy stood to the other side, face set, gun trained on the dark-haired man who sat on the bed at the side of the room, cradling a still, small form in his arms, a massive pistol in his right hand. He was sobbing and rocking the child but as soon as Father Matt entered, he brought the pistol up and pointed it. "Stop right there. No more. You aren't taking my baby away."

"I'm not here to do that," Father Matt said in his quietest voice. He noticed a nurse cowering in a corner, shaking, her hands covering her head, a graying braid falling against the back of her floral-patterned scrub shirt.

Oh, dear God, he thought. *What am I doing here?*

The deputy to his right spoke in a toneless voice. "Clint, let Mavis go."

The man rocked back and forth again, the gun still raised. "No. I need her to take care of Josie. She's so sick. I brought her here for help. She needs help."

A single sob came from the direction of the nurse, who curled into a tighter ball and pushed herself against the wall as though it might open for her if she pressed hard enough.

"Josie. Is that your little girl?" Father Matt was surprised to hear his own voice. The man nodded. "Tell me about her."

More rocking, but the man still held tight to the gun and the child. "She's bad sick. She has lipid disease, that's what they say. I don't understand it. She got the tummy flu. She couldn't eat. I brought her in because she was so sick. They tell me she died. But she didn't. She can't die from the tummy flu. The nurse just needs to take care of her." Tummy flu. The words of a father to his child, at odds somehow with a grown man holding a clinic hostage to his grief, yet somehow also appropriate.

Father Matt's mind raced. The deputy behind him to his left started to speak, but Father Matt waved a hand to silence him. "The receptionist told me Mavis needs to get something from the cabinet outside. Let her go. Clint, is it? You want her to take care of Josie, don't you?"

As he spoke, he motioned to the nurse who had turned to look in his direction. He motioned with his hand, his eyes still fixed on the man with the gun. "She's standing up now, Clint. I'm going to move over this way. You point your gun at me, not her. She's pretty scared. She can't help you if she is so scared and if you won't let her go."

Before the deputies could protest, Matt Gregory put his six-six frame in the middle of the room, extending his arm in the direction of the nurse. His fingers waved her on, and he whispered, "Come on, come on. It's okay." The nurse slid up the wall, dashed for the door, and was gone. The man stiffened, and his grip on the gun tightened, but he did nothing more. The front of his blue sweatshirt was wet and his eyes open, round and staring. A stuffed brown bear slid to the ground from the side of the bed.

Keeping his back to the deputies, Father Matt spoke in an even voice, "I want you two to leave." *What am I doing?* he thought to himself. But he repeated the request.

"No can do, Father," one deputy said. "Too dangerous. The hostage team from Montrose is on the way."

"Leave. Now." Father Matt was surprised at the authority in his voice. "Wait for them outside the door."

"Can't leave you at risk, Father."

"I'm already at risk. Get out of here. Leave us alone." He felt — rather than saw — the vacillation in their will and took advantage of it. "Now," he repeated. "You can see through the glass in the door. Crack the door. Just stand right outside."

He heard the soft sound of the door closing, but the click of the lock did not follow. He was alone with the man and his child, and he was afraid. He took a deep breath and gathered his thoughts. The man looked away from Father Matt to his child, crooning something to her, but the gun remained steady and pointed right at his chest.

Sweet Jesus, Mary, and Joseph, help me! Weren't the police supposed to ignore the ranting of a madman? Weren't they trained to keep interlopers like him away from things like this? *What have I done?*

Saved at least one life, came the answer. *Now save another.*

"Are you Catholic, Clint?"

"Not anymore." The man looked up again. "Don't believe in God. No God would make this happen to my little girl."

"I agree," Matt said with conviction. "But I believe. Do you mind if I pray? It's what I do, you know."

The man nodded slowly and looked back at the child. His gun never wavered.

Now what? Father Matt thought, his mind suddenly blank. A man who prayed for hours every day could remember nothing. The silence in his mind was so deep, it was like a living thing, taunting him as he watched the man still rocking, felt the aim of the gun, and marked a trickle of sweat between his shoulder blades. Behind him, he heard muffled voices and caught a few words of conversation through the cracked door. "ETA seven minutes. Can't find the wife. Get that priest out of there."

Improbably, he heard himself begin to speak.

"Blessed be God. Blessed be His Holy Name. Blessed be Jesus Christ, true God and true man."

Why am I praying the Divine Praises? he thought wildly,

but he could remember nothing else. He kept going. "Blessed be the name of Jesus." The man looked up, incredulous.

"Blessed be His Most Sacred Heart." He continued in spite of himself, his voice soft, his heart racing and his mind in chaos. *This is not right!*

"Blessed be His most Precious Blood. Blessed be Jesus in the Most Holy Sacrament of the Altar." The voice came from the man, almost a whisper.

"Blessed be the Holy Spirit, the Consoler." The two of them together. Clint must have been an altar boy. Father Matt suspected he'd learned those responses by heart at the behest of a priest. Catholics his age rarely knew them otherwise.

"Blessed be the great Mother of God, Mary most Holy." Father Matt took a tentative step forward, and the man dropped his arm, placing the gun carefully on the bed, heaving a great, ragged sigh. They said the rest together, and by the time they got to the last line, Father Matt had the man in his arms, holding him even as the man held his little girl with the blond curls.

He was still holding him when the hostage team arrived. The man surrendered to the deputies peacefully, to have his hands cuffed behind him, but not until Father Matt anointed his daughter at his request. Even as he traced the Sign of the Cross on her forehead, he recalled his professor's thoughts on the subject of who should receive the sacrament of healing.

"Many's the dead body or Protestant I gave Last Rites to in those days, I'm sure. No matter. Let God sort it out. Sometimes the oil is for the survivors."

So it is, he thought as they led the man out of the room. *And,* he thought to himself, *there's a good deal of latitude when death occurs.* He shrugged off his doubts.

One of the deputies cast a backward look as he closed the door. "Good job, Father. Where'd you get your hostage training?"

A laugh threatened to surface inside him. "Right here," he managed to say before the door closed, leaving him alone. He reached down and picked up the stuffed bear. It had been left behind in the commotion of the arrest, and it was precious. He would see it got back to the man – Clint? Suddenly wobbly, he laid back on the gurney and closed his eyes. He shifted uncomfortably, feeling something hard and small in the middle of his back. He sat up and rummaged in the sheet to find the offending object. Maybe it was something else of the little girl's or something from her dad's pocket.

He retrieved a small vial with a rubber gasket on top. He recognized it as the kind of thing vaccines come in. He smoothed his finger over the top, where a needle would permit withdrawal of the contents. It was almost empty, with only a few drops of clear liquid still in the bottom. He turned it so that he could see the label. Potassium chloride. *For intravenous infusion after dilution,* it read.

He remembered the father's words. *She can't die from the tummy flu.* And the receptionist's. *I don't know why they even brought her in, a kid like that.*

A gorked-out kid like that. The words were so impersonal, as if the child were something less for her sickness. It was so wrong, especially in a place meant to be the very place the sick belonged. In clinics, it was the well who were out of place, except when they were there to help the ill and infirm.

He pocketed the vial, uncertain what it meant but vaguely aware that this might not be usual for this kind of situation. As he was leaving the clinic, the gray-haired nurse, still shaking, came up to him to thank him. He barely heard a word she said. His attention was fixed on a small, gold pomegranate pin on the collar of her scrubs. He smiled and nodded and excused himself as quickly as he could, ignoring the call of a reporter who wanted to talk to him.

He hurried out into the cold, the stolen vial suddenly heavy in his pocket. He remembered where he'd heard about potassium chloride before and why. He looked at his phone. A little after five. It could wait until daybreak. Jane Wallace would be up by then. He offered a prayer of thanks that he and the local medical examiner were good friends. He needed someone to bring this to.

CHAPTER ONE

Father Matt blew into my office first thing in the morning without even knocking. He shed his coat and gloves as he strode to my desk, talking the whole way.

"Jane, a nurse from Proserpine just killed a patient down at the clinic. You need to do something." He dropped his wet gloves on my desk. They plopped onto a stack of correspondence I had just signed. The melting snow dripped water onto the top letter and smeared my signature, written in fountain ink.

"Father!" I brushed the gloves aside and rescued the other letters. "Slow down. What's happened? And who is Proserpine?"

"Sorry." Father Matt tossed his coat over the back of the green leather couch. "I was called down to the clinic. A little girl died there this morning, Josie...Josie..." He paused. "I don't know her last name."

"I do. Josie Beck. She was a client." I breached two flavors of professional confidentiality without a second thought. So we'd lost the race to get Josie her care. The insurance company won. For once, at news of a death close to me, I didn't feel like the earth had fallen away. I was just so very sad. "Tell me what happened." We sat down in the sitting area, he on the couch, I in my favorite overstuffed chair. I had to move some books aside first.

"She got sick with some kind of stomach virus. Her father brought her into the clinic. They were treating her, IVs and all, and getting ready to transfer her to Grand Junction. The receptionist said that that kind of thing could be bad for her."

I considered all of this for a moment. "I suppose. I don't know enough about the details of her particular disease, to be sure. But her health was pretty fragile, so I suppose that anything might have tipped her over the edge."

"Would *this*?" Matt rummaged around in his pocket and handed me a plastic bag. In it was a small vial. "I found it in the sheets where Josie was lying."

Potassium chloride. I turned it over in my hands for a moment as I ran the probabilities. "It could. Certainly a bolus of this is enough to kill anyone, and it is untraceable at that. But if she had been very sick and her electrolytes were off balance, the clinic staff could have added this to the IV just to bring her numbers back in order." I set it carefully on the table beside me. "Matt, that was one sick little girl. This isn't much to go on."

"How about the fact that the nurse taking care of her is a member of Proserpine?"

"Proserpine?"

"It's that...that...group that advocates assisted suicide. Calls it 'compassionate death.'" Father Matt almost spat out the words.

I couldn't blame him. I had no use for the groups pushing assisted suicide, especially since a few states, including Colorado, had legalized it. It bothered me enough on its own; now I was finding that insurance companies were reluctant to cover expensive terminal care, like Josie's, but were more than happy to cover the cost of drugs to end a life. At its best, it was medical ethics gone mad. Personally, I considered it the worst kind of victimization of the most vulnerable, and crass profiteering at its worst. "And you know this, how? Are you spying, Father Matt?"

"No. Well, yes, but that's not how I know. She was wearing a pomegranate pin on her scrubs. That's their logo."

I considered the situation. Josie was terminally ill; we all knew that. She was at the center of a fight to get her insurance company to pay for new, cutting-edge care that promised to extend her life, at least a bit, and make it more comfortable. It wasn't experimental but it was expensive, and the insurance company balked. All they had to do was play a waiting game and they'd win; they had. No real possibilities there.

Josie's father doted on her and had given up everything to care for her, even selling the family ranch to have enough money to get her everything short of the treatment he so wanted her to receive. No motive there. Her mother, unable to handle the stress of a sick child and without the strength of her husband whose attention was focused only on his daughter, had bolted. She lived in Montrose now with a new boyfriend, and Clint Beck had confided that he thought she was into drugs and drinking alcohol. Not an uncommon way to deaden the pain of having a dying child and a dead marriage. A great deal of sadness but no one I could see who would seek the services of Proserpine, and I said so.

"Jane, I'm telling you that child was killed. Can't you even investigate?"

I considered his request. I could stretch my jurisdiction to reach that far without doing complete violence to it. It was, after all, the unexpected death of a small child. I pondered what that would do to Clint. I picked up the vial again, gingerly this time, by the edges of the crimped top. Finally, I answered.

"I don't think I can justify it. I really can't. Besides, I'm not sure I could prove it if I did take the case. Even if someone injected her with this, there'd be no way to trace it. And anyone smart enough to use potassium chloride would be smart enough not to put it in the IV fluid, because it's too much and too easy to trace. Inject it, and there's a quick, easy death, with nothing to prove except by circumstances. And the circumstances just aren't there."

Father Matt wasn't listening. He was already putting on his coat, a distracted look on his face. As he bent to pick up his gloves, he muttered, "Thanks, Jane," and left as quickly as he had come.

I turned the vial over in my hand once more and then picked up the phone to call the clinic. Nothing ventured, nothing gained, and I trusted Father Matt's instincts more than I let on. I picked up the phone to call the clinic just as it rang. Half an hour later, I hung up and forgot all about Josie in the press of the day's work.

***

Father Matt ran the few blocks to the clinic, slipping on the ice and nearly — but not quite — falling. He was out of breath when he barreled in the door. The same receptionist was still on duty. It was a wonder they had not sent her home; surely her shift was over by now. A wonder they had not closed down the clinic, for that matter, though he supposed he could see the logic. It was the primary source of care for the town, the newer doc-in-a-box at the other end of town notwithstanding.

"I forgot something in the room; can I go back?" He spoke in a rush, gasping a bit for breath.

The woman smiled at him. "Sure, Father. Nobody is in there. And thanks for coming. But what did you leave? We cleaned that room hours ago. Nothing was turned in."

He couldn't think of a plausible lie, so he didn't reply. He rushed to the room he'd so recently occupied with Clint Beck and Josie. It was clean and tidy, no sign that almost-murder had taken place earlier in the day. He cast about frantically for the trash can. Clean and empty, like the room.

He stood for a moment in the middle of the room and then went back into the hall. The gray-haired nurse was just about to enter the treatment room next door. *It's a surprise she's here,* thought Matt. Maybe they have long shifts. Twelve to twelve or something like that.

"I dropped something when I was here; I can't find it in there," he stammered to her. "Where do you put the trash? I need to look for it. Very important." His cheeks flushed; he was unused to prevarication.

The nurse pointed to an open door at the end of the hall. "Down there. But I didn't see anything unusual when I cleaned the room. You are more than welcome to look, though." She entered the exam room with no further word, leaving Father Matt in the hall alone.

He walked casually to the open door, looked around to

make certain he was unobserved, and entered the room.

The trash held only tissues, papers, and wrappers, but he noticed a large, covered, red container labeled "biohazard." Feeling as guilty as a schoolboy nicking a test from the teacher's desk, he removed the lid.

There it was, lying on top, an IV bag half-empty, labeled with Josie Beck's name. He pulled it gingerly out of the can, dropped it into one of the extra red bags out of an open box on a nearby counter, and tucked it inside his jacket. He replaced the red lid and backed out of the room.

As he passed the desk again, the receptionist smiled. "Did you find what you were looking for, Father?"

Father Matt smiled back and nodded. "Thank you," he said. "God bless." *I hope I found it*, he thought, as he started out the glass door and back home to think.

CHAPTER TWO

Medical examiners come in two categories: the hyper-organized and the incredibly slovenly. I fall, at least in the professional part of my life and on my better days (which are few and far between), in the former category. Sadie Jackson, the new M.E. in the office, falls squarely in the latter. Her office, even though she'd been part of the team for a few short weeks, was a rat's nest of papers, files, books, and slide folders. I could barely see her microscope amid the rubble. She and my son Ben were clearly cut from the same bolt of cloth.

I opened the glass door to her office gingerly, not wanting to send tumbling a precarious stack just outside its clearance. Sadie sat with her back to me, head bent over a book, brown hair in a bun at the nape of her neck that was as messy as her desk. Another difference. I can't sit with my back to a room.

"Sadie?"

Her tousled head jerked up, and she swiveled her chair around. "Hi, boss."

"Sadie, I'm about to head out. I was just wondering what was on the table today."

"Not much. Just one F.D.I.B., old lady about eighty or so."

"F.D.I.B.?" It was taking me some time to get used to

Sadie. She came with excellent credentials, good training, and fine recommendations. Now that I was coming out of the fog of mourning the murder of my husband John and finding a life again, I had little desire to spend every waking moment in the Center, so I hired her on a trial basis. I'd been working with her a little over a month. Her skills were excellent, but I found her manner hard to take, a little too cavalier for my taste. There was something unsettling and freewheeling about her, though I couldn't put my finger on it. I wrote it off to my age and idiosyncrasies; the other staff, more of an age with Sadie, got along fine with her.

"Found dead in bed. Nothing to angst over."

"What did you find?"

Sadie cocked her head. "Nothing. I didn't do a post. External exam was normal, at least for someone that age. Nothing suspicious in the report. Family didn't want an autopsy if we didn't have to do it."

"But you took blood and urine and photographs."

The cant of her head increased, and she looked puzzled. "No, I didn't. Why should I? It's a waste of resources."

I suspected Sadie was more interested in protecting her free time than the Center's budget but refrained from saying so. "I realize you come from a different environment, Sadie," I said. "But here, there's a minimum for every case. Blood, urine, photos. Did it ever occur to you that the request for no autopsy might be because there is something to hide, rather than because there isn't? Is the body still here?"

"I think so. I'll go get those samples now."

"And when you are done, re-read the handbook. Make notes if you have to. No cutting corners." The memory of cut corners that obscured a serial killer last summer still poked at my pride, even though it worked out in the end.

Sadie turned back to her book, dog-eared a page (I cringed again), and stuffed the book back on the shelf over her desk. As she did, my attention was drawn to a small wooden statue of a figure dressed in an elaborate white gown. The carving was intricate but very much of the folk style so common in Mexico. The carved dress was decorated with bits of lace and seed beads, and the veil was made of sheer fabric edged with the same lace. The figure held a bouquet of pink roses in skeletal hands. I recoiled. Instead of charming, the face was a skull with empty sockets. A scythe and a globe rested at her feet. I stared at it in disbelief. Santa Muerte, so-called "Saint Death," a hideous caricature of a bride and legitimate Santos. It made my skin crawl.

Sadie noticed my interest. "Cool, isn't it? I got that at a medical meeting I went to a few months ago. Good symbol for a medical examiner, isn't it?"

"Get rid of it."

"What?"

"You heard me. Get rid of it. Now. I want it out of this office before you do anything else."

"No. This is my office and I like it. You can't make me take it out just because you don't like it."

"It is an office in the Center. You really do need to read the handbook. No personal items in offices." I'd written that particular passage in the rules and regs out of an abundance of paranoia. I'd had enough brushes with H.R.

law to know that I just did not want to deal with claims of offense of one employee by another. The easiest way to solve that was to sterilize offices of personal décor.

"Your office has personal stuff in it."

"My office is not part of the Center. It's a common mistake. It has been made before. This is part of the Center. Get rid of it, or I will. And remember that I have the master key, and all offices are subject to random search for security purposes."

Sadie shrugged her shoulders, knowing she was bested. "Jeez. No need to get so bent out of shape. It's just a statue."

I softened a bit as I saw her take the figure off the shelf. "It's not just a figure. It's…" I struggled with how to make this woman understand. I settled for taking the coward's way out. "It's associated with criminals, drug trade, assassination, all sorts of things we work against, Sadie. Black magic, voodoo, Santeria. Plus, it is a mockery of better things. It has no business in a medical examiner's office." *Especially as long as I am in charge*, I thought to myself. No sense tempting evil here any more than it already is.

"Okay, boss, I get it." She smiled an easy smile, one that I somehow didn't trust. "But I bought it because it seems that death is the M.E.'s bride. No death, no job, after all. Best we can hope for is that the deaths we see are good ones, don't you think?" Her comment was off-handed; Sadie was already rummaging in her backpack. She brought out a wad of keys as disorderly as her office. "I'll be right back. I want to put this in the apartment. Then I'll get on that autopsy." She brushed past me, toppling the pile I had been so careful not to disturb.

Best we can hope for is that the deaths we see are good deaths. I bent to pick up the scattered papers Sadie left in her wake. Computer printouts of articles and reports were interspersed with unopened junk mail. Trying to give the pile stability it did not deserve, I stacked the mail on top of the printouts.

I paused at the last piece. Not a mass mailing like so many of the others, this was a fat envelope with an individual address, handwritten, and it had been opened and re-stuffed. On the outside of the envelope was a scrawled note: *Call Jake*, in Sadie's unmistakably sloppy hand.

The return address was for Proserpine. This organization I'd not heard of before was mentioned twice in a day, and if Father Matt was right, one that gave me cause to be suspicious. It made me wonder what Sadie meant by a "good death." And I wondered just what kind of medical meeting offered Santa Muerte statues for sale.

***

Fiona Idoni, née McLaughlin, formerly Countess of Maldoino, brushed the dark auburn hair the hairdresser had touched up that very afternoon into an elegant knot at the back of her head, smoothing it into place with hands still a bit tender from the ministrations of the plastic surgeon. Still, she was glad someone had invented the technology that gave physicians the ability to make her hands look as smooth as her tucked faced and revised neck. Nothing worse than a woman beginning to show the advance of age and staving it off with bright eyes, smooth cheeks, and wrinkled neck and hands. At least all her parts matched, and she took care to wear dark stockings or slacks, so that the small purple veins emerging on her once-perfect legs did not show.

The image that looked back at her from the mirror smiled: even white teeth, clear pale skin that had never freckled up, pale blue eyes in a round face, full lips, and a nose that had once been cute as a button but now was just the right shape to have made her peasant face suitable for an Italian count. She saw a place on her temple where the hairdresser had missed an infinitesimal patch of faded and graying hair, and she scowled. She would have a word with her tomorrow.

A pain as sharp as a sword passed through her head when she touched the line of scar the surgeon had left behind in the hairline, almost as though she had touched a trigger. She grabbed the marble basin and closed her eyes against it until it passed as quickly and sharply as it had come. She looked up again. The trickle of the tear at the corner of her right eye had not yet blurred her carefully applied mascara, and she dabbed it away. She looked down to find that one bright red nail was broken, snapped against the side of the bowl, and she frowned. A few minutes with a file and a bottle of polish, and it was acceptable. Still, the nail should not have broken. Another reason to have a word with the woman at the expensive shop where she had spent all day.

The ivory sweater she donned was shot through with gold threads like the thin, sleeveless shell she was wearing, and it was crusted with beads at the neck, hem, and cuffs. She fastened a long, unadorned gold chain around her neck and let it drop against the silk of the shell. She regarded the whole effect in the mirror as she smoothed almond-scented cream on her hands, turning her head this way and that until she was satisfied that she was as elegant and attractive as she could be. Pursing her lips together, she turned from the mirror, threw her mink jacket over her arm, and picked up the gold purse lying on the brocade seat of the overstuffed chair in the corner by the door.

The Maître d' at the Chop House said that he had reservations for eight. They had not laid eyes on each other since that day, so many years ago, when she fled that dreadful, cold-water flat in the arms of Antonio, the first in a string of lovers, each increasingly wealthy and demanding. She played her hand well, extracting from each a piece of a fortune until here she was, agreeably alone. She thought that she could leave behind the comfort of men and their beds and their demands on her time and her body. She divorced her most recent husband in a display of cold-hearted avarice that left even the tabloids aghast. She took with her money, a home on the coast of Capri, and a sweet little maid to pick up the pieces of her life.

She hadn't counted on the loneliness. After years of defining herself by the man whose arm she adorned, she found herself suddenly longing to find the man who had started it all: the first one, whom she had abandoned to fate and followed with fascination. He had never married again, and not even the ugliest gossip magazine ever linked him with a woman, at least not until word reached her of this medical examiner in Colorado. She wondered whether she would be too late, whether he had finally fallen in love again. Would he recognize her?

There was but one way to find out. She turned the big

brass doorknob and stepped out in search of a man she could attach to. Now more than ever, that mattered desperately to her.

CHAPTER THREE

"Señora Doctora!" Pilar's voice interrupted me in my attempt to dress my stubby lashes with mascara. I jerked, leaving a stinging dollop in my eye and a rake of black lines across my cheek. I sighed and dampened a washcloth to remove the damage as I called back to her.

"Yes, Pilar. What is it?" I tried to dab the black marks without disturbing the foundation I had laid, but to no avail. A beige streak of, improbably, sunset rose discolored the white terrycloth. My reflection peered out at me from the mirror. I looked like a child playing in her mother's makeup, which wasn't far from the truth. What had possessed me to try to pretty myself up? I tipped a bit of the beige makeup onto my finger and attempted a repair.

Pilar appeared at my elbow and regarded me, her dignified face wrinkled in curiosity. My attempts at camouflage only made the spot on my cheek more noticeable, and my right eye was beginning to tear. There was a dark line on the inside of my lid, and my eye was getting bloodshot.

"Why do you bother with that?" Pilar echoed my own frustration. "Señor Eoin likes you as you are. A woman who is beautiful has no need of paint." She looked at her own unadorned face in the mirror. The eyes in her reflection turned to me, and she smiled.

Pilar had a point. Her iron-gray hair was pulled back in

her habitual bun, her aquiline nose was raised in the tiniest gesture of disdain, and her brown face, unadorned by so much as a trace of lipstick, was striking. Crow's feet wrinkled the corners of her eyes, and fine lines marred the line of her mouth. She is just Pilar, and I am just Jane, and neither of us has much desire for enhancement. And in my case, even had I the desire, I lacked the requisite skill. I abandoned the quest for even skin tones, shrugged at Pilar's image in the glass, grinned, and soaped up the washcloth.

"What's up?" I bent over the sink, lather dripping from the cloth and running down my bare arm.

"You cannot wear this tonight." Pilar held up the denim skirt I had asked her to press for me. I saw the proffered skirt in the mirror. A stubby brown finger waggled through a hole in the seam up the front. "I would fix it, but the machine is still broken. Maybe these instead. They are just clean." Pilar held up a pair of soft corduroy jeans the color of good-morning coffee.

I stood up, drying my face with a rough cotton towel. "Sure. Just leave them on the bed. Thanks."

The hole was only an excuse, and I was fully aware that those nimble brown hands could have stitched up the rent in record time. Pilar had taken a proprietary interest in my dinner date with Eoin Connor, hovering as anxiously as a mother sending her daughter off to her first prom.

"He is downstairs. He came early. You should hurry. It is not good to keep such a man waiting."

I glanced at the watch on my wrist. Eoin Connor was a full half-hour ahead of his time. I ran a brush through my curls. I remembered now why I hate makeup so much. I prefer the feel of a clean face. "I'll be down as soon as I can. Please pour him a drink, would you?"

"He is already drinking your whiskey." Pilar's brown eyes crinkled, and her smile reminded me that I needed to get her an appointment with the local dentist. "In your best glass. I told him not to break it."

"Thank you."

She laid the jeans on my bed, smoothed them, and stood up to face me as I came out of the bathroom, the damp towel still in my hand. She held up a sweater in tones of burnished gold and red, one I had purchased at a local shop earlier in the week. I had not even taken it out of the bag, red and white with a deer on it, now lying discarded on the floor beside the bed.

"Wear this. Señor Eoin has been away a long time. You should look your best for him." She dropped a pair of boots by the bed for emphasis. "I polished these for you. It is not snowing today. You can wear decent shoes."

"Anything else, Dueña mía?" I smiled. Pilar had taken good care of me since the first day she arrived, a little over six months ago in the midst of a string of killings and my own raw grief. She had simply arrived, settled in, and had been fussing over me ever since: mending my clothes, cleaning my house, making my dinners, and dispensing advice to me and to Isa and Lupe, the other two Mexican women who shared my house. She is the resident matriarch, and we all love her.

"Wear perfume. You do not want to scare him away, smelling like that place." Pilar understands how I make my living, but she disapproves, and not always vaguely. She turned from the bed to give me a final, stern look, and stopped at the door before disappearing downstairs. "And earrings. Nice ones. Big ones." I heard her footsteps on the stair runner as she descended slowly, her knees no doubt troubling her. Her arthritis was one reason I had abandoned the first floor master suite in favor of Pilar and had taken this smaller room on the second floor, the one with a view of town.

I glanced out the window as I pulled on the sweater and jeans, confirming the weather forecast. No white flakes reflected in the streetlight, and the sidewalks were clear of snow, though there was an accumulation that kept the lawns and peaks white this winter evening. I had missed Eoin Connor's company these last weeks. He had been my constant companion since a string of murders in June that brought him into my life. Business with his editor in New York and the completion of his latest book had kept him away for more than a month.

I pulled on the boots and brushed my hair. In deference to Pilar, I added a pair of tasteful gold earrings and dabbed a bit of scent behind my ears and on my wrists. I checked my appearance one last time: taller, thinner, and older than I wanted to be, silvering hair in random curls shaped and organized into a chin-length bob, black eyes under dark brows and nearly invisible wire-rimmed glasses perched on my crooked nose. *As good as it gets,* I thought, and left my room, more excited than I expected to be, to take the stairs down to the parlor two at a time.

I stopped at the last landing to collect myself, but my subterfuge was unsuccessful. I heard a familiar voice boom up from the sitting room.

"Woman, I'm not off to anywhere. Don't be breaking

your neck in your hurry to see me." Eoin Conner rounded the corner, glass of Jameson in hand. He smiled up at me, genuinely pleased, and offered me his free hand as I came down the last four steps at a more dignified pace. He pulled me into a quick embrace, careful not to spill his whiskey, then stepped back to keep me at arm's length.

"You're a sight for sore eyes," he said. "It's a pleasure indeed to see a woman not wearing a black suit and painted up like a jam tart." He hugged me again, and I caught a familiar whiff of peppermint and tobacco.

"You, too. I've missed you." *More than I would have thought,* I reflected. I was still recovering from the death of my husband, and I found my growing affection for Eoin Connor confusing. No, not confusing, I corrected myself. Unsettling, precisely because it was *not* confusing. I found him attractive in a mysterious sort of way, and on more than one occasion found myself daydreaming about what might lie ahead for us. I had missed our long evenings together, sipping good whiskey and talking about our lives; walks in the woods and in town; the feel of his calloused hand in mine; and his strong presence at my side during Sunday Mass. I had scarcely heard from him during his absence, but I understood his writer's need for solitude and concentration, not unlike my own in the days when I prepared for court cases. Eventually I would resurface into the world, and now he had, too. I wondered once again what would come next.

"How did the meetings go?"

"The book is ready. Dan didn't find much to quibble about. I have to admit, it's one of my better ones. There's talk of a mini-series already, and if that comes through, I'll be off to California to hammer out a screenplay. Still, considering that I was sorely distracted in the middle of it, it's not a bad end." He smiled and winked as he drained the last of his whiskey.

I was all too aware that I had been the distraction, between trying to solve serial murders and nearly getting killed myself. Even so, it had ended well and with Eoin in my corner. His absence had made me wonder if he'd wormed his way into my heart. I had missed him much more than I expected.

Two steps into the parlor, Eoin laid his glass on the sideboard and then returned to hold my down coat for me. "I'll buy you a wee dram in the bar before dinner," he said, as he shrugged into his own shearling jacket and held the door open for me.

The air was crisp but not too cold. I pulled on my gloves as we walked and talked about all the things we had missed together in the last weeks: book gossip, my new assistant, the latest crisis in Telluride politics, and the news of my six children scattered to the four winds. As we turned the corner onto Pacific Street, he took my gloved hand in his.

I relished the comfort of his grasp at the same time that I wondered about it. We had been together nearly every day since the series of murders of trust fund beneficiaries was finally solved, save for his visit to New York. I felt certain that he harbored affection for me, as I did for him, and yet, aside from holding my hand and the occasional hug, he was as chaste as a schoolboy on his first date. Actually more so, considering the public displays of affection I saw among even the youngest of Telluride's dating population. My heart was warming to Eoin, but I wondered whether his interest was merely polite and platonic. My daydreams and I were increasingly interested in the answer.

The Chop House was not crowded. Georges, the Maître d', was by now an old friend; when we ate out, it was nearly always at the Chop House. He escorted us to our usual table in the corner just off the window. It gave Eoin a good view of town, to satisfy his voyeur instincts, but was not a spot easily seen from the street. The perfect combination of vista and privacy. We soon settled in with a bottle of good merlot between us and steaks on order.

"You really are a sight for sore eyes, darling Jane," Eoin said. "New York was a lonely place without you there." He reached across the table to take my hand in his. A month in the city had nearly banished the calluses that testified to his habit of hard and manual labor to keep his mind clear and his body in shape. His hands were almost soft, and they were warm.

"You can thank Pilar for that," I said. "She picked this out for me. She's a hard woman to resist."

Eoin cocked his head and his eyes glinted. "And a fine job she did," he said, trotting out his Irish accent for effect. "Provided me a grand canvas for this." A long, thin package wrapped in teal paper with a tidy white bow materialized on the table.

I felt my face flush. A gift. I had not expected this.

"Go on," he urged. "Open it."

I hesitated. I wasn't sure I could pick it up without my hands trembling, and that annoyed me. He had purchased one present for me, early on, on a lark: a shawl and a brooch that had proved the key to solving a series of murders. This was different. He'd clearly thought about this, and I recognized the very expensive shop the box was from. I looked up at Eoin's expectant, serious face and cautiously picked up the package.

I slit the meticulous wrapping with the knife at my place and carefully unfolded it to reveal a flocked, hinged box. I opened it slowly, almost afraid of what I might find. What I saw glittering in the light from the candle on the table made me gasp.

"Don't you like it?" Expectancy turned to concern.

I couldn't answer for a moment. Nestled on the velvet lining was a simple gold chain on which was hung a briolette emerald the size of a grape. It was simple and elegant and absolutely gorgeous. And, I suspected, ridiculously expensive.

"It's been a long time since I bought a real present for a woman." Eoin hurried to fill the silence. "If you don't like it, you can exchange it, get something else." He now sounded like the schoolboy I had compared him to in my mind as we walked down the street.

I reached my hand across and touched his arm, looking straight into his eyes, almost as green as the stone. "It's beautiful. I love it, but it's far too extravagant."

Relief flooded his rugged features, and his good nature returned. "Can you not just accept it, Woman?" he teased, using a nickname he knew to employ judiciously.

"I can. Thank you, Eoin, it's really lovely." I pulled it out of the box and fastened it around my neck. It felt heavy and comfortable, several inches below the scoop neck of the sweater, and the green against the red was, indeed, striking. "Pilar knew," I said, remembering that she had encouraged earrings, but nothing else. The gift pleased me a great deal, if only because it proved Eoin Connor had thought about me in the long weeks he was away with only the odd email and no phone calls to keep in touch. It pleased me more that he had engaged my makeshift family in a surprise, because it bespoke an affection that was more than just friendship.

"A man has to take his aid where he can," Eoin replied, smiling, and taking a sip from his glass. He looked at me for a long moment with a satisfied smile on his face. Abruptly, it faded, and he was serious, enough to make me finger the emerald and worry that I had overestimated the meaning of this expensive bauble.

"Jane, darling girl, I have something to tell you, something that affects you and me." Eoin took another sip of wine, and I felt my blood run cold. Conversations that start out this way never turn out well. "There's something about me that you need to know. I've been trying to find a way to tell you…"

I turned to see one of the most attractive women I have ever encountered. I had caught her out of the corner of my eye as Eoin was starting to speak, my restless gaze no longer able to hold his for fear of what I would see in their depths. The Maître d' escorted the woman down the three steps to the main floor of the dining room and gestured in our general direction. She was not tall, perhaps five-three, but she moved with the grace and authority of royalty, oblivious of the fact that every eye in the dining room followed her; at the same time she was clearly enjoying it. She was dressed in an ivory sweater set and gold silk slacks, and her dark red hair was pulled into an elegant bun. As she approached, I realized that she was older than she looked, but her surgeon had been a good one. She looked refreshed and attractive, not nipped and tucked, but there was something about the smoothness of her face that just didn't fit.

Eoin noticed my distraction and looked over his shoulder just as she approached. I heard him whisper, "Oh, no!" under his breath as he stumbled to his feet. He gained his balance just in time for the woman to throw her arms around his neck and, standing on tip-toes, kiss him in a familiar way I had yet to experience.

"Eoin, darling!" Her accent was impossible to place, the sort of neutral, upper crust European inflection of the aristocracy. "How are you?"

For the first time since I met him, Eoin Connor was speechless. He stood flatfooted as the woman ran her hands across his shoulders, then took his face in her hands and kissed him again. I found myself fuming.

Finally, I heard him mumble. "Fiona, what are you doing here?" He took her hands and pushed her away, taking a step back.

The woman cocked her head and pursed her lips in a calculated little-girl pout. "Eoin, how could you? Where else should I be?" She ran her hand up his arm, and he pulled it away as though he had been shocked. The woman smiled and leaned across him to look directly at me. I had the same uncomfortable feeling I often experience in the reptile hall at the zoo.

"This must be the famous Jane Wallace." She reached her hand across to me, and I regarded her cautiously as I took it. It was soft and manicured. "Fiona McLaughlin

Connor. And what, Dr. Wallace, are you doing having dinner with my husband?"

***

I replayed the scene over and over again in my mind as I downed a stiff whiskey. I am familiar with the concept of time standing still; I had experienced it when the security guard came to tell me that my husband had been killed. I never expected to experience it again, but I had, right there in the restaurant.

I had no recollection of what I said in response to her announcement, except Eoin's shocked face, his hand reaching out to me as I shoved back my chair and threw down my napkin. My clumsiness jostled the table, and my glass of wine toppled. I watched the spreading red stain for a moment, hearing Eoin's voice only faintly through the buzzing in my ears. "Jane? Please, Jane!" Then, "Fiona, damn you, what do you think you are doing? You haven't been Connor for 30 years..."

A marriage half a world and half a lifetime ago, the rational part of me thought. His *wife* was all the rest of me heard. I remembered most of all the brush of his hand, the soft one, the unfamiliar one, as he tried to stop me from leaving. I remembered the heat in my face as I ran out of the restaurant to the stares of the diners along the way, leaving my coat and my shame behind.

Pilar was downstairs when I arrived back home, and taking one look at my face, she shepherded my extended Mexican family upstairs. I sat now in my favorite chair with a cat in my lap, a Waterford glass in my hand, a knot in my stomach, and an ache in my heart. I didn't hear the front door open behind me, but I recognized Eoin's tread in the hall.

The cat protested when I stood to face him. He held my down coat in front of him, a penitent look on his face. "You forgot this." When I failed to respond, he placed it gingerly on the federal chair in the front hall. "Jane. Please, let me..."

He had taken no more than a tentative step toward me when my anger erupted, and I hurled the glass, still half full of whiskey at him. I have a good arm, but Eoin has better reflexes. He caught the glass and set it carefully on the sideboard as he continued his cautious advance in my direction.

"It's me you want to break, Jane, not the glass. Don't waste good crystal over me."

I closed my eyes, hoping to master my emotions. I heard him stop in his tracks, waiting for me to continue. The clock in the front hall ticked the time away for half an eternity before I was able to speak.

"Why didn't you tell me?" I opened my eyes, preternaturally calm, the anger spent for the time being.

Eoin was silent as he covered the last few feet that separated us, and he held my gaze for a moment before he answered. His green eyes were sad, his voice subdued. "At first, there was no reason; you'd have nothing to do with me. Then, I was afraid...you'd been through so much." He stopped and took a breath. "That's not true. I was afraid because I knew you'd have nothing to do with me, and I enjoyed your company." Another pause. "For what it's worth, I was trying to tell you when Fiona walked in."

My temper flared again. "So you bribed me with an emerald necklace to soften the blow?" I grabbed at the necklace, but Eoin stopped me before I could yank it off and throw it at him, even as some small, residual, sane part of me wondered when I'd gotten to be such a little girl.

"Please let me explain. The necklace was just a gift. To work up my courage, not to buy you off. A stiff glass of Jameson would have been cheaper."

It was a weak jab at humor, but it worked. "Might have worked better, too." I mustered up a bit of a smile.

Eoin matched it, and I could see the tension ebb out of his shoulders. He took my hand and led me to the loveseat, dropped onto it, and patted the seat next to him. We sat for a moment in silence, regarding our shoes earnestly. Finally, Eoin eased his arm around me and pulled me close enough to kiss my hair before he spoke.

"I met Fiona in Belfast, when I was working at the docks. She was — is — a beautiful woman. I couldn't believe she'd have time for the likes of me, but she did." He shifted his weight to look down at me. "I was young, Jane, and lonely. Belfast was a hard place then. It was still during the Troubles..." His voice trailed off, and his expression told me he was back in Belfast even as he spoke.

He squeezed my shoulders as he took up the story again. "She did so because she thought she was pregnant, and not by me. But I didn't know that. We got married and set up house in a little flat on Falls Road. I think we were happy for a while. I was; I know that." He paused a moment as though collecting his thoughts. "Fiona was from as poor a family as I am, but she had no intention of remaining poor. She worked as a receptionist in a bank. I think they hired her for her looks. I would have."

"She's pretty, Eoin. I get that. I saw her."

Another squeeze. "Pretty isn't everything, Jane. It isn't enough, but it was enough to get Fiona out of Belfast. She met an Italian journalist, a wealthy young man, and a dilettante playing at being a reporter in a pretty tough spot. I came home one day to find she'd run off with him, and I haven't seen her since – until today. She divorced me as soon as she could."

I sat up to look at him. "And you?"

"I left. I went to England, worked for a while, licked my wounds, and started to write. And when I returned to Ireland, I asked for a decree of nullity. It was denied. Fiona lied to the tribunal, and at the time, I was suspected of being a collaborator with the R.U.C. Afraid or honest, no matter. They ruled the marriage valid. End of story, at least for me. Not for Fiona. She's had five more husbands along the way. For the record, it is Fiona McLaughlin Connor Fontini Haller Dulac Semphill Idoni."

"You kept track."

"I did. I'm not sure why. It doesn't matter. Really, Jane, it doesn't."

I struggled to take in all he had said. Eoin was married in the eyes of the Church. It explained a lot. It explained why he remained single in spite of celebrity and more than an honest man's share of attractiveness. It also explained his chaste behavior with me. Many — most — maybe almost all — men I know would have simply ignored the Church and married again. Not Eoin. I struggled to wrap my mind around the implications of his admission. Finally, I asked the only question I could think of. "Why is she here?"

"She says she wants to try again. I'm not sure I believe her — though I probably have enough money now for Fiona to be interested. I suspect it is something else, but I have no idea what."

I let the statement lie between us for a long while, a numbness I thought Eoin had helped me banish settling into my soul again. I was weighing my desires and the equities of the situation and enjoying the warmth of Eoin's embrace until I realized it was an illicit pleasure. I sighed and sat up.

"That's it, then."

"I asked about a rehearing when I was in New York. I've an old mate who's a monsignor there. Different times, a different tribunal. He's helping me with the paperwork. It ought to be a simple matter, though it will take time. Will you wait for me?"

For an instant, hope sparked in me, then just as quickly, it died. I knew something about the process from friends who had gone through it. Witnesses, investigations, questions, answers. Eoin's marriage had been half a world away. People move or get lost or die. Or, apparently, lie. "Do you think she'll tell the truth this time, if she wants you back?"

Eoin shifted, and his face grew weary. My heart ached, and I looked at every detail of his features, afraid I might not see him again. The scar on his cheek made him look surprisingly vulnerable. I'd never asked him how it happened. Now I'd probably not get the chance.

At last, he answered me with another question. "Are you not willing to fight for me, Jane? Am I not worth it?"

Tears finally spilled onto my cheeks. "Of course, you're

worth it, Eoin. But whom do I fight? The Church? She's your wife."

His voice sounded a hundred miles away when he replied. "So she is. So she is." He left me on the couch. By the time the front door closed behind him, the cat had reappeared in my lap. I petted her absently as I stared at the empty glass I had thrown at Eoin Connor.

***

"Open the door, ye bastard son of Peter! Open up!"

Father Matt sat half-upright in bed, bleary-eyed, trying to place the source of the commotion that had yanked him from a sound sleep. He strained and rubbed his eyes. The sound, whatever it was, stopped momentarily. He started to recline again when it resumed with a ferocity the priest thought would bring down the very building. And the roar was enough to wake the dead: a great bellow, rough-voiced, slurred, and insistent over the racket.

"Open up, damn ye! Or are ye afraid to face me, ye miserable excuse for a man?"

Crow-hopping as he pulled on a pair of sweatpants, Matt Gregory headed for the door, calling vainly that he was on his way. He stuck his head through the tattered neck of a stained tee shirt as he took the stairs down, two at a time, to the back door that was his customary entrance. The pounding ceased for a moment as he reached the landing midway down. He could see the door bend inward with the force as it resumed yet again, and heard the crack of breaking board.

"If ye don't open up, ye..."

Father Matt interrupted the tirade by complying with

the request, to find Eoin Connor in mid-bellow and mid-strike. The unexpected absence of the broken door he had been assaulting threw him off balance. He fell headlong against the priest who stepped back to keep from falling himself. Regaining his balance, Eoin Connor cocked his head and regarded the tall man in front of him with great gravity for a moment before he swung his right fist at him.

Good God! Father Matt thought as he ducked and blocked the blow. The priest could smell the whiskey on Eoin Connor's breath, and the wide plant of his stance bore testimony to his condition. Even so, the blow was a hard one that sent a wave of pain up Father Matt's forearm, and another in quick succession, blocked by a tucked shoulder protecting his bearded chin, followed it.

"Eoin, what's gotten into you?" Four inches taller and thirty years younger, the priest had a physical advantage, but not much, he reflected, as he shouldered himself into the man in front of him, pinning him against the corner of the vestibule — only because the man was too drunk to think clearly, and a good head was the better part of a good fight.

"It's your damn fault she won't have me, ye and the wicked whore of a Church ye serve." Connor shifted and gathered himself to deliver another blow.

Father Matt planted his own fist in Connor's midsection, finding it surprisingly hard, harder than his own. He heard the air go out of Connor's lungs and he crumpled, hands against his stomach as he fought for breath.

Father Matt pulled Connor through the vestibule into the empty hall, hitting the light switch with his elbow as he passed, and shoving Connor into a tattered chair that was surrounded by children's books. It was the chair the head of the parish daycare center used for reading to the children. It would have to do for this great lout for the time being.

Connor's ragged gasps began to subside, and he bent slowly forward, holding his head in his big hands. Father Matt watched him warily until he ran his fingers through his coarse gray hair in a gesture of despair so palpable, it filled the room. The knuckles were bruised, swollen and bloody. Matt's forearm still ached where his blow landed.

At length, Eoin Connor sat upright in the chair and looked at the priest with bloodshot eyes, anger spent and a single tear following the course of the scar on his left cheek. When he finally spoke, his voice was tenuous and broken. "She'll not have me."

Father Matt pulled a folding chair up and sat in it, meeting the man before him eye to eye. Still, rubbing his left arm, he made sure that he was more than a swing away. "Eoin," he said calmly, "what are you talking about?" It had to involve Jane Wallace, surely, but as far as Matt knew, she was fond of Connor, probably loved him, though Father Matt doubted she had ever considered it in so many words.

"Did I hurt ye, Father? Ye've got a mean fist yourself." Connor rubbed his midsection. Father Matt recognized stalling tactics and brushed them aside.

"I'm fine. But you're a man I'd rather fight beside than against." The priest leaned back in the chair, satisfied the drunk in front of him posed no more threat. "Who won't have you, Eoin?"

"Jane." The single word cost Connor his bravado, and he dropped his head into his hands again with a sigh. The two men let the name lie between them. Connor lifted his head, sighed again, and shifted his weight to feel in his hip pocket, only to find what he sought gone. "Damn," he said softly, more to himself than to the priest. "Not bad enough to lose the woman, now I've lost my f...my pipe."

Father Gregory looked at him in disbelief — as much at the words as the fact that Eoin Connor was still able to censor himself. He laughed, a short bark of a sound, more relief than amusement. It was enough to break the tension. "Come on, Eoin," he said, offering his still-good right hand, "I think I've got one you can borrow." He pushed the back door closed as the two of them climbed the stairs to the apartment that served as rectory and retreat for the parish priest.

Without a word, Eoin Connor settled himself on the leather couch as Father Matt first started a pot of coffee in the small kitchen, then pulled a pair of pipes from a stand on a desk cluttered with books and papers. He passed one to Eoin Conner, who saluted him with a lift of it and waited patiently for Father Matt to pass the black leather pouch.

The priest took his own seat in the wooden rocker reserved for watching television and praying his rosary. The two men tamped and puffed and fiddled until pipe smoke competed with the smell of brewing coffee. Satisfied, Father Matt posed his question again. "What happened, Eoin?"

Strong shoulders lifted, and the bowl of the borrowed pipe glowed red. Eoin Connor took the stem from his mouth and looked squarely at the priest. "I had dinner with Jane."

Father Matt noticed that Connor's brogue was gone, an indication that the man was in control of himself once again. "That sounds like a good thing," he offered tentatively.

Connor took the pipe back into his mouth, puffed and spoke around it. "So you would think. And so it was, until Fiona showed up."

"Fiona?"

This time the lift of the shoulder came with a sigh. "My wife."

"Your *what?*"

Another sigh. "I don't suppose you'd have a wee dram to help me tell this tale, would you?"

Father Matt's eyes narrowed and hardened. "You've had more than enough."

"I suppose so." Eoin Connor offered no more explanation. The noise of the coffeemaker filled the silence until the last gasp of steam indicated the brewing was done. Father retreated to the kitchen and returned with two cups.

"Your *what?*" he repeated as he offered one to Connor.

"My wife."

Anger flared in Father Matt Gregory. "Your wife? Just what the h...just what were you thinking? Hasn't Jane been hurt enough? She's just over John, and she's fallen in love with you, and you have a wife?" He clenched and unclenched his free hand as he took a long drink of the hot coffee, hoping it would calm him.

"I was thinking I'd never see Fiona again. She lied to me to get me to marry her, then abandoned me nearly thirty years ago. Ran off with another man."

Father Gregory's anger abated as quickly as it rose, and he took his seat again, relief flooding over him. "Well then, that ought to be a simple matter. It's no marriage at all. Fraud in the inducement. If you can prove it."

"Not according to the marriage tribunal." Connor took a deep breath and hurried to finish his story before the priest's anger rose again. "I asked, almost as soon as Fiona left me. But Fiona lied, swear and be damned; she lied and I suppose other witnesses did, too. I don't know why, I don't know what, but the petition was denied. As far as Rome is concerned, I'm still married. Fiona, on the other hand, divorced me as soon as the ink was dry; it was her ticket out of Ireland, and she married the man she left me for. He apparently had no scruples about taking up with another man's wife."

Father Matt took in this news with some surprise. "But you've not remarried yourself?"

"Chaste as a monk. I hurt too much at first, and I was too selfish to deal with a wife later on. Not to mention the peril to my immortal soul." Eoin looked sheepish, and Father Matt was aware that he meant what he said. It surprised him. "Fiona went through five more marriages and God only knows how many more men. She just divorced her fifth husband. A count."

Pipe smoke swirled around Connor's head as he gathered both thought and temper before he went on. "Now, for some reason, she shows up out of the blue and wants to make it up to me. Claims she's seen the error of her ways and wants to make it all right by me, be the wife I've never had." Eoin's big hand clenched the coffee cup tightly, then set it carefully on the side table. "There's been enough hurled dishes tonight. Jane shied one of her good glasses at me when I went by to explain."

"Explain? Eoin, you've lost me."

Another sigh. "I took her out to dinner. When I was back in New York, I asked about the possibility of a rehearing. Seems I ought to be entitled to one. I took Jane out to tell her about that and come clean about my past when Fiona showed up at the table and announced to all the world that she's my wife."

Father Matt gave a low whistle. It wasn't hard to imagine the scene. Jane Wallace had a temper.

Eoin's face creased in pain, and he continued. "I tried to explain to her, but she'll have nothing to do with me. I'm married, and that's it as far as she is concerned." He reached in his breast pocket and retrieved a piece of lace, and unfolded it. Caught in the folds was a gold ring. He picked it up and examined it closely, his eyes sorrowful and distant. "My ma's ring and a bit of her lace. I was going to ask Jane to wait for me, until things could be straightened out. I never got the chance." He passed the ring over.

Father Matt felt it in his hand, slight and delicate. It was a plain gold ring, thin and worn, the ring of a poor woman married a long time. He turned it over a few times himself, then looked up.

"Eoin, I think your friend is right. It may take time, but I think..."

"Doesn't matter. She'll not have me, and I'll not have

Fiona." Eoin paused, sadness in his eyes and defeat in his shoulders. "I'm tired of spending my nights alone." He shook off the restraining arm, took a final puff from the pipe and handed it back to Father Matt. "I thank you for your kindness. I'm sorry I hit you. I'll fix the door."

Father Matt cast about for a decent reply and found none. He was saved the trouble of answering when the pounding on the downstairs door resumed. This time it was the voice of the town marshal, angry and demanding entry.

Father Matt pushed Connor aside with a warning look and took the stairs two at a time once more. The door creaked a bit as it opened, a tiny bit off-kilter from Connor's assault on it. The marshal regarded both the battered door and the weary priest with a sympathetic look.

CHAPTER FOUR

I was just rearranging the bookshelves in my office in alphabetical order — having tried size, color, and subject already — when my cell rang. I flipped open the leather case as I placed a volume by Eamon Duffy next to one by John Dietzen. I noticed as I slid my finger across the screen to accept the call that it was after three. I had tried sleeping after my disastrous dinner with Eoin but gave it up as a bad attempt.

I recognized the voice of Jasper Quick, my factotum at the center.

"Doc? Did I wake you up?"

I wished. I ran my hand over my forehead. "No, I'm up. I couldn't sleep."

"Hmm. Anything to do with that Connor fellow?" he asked suspiciously.

"As a matter of fact, yes." I sighed, hoping that my firm voice was enough to tell Quick that this was a subject well past the limits of our friendship. He'd nursed me through the loss of one love. I wasn't looking forward to his doing it again. "What's up? Lucy's on call, not me, and so is Sadie." Not for the first time, I recalled Sadie's showing up on my doorstep on a lark while visiting town two months before and my hiring her, thinking I might want to ease off and enjoy life a bit. *Silly me.*

"I know, Doc. But you might better come down to the Center. Cops are here. There's something you need to see." His voice was cautious but left no room for doubt that my presence was required. I told him I'd be there soon and heard his speaking into the distance to someone as I hung up.

By three in the morning, even Telluride's nightlife had wound down. I tightened my scarf against the wind that was beginning to pick up, and a few snowflakes stung my cheeks. I slipped on a patch of ice crossing the street and landed in a half-thawed puddle of mud at the corner of Pacific and Aspen. Swearing to no one in particular, I picked myself up, brushed the dirt from my coat, and hurried on toward the Center.

When I arrived, Quick was standing outside, bundled against the cold, talking to one of the town deputies. They fidgeted in a way that told me they'd been standing in the cold too long. As I hurried up, I saw what had prompted Quick to call me in the middle of the night. The two-plate glass doors of the front entry were a spider's web of cracks. I mentally assessed the damage as I approached. At least three hits; the lowest of the three was probably the last. Mindful that medical examiners are not always everyone's favorite public servant, I had made sure that all the glass in the building was sturdy, layered glass that would resist breaking outright in a situation like this. Whoever took after the doors certainly had a grudge against me — or the office.

I nodded and smiled curtly to Quick as I extended a gloved hand to the deputy and asked, "What happened?"

The deputy deferred to Quick.

"The alarm went off a little before two. I heard something over the noise, and I came downstairs." Quick, like the others who work in the Center, lives in an apartment on the top floor, housing in Telluride being too expensive for the likes of ordinary folks.

I scowled at him. "That was stupid," I said with no preamble. "The alarm's there to warn of trouble. It rings into the police. You should have sat tight."

Quick shrugged. He'd been an army medic before coming to work with me. I suspected that his tolerance for danger was higher than mine. "Probably so. Anyway, I got to the front just in time to see that Connor fellow hit the door with a baseball bat, right there." He indicated the lowest of the blows, the one I reckoned as last. "It was something fierce, because the bat snapped. He was hollering, loud, but I didn't understand him. He punched at the door with his hand once, and that must have hurt. He stumbled back, and I saw him tuck his hand under his arm, then he went off. Staggered. I think he was drunk."

The deputy interrupted. "I got here just a little after. Nobody around. John and I searched up and down the streets, but no luck." He shrugged in the direction of the wall, where a broken ball bat lay. It was a Louisville slugger. Eoin had nostalgic tastes. I wasn't sure you could even buy wooden bats anymore. I wondered where he got it. I suspected it was old; no other reason for a bat to break. I wondered why he had it. He didn't strike me as a baseball fan.

I sighed wearily, and the deputy continued. "I'd like to take a look at the surveillance tape, if you don't mind. Just to make sure."

I nodded. "Come on in." Quick held open the mangled door, and I showed the deputy the console behind the big desk in the office foyer. I paused for a moment, unsure how to bring up the pictures he wanted. The Center is my baby, all right, but I leave technical details like this to others. At present, all that was visible of the front of the building on the black-and-white, four-panel security screen was a blurry image of the broken door, just swinging closed on its pneumatic hinge.

Quick eased me aside and quickly accessed the video from the camera over the door. At precisely 1:56 by the tracker on the tape, Eoin Connor came into view, baseball bat in hand. He seemed to be yelling something, but the video was image-only. He shook his fist at the sky, stepped back from the door, and let fly with a blow so fierce that I could see it jar him as the bat connected with the sturdy glass, and cracks emanated from the center of impact. Another, then the third − I was right, the lowest was the last. Just as Quick said, the bat dangled broken, and Eoin took a last desperate swing at the door.

I saw something Quick didn't. When he pulled his right hand back, first grabbing it with his left, then tucking it under his arm for relief, I saw anguish, not just pain, in his bearing. He looked upward for a moment, then inside, and, presumably seeing Quick, hurried away.

I sat heavily into the receptionist's chair, head in my hands. "Not much doubt," I finally said. I looked up at Quick, whose glance told me he understood.

"Not that I doubted you." He shrugged.

I sighed and looked at the deputy. "What now?"

"Can you come down with Quick to make a statement?"

Before I could answer, my cell rang. I pulled it from my jeans. Caller ID told me it was Father Matt. He didn't even wait for me to say hello before he rushed to speak.

"They've arrested Eoin. I'm at the marshal's office. Seems he took a disliking to your office door." There was a pause; his voice was quiet and muffled as though he were trying to maintain privacy in a crowded place. "They're fingerprinting him now. Jane, can you help? He's in terrible shape. Showed up at my door drunk as can be. He almost broke it down, too." Another pause. "Please?" A further hesitation, then, "I have to go. The marshal wants to talk to me. Hurry, Jane; please, hurry."

I wanted to cry. Instead, I pinched the bridge of my nose and answered in as flat a voice as I could muster. "I'll be right there," I said, and gestured to the deputy. "Let's go," I added, as I slid the phone back in my pocket.

The wheels on the chair creaked as I slid it back to stand. "Can you make that door secure?" I asked Quick.

"No problem. I'll run a little duct tape over the breaks just so no damn fool gets cut on the glass and decides to sue you. I'll call about getting it fixed in the morning." He walked with the deputy and me to the door and held it open. It was snowing harder. I heard the click of the lock when Quick pulled the door and turned the key.

Father Matt was talking to the marshal in hurried, hushed tones when I walked in. They both turned when they heard the door open, Father Matt with an expectant look on his face, and the marshal just looking tired.

I gave them both a no-nonsense look and took the advantage my unannounced entry had given me.

"No charges, Grant. Let him go."

Weariness turned to incredulity. "Jane, we've got a witness. I know you and Connor are..."

"So what? I am not pressing charges. As far as I am concerned, he did nothing."

Grant Holmes raised his chin and narrowed his eyes. It wasn't like him to spoil for a fight, but I could give him one. "Sorry, Jane, the State is the victim here, not you. There's enough vandalism here I can't get a handle on. This I can. And just because this fellow is your..."

I cut him off. "He's my nothing, Grant, other than I asked him to test out our doors to be sure they are what they say they are. I've had a series of threats, the last one pretty serious. I needed to know my staff is safe. I asked him to check it out." It was a bald-faced lie, and I squared my shoulders, looking at him without blinking, keeping my hands still at my side in an effort to avoid my physical tells of fibbing.

"That wasn't his story."

Father Matt jumped in. "He didn't have a story, Jane. He just came along quietly. I told him not to say anything." Bless Father Matt; he'd been watching too much television, but his interruption worked.

Grant Holmes closed his eyes and shook his head, knowing that he'd been outmaneuvered. Then he opened them again and cocked his head to the side. "Fair enough, though I don't believe either of you for a moment. I've still got him for drunk and disorderly."

"No, you don't." It was Father Matt again.

"The hell, I don't. He's drunk. I had two calls from your neighbors complaining of the racket; it's how we knew where to find him." Grant rarely swore. His temper was wearing thin. Time to proceed with caution.

Father Matt drew himself up to his full six-six, looming over the marshal, which was impressive, despite the fact that he was clad in scroungy sweatpants, a tee shirt and a fleece jacket open, now against the warmth of the room. "Language, Marshal, please, language. He was trying to wake me up. I'm a sound sleeper."

"He's still drunk. Drunk and in public and disturbing the peace."

My turn, and I gauged my reply carefully. "No more drunk than the average resident on a Friday night, and you don't arrest them." It was a gamble but not much of one. Telluride sported its fair share of inebriates once the bars closed. We are blessed that almost all of them can walk home. I avoided Father Matt's eyes.

"Besides, we had a bit to drink together before you arrived, Marshal. If he's drunk, how do you know it isn't my own fault?" I noticed Father Matt carefully avoided an actual claim to have over-served Eoin. Lying is a sin. Carefully stating the facts isn't. Father Matt seemed to be pretty close to the line. Then again, he didn't actually say what he gave Eoin to drink.

Grant Holmes looked from me to Father Matt and back again. I struggled to keep my expression neutral, a habit perfected in years of trial work. Father Matt simply hid behind his bushy beard and looked down with placid eyes. Eventually, the marshal gave up, shaking his head.

"All right, Doc, I'll let him go for now. But it better not happen again. And I'm going to need this in writing from you. I can't be accused of favoritism, letting this go."

I suppressed the urge to sigh with relief. "I'll be happy to. Type something up, and I'll drop by tomorrow to take care of it."

Holmes nodded and called back to the booking room. "Turn the Irishman loose. No charges." Then, to me, "Be here at nine sharp, or I'll arrest him again, and you too for obstruction. And, you," he nodded at Father Matt, "as an accessory. You be here, too. I want your statement, signed, sealed, and delivered."

I wondered how much fine-tuning Father Matt would have to do with Holmes' verbiage for it to be able to pass moral muster, but no matter. That was his problem. I was prepared to lie outright. I skipped over the implications of that for the moment. I'd have to find another priest to hear that particular confession.

The green metal door that led to the booking room opened, and Eoin Connor walked through, his shoulders bent, shirt dirty and disheveled and looking suddenly old. He looked around the room, blinking a bit, and raised a bruised and swollen right hand to brush a bit of his unruly gray hair out of his eyes. He stopped, motionless, when he saw me.

Before he could say a word, I pushed my way past Father Matt and back into the cold night.

***

"What in the name of all that's right and holy were you thinking, Eoin?"

Eoin Connor passed a bruised and bloodied hand over his face and said nothing.

Father Matt pressed him as they walked through the

last of the night. He was tempted to lend him the mittens Pilar had knitted for him. Made of scraps of yarn, they were as colorful as Joseph's coat, but so warm that, once he tried them on, he promptly abandoned all other hand-wear in favor of them. He decided against it. Eoin would get them dirty, and besides, he deserved to suffer a little in penance. "Eoin, I asked you a question. What were you thinking?"

"Leave me alone, Father," Eoin growled. "I'm in no mood to talk about it. It's none of your affair. You can't help."

Father Matt stopped in his tracks. "None of my affair? After you almost break down my door and punch me out? None of my affair? Once again, Eoin — what were you thinking?"

The older man continued to plod along the street, head down, walking carefully, as though every motion hurt. Which, Father Matt reflected, it probably did. Either in his head or the rest of him. "You're getting a little long in the tooth to be brawling, Eoin."

"I've lost them both," Eoin said. He stopped, looked up at Father Matt, and said it again. "I've only ever loved two women in my life. An Italian took Fiona, and that damn morgue is taking Jane away."

Confused, Father Matt shook his head. "What are you talking about, Eoin?"

"That damn morgue. The one Jane Wallace won't leave, not now, not ever, to be with me. The one, that one or another, Fiona will end up in, not soon enough for me. And me alone, no wife, no woman. I hate that place."

"Well, that explains the baseball bat...I guess." Father

Matt was still trying to put the pieces together. Eoin didn't sound drunk anymore, but he still talked like a drunk.

Eoin straightened up and extended a hand to Father Matt, who hesitated, then removed his mitten before taking it. "I should know better than to fight against anything other than another man. Church, morgue, government, I.R.A. — it doesn't matter. They don't fight fair. They always win." He sighed and walked away without another word. Father Matt watched him until he turned the corner. There would be time to talk more tomorrow. The hurt was too great just now.

Father Matt looked up the street at the sound of a car door closing to see a taxi idling in front of St. Patrick's parish hall. As he approached, he saw a figure lean into the window and hand something to the driver. Money, Father Matt assumed. He noticed the cab was from Montrose. Expensive trip. He wondered which of the houses along the street was getting a visitor at such a late — or early — hour.

Probably a delayed flight, he thought. *Ah, well. If he's visiting here, he can afford the fare.* The driver's door swung open, and the cabbie went to the trunk to remove luggage. Matt counted by habit the three lilac bushes on the side of the road before he turned the corner for the back entrance of the rectory. He had reached the small courtyard that framed the side entrance when he heard a voice behind him.

"Father Gregory!"

Father Matt turned in astonishment. He would never forget that voice, the bane of his existence in seminary. Monsignor Charles Jamais.

A short, rotund man was hurrying toward him, slipping a bit on the icy walk. "My bags are back there. Please get them for me. There's a good man." Monsignor Jamais covered the distance between him and the now open-mouthed Father Matt in the course of those few words. He extended a hand, gloved in soft, black leather.

What in the world? thought Father Matt. It was a night of confusion, that was for sure. He extended his hand, still clad in Pilar's mitten. "Monsignor?" he asked cautiously. "What brings you here so late?"

The gloved hand waved dismissively. "Oh, the plane was late. Travel in America is so tedious these days. Did you know there isn't even a first-class cabin from Denver to here?"

"It is a small airport, Monsignor." Silently Matt added, *you pompous jerk.* Father Matt remembered all the arcane references Jamais had made to his time in Rome as a seminarian, then in training to be a canon lawyer. It was a severe and eternal disappointment to him that he had never been tapped for more permanent service there, or to the purple, either. Only to the honorific of monsignor. Matt remembered him as a bitter man who delighted in tormenting his students, narrow to the point of nitpicky, and never satisfied with anything or anyone. *Least of all yourself,* Matt thought, then sighed and smiled again, forcing himself to be pleasant. He hoped his hypocrisy didn't show. He was about to ask what brought Monsignor Jamais to Telluride when the man himself solved the mystery, albeit by creating a larger one.

"It was so good of you to offer me a place to live," the short man replied. "Bishop Herlihy" — Father Matt recognized the name of the new bishop of the diocese where the seminary was located and knew he was a good man — "offered me several options, but not one was remotely suitable. So tiresome to live with old, cranky priests, don't you think? And none of them with a life of the mind, just peasants, all of them. You always had a good mind. I hope you haven't let it languish in this God-forsaken part of the world."

Father Matt closed his mouth with determination and swallowed hard. *Some people think this is God's country,* he thought to himself with a bit of righteous anger and a larger measure of confusion. He had not asked this abrasive, arrogant excuse for a brother priest to come to Telluride, not unless he'd lost his mind, and he didn't think he had. Although at this particular moment, he wasn't sure. He considered for a moment what was going on but was brought out of his thoughts by that voice again.

Monsignor Jamais was standing by the door. "Don't forget my bags, Matthew. Please let me in and show me to my room. It's really rather cold out here, and I am tired. I should be up by nine, though. I like my eggs poached, if you please. And my bacon soft. Please tell your good housekeeper. I expect you'll already be at work by then. A pastor has a lot to do, I expect, even in a backwater like this."

I don't have a housekeeper, he thought, gritting his teeth with increasing annoyance in an attempt to refrain from saying what he was thinking, but he opened the battered door. He saw a passing look of disapproval in Jamais' face, but the man said nothing. He escorted Monsignor Jamais to the easy chair. "Wait here," he directed, as he disappeared into his room to make up the bed with new sheets. Hearing a lecture on his slovenly habits would have been too much to bear, and there'd already been one visit to the hoosegow this night. He didn't need to be the focus of another one for decking a monsignor, even for good reason. Besides, if he remembered correctly the lore from seminary, anyone who hit a priest would have a hand sticking out of the grave in eternal accusation. He was pretty sure at this moment that the tale had been invented to keep obnoxious professors out of the hospital.

When he returned, Monsignor Jamais handed Father Matt his overcoat, gloves, and black scarf. In the light of the ceiling fixture, his face was shadowed and fragile. He was thinner than he appeared on the sidewalk, having shed a jacket and sweater, as well as the coat. Matt struggled to balance them. *He's an old man!* Father Matt realized with a shock, then did the math and mentally shrugged his shoulder. In his early seventies, he supposed. Not that old these days, though he supposed the crabbed life of a seminary professor beset with students he didn't like and a steady diet of disappointment might make a man look older than his years. Even the blond hair he remembered was gone and had turned white in the thin fringe that remained.

"This will do nicely. Thank you, Matthew. You are very kind. I think I'll go to bed now. Goodnight."

"Goodnight, Monsignor." Father Matt eased the door closed behind him and headed for his overstuffed chair and his pipe. He needed to think a bit. The voice was familiar to him, and the figure, accounting for age, except...

Except the arrogant little man who had once drilled

canon law into Father Matt's thick and sometimes unwilling head was now diminished and afraid.   His words had been as confident as ever, but under the lights, the pale blue eyes were wide and confused, and that face, ever confident and demanding, seemed uncertain and timid. *Well,* thought Father Matt, as he drew on his pipe, *I suppose a call to Bishop Herlihy is in order in the morning.*

Matt finished the pipe and laid it in the stand before he searched out an afghan from the hall closet. He debated which was more comfortable, the couch or the chair. He sat down in the chair and stretched out his frame, long legs crossed, and settled himself into the soft curve of its side. It had been quite a day.   Disruptions usually came in threes and fives.   Josie, Eoin, Jamais, what next?   He shuddered to think. *How long it will take him to figure out that there's only one bedroom?* he wondered before he drifted off to sleep.

CHAPTER FIVE
January 10

I slept in after the evening's festivities and awoke with a headache. Pilar fed me in cautious silence, pressed a travel mug of coffee into my hand, and shoved me out the door. I suspected she had no desire to deal with me just yet. I walked the few blocks to the Center but hesitated before I pushed open the big, glass door. True to his word, Quick had duct-taped the broken window, but it was going to be several days before the special order glass would be here to repair it even with a rush on the order. Until then, it would be an unpleasant and unavoidable reminder that I was, once again, a woman bereft of male companionship. I had grown fond of Eoin and missed him already, even though I was furious at his deceit.

The office held no appeal this particular morning, but it was familiar and was the only place I had to go. Work has always been my best narcotic.

I stepped in to ask our new receptionist what was on tap. Tim pulled up the computer log and perused it for a long minute before he answered, a note of uncertainty in his voice. "Not too much, I think. No, wait, there's one body here, and it says 'sign out.' But there are three or four other names...I'm not clear..."

I moved behind the desk and nudged him out of the way. Aside from the fact that I can't make my glasses work while I'm looking at the computer from a distance and while standing, I despise it when people read over my shoulder. I will not do it to anyone else.

Tim stood aside as I sat down, aware of my idiosyncrasy. "You're right. This one body is in house, and it looks like a natural death. Dr. Jackson will take a look later this morning if she hasn't already. Two of the other names are reports in from the field. Look here." I indicated the final column in the spreadsheet. Tim leaned in between me and the screen to see what I was talking about. His position gave me a perfect view of the large, hollow plug in his left earlobe. It was so large that I could see part of the computer screen through it. One of these days the plastic surgeons were going to be making a mint fixing deformed earlobes. That and revising tattoos. Tim had one of those, too. I could see it crawling up his smooth, brown neck: a green and yellow snake, mouth open, red-forked tongue flicking out as if to catch the bottom of the earlobe that was now artificially close.

"Got it. Sorry, Dr. Wallace. I'm not sure why that gives me so much trouble."

Could it be because you are recovering from a brain injury, thanks to riding your Harley without a helmet? I thought. Tim was the latest in a series of receptionists for the Center. The back office staff has been stable since day one, but we seem to go through receptionists with some regularity. When I lost the last one, Father Matt convinced me to hire Tim. He isn't the quickest at picking up the job, but he is pleasant and he works on powder days. The accident ended his skiing, as well as much hope of gainful employment. We could manage. He needed a job, and I need someone reliable. Match made in heaven.

"You'll get the hang of it." I leaned forward again. The last name on the list caught my attention: a child. Deaths of children unsettle me, and here was a second one in two days. This one was from the Medical Center, as well. Skye Gleason, two years old. From the Medical Center, just like Josie. I abandoned my plans to take the day off and decided to head upstairs. As I straightened, I clapped Tim on the shoulder. "That last name, Tim? There's another body on the way. Let me know when it gets here. And ask Lucy to give you another lesson."

He was already writing himself a note. The trash basket would be filled with the tiny, crumpled pieces of paper by the end of the day. Tim lived and died by his notes, another side effect of the accident. "Sure thing."

I would have preferred a "yes, ma'am," but I've learned to take what I can get here in the casual mountain west. "Thanks, Tim. Take care."

He grinned. I saw him touch the mic of his headset as he relayed my request to Lucy.

I am a creature of habit. The first order of the day is to go over the cases waiting for me, the second is to review the reports from the previous day. In the past, that meant proofing my own work. These days, it meant keeping a weather eye on Sadie Jackson. My conversation with her yesterday surfaced in my mind, pushing out all thoughts of Skye Gleason. I flipped through the stack of papers, looking for toxicology. Nothing. I frowned and picked up the phone.

Quick answered on the first ring. "Yes, Boss?"

"Morning, Jaz. How's things?" Quick preferred being addressed by his nickname. I don't think I ever heard anyone actually call him Jasper, least of all, me.

"Busy. You got a case down here this morning. Little kid. Just got here. His sister is in the hospital sick, too, and they don't think she'll make it. Sounds like a poisoning."

No need to pull up that file, after all. Quick would have all the details when I got downstairs. Of all the cases I had to do, children bother me the most. So out of the expected way of things. "I'll be there in a bit." I paused a moment for decorum. "Tell me, did Sadie ever get blood and urine on that woman who was found dead the other day? Elsie Teague, I think." One of the side effects of having another medical examiner handling cases is that I was starting to lose track of names. I disliked that.

"I think so. Let me check." I heard the receiver hit the desk and bided my time, seeing in my mind's eye Quick rustling through the rack of tubes in the refrigerator. It wasn't long before he returned.

"Sure did."

"Send it for a screen, please," I requested. Another talk with Sadie. 'Get samples' meant run samples in my lab, especially when corners had already been cut.

"Slow down, Boss. She did. Well, she sent it for a basic screen. It came back negative except for nicotine. Don't you have the report?"

I leafed through the stack again and was about to vent when I noticed a sheet face down on the floor. I picked it up. Sure enough, Elsie Teague. A whopping level of the major metabolite of nicotine, but all things considered, not too high for a heavy smoker.

"Sorry. It slipped out of the folder. I've got it. I'll be down in a few." Tox report or no, something still bothered me. John used to call it my mesenteric baroreceptors, which was his overly arcane term for gut feelings. I shook it off and waded through the remaining reports, initialing each one as I went, before I headed down to the morgue.

Quick already had things laid out for me. As I dressed out, I called over to him, "What's the history?" Time to get to work.

***

Father Matt was awakened far too soon by a crash from the kitchen. He forced his sleep-clogged eyes open and tried to unfold himself from the embrace of the chair. He caught his pant leg on a protruding nail, heard the fabric rip, and felt a trickle of blood down his left leg.

"Matthew!" came an accusatory voice from the kitchen. "Where do you keep your tea?"

"I don't have any. Don't drink the stuff!" Matt Gregory shouted back and peered at his watch. Half past six on his supposed day off, his only day to sleep in. "I thought you were sleeping until nine," he added.

Monsignor Jamais was chirpy, which Father Matt found even more irritating. "Matthew, dear boy. It's almost nine. Your housekeeper being in absentia, I thought I'd make tea. You should look for someone more reliable, Matthew. This really is unacceptable." He rooted around a bit more in the cabinet. Then he added, "Where did you say the tea is?"

Father Matt stepped around a broken mug in the middle of the kitchen floor, the source of the crash. "I didn't. I don't have any." *Almost nine? In what world?* he thought, feeling the irritation rise. The cut on his leg was beginning to hurt.

He must have said it aloud, because Monsignor Jamais pulled out the gold pocket watch Father Matt remembered well. The monsignor would stand at the podium waiting for the precise hour for class to begin. When the hands of his watch reached the hour, he would snap it closed with great ceremony and walk to the classroom door to close and lock it. More than once, Matt, perpetually late, was treated to the door slammed in his face. Monsignor Jamais brooked no tardiness.

Father Matt looked at the watch. Past eight-thirty, creeping toward nine. *Eastern time,* Father Matt thought. He forgot to reset his watch.

"You really should have bought some tea when you knew I was coming, Matthew."

"I didn't know!" Father Matt exploded. He moved toward the coffeepot and felt a sharp pain in the sole of his foot. Great. Now he was bleeding there, too. He bent to pull a sliver of the cup out of his foot. Monsignor Jamais was oblivious.

"Of course not; who would have known the plane would be late? No matter, we'll get some today. I suppose I can make do with coffee. Do you have cream? I like mine light."

"Get out of my kitchen!" Father Matt's voice was nearly a shout again. Then, feeling a bit guilty, he added as nicely as he could, "Please." He ushered the priest out of the narrow galley and sat him down at the tiny dining table. "Just stay put," he warned as he walked on tiptoes to the bathroom to wipe the blood off his foot and leg. He only had one bandage; this he applied to his leg. The bleeding from his foot had almost stopped. He recovered slippers from his room, tucked some toilet paper in the bottom of the one — the better to absorb any residual blood — and set about cleaning up the broken mug.

All the while, Monsignor Jamais kept up a running chatter. Father Matt ignored the commentary on the monsignor's flight, the dreadful service at the Denver Airport, the food at Pan Quotidian, and assorted seminary gossip as he started the coffee and put in some bread to toast. He laid a few slices of cold meat and cheese on a plate, quartered an orange and halved a banana, and put them alongside. He put the plate in front of Monsignor Jamais, buttered the toast, opened a jar of raspberry jam, and poured two cups of coffee. One light.

"Thank you, Matthew. A light breakfast is always good, but really, you are too kind to your help. Your housekeeper should be here to cook for you."

"I don't have a housekeeper. A maid comes once a week, but I don't have a housekeeper. I can cook for myself," Father Matt growled, as he reached for the remaining slice of ham and a piece of Gouda. Monsignor had already helped himself to most of the food.

At least he is enjoying it, Matt thought, as he spread thick, red jam on his toast. Suddenly, Monsignor went pale and dropped his knife, swallowing quickly before he spoke.

"Matthew! I completely forgot. What time is Mass? I hope we haven't broken the fast," he said. "Matthew? When is Mass?" Monsignor Jamais repeated.

"Not until noon, Monsignor. You have plenty of time. It's not even seven yet. You forgot to set your watch for

Mountain Time."

The words went unacknowledged, even though the little man looked at his watch. "I still must hurry. I like to keep three hours, you know. Far more meaningful than the sixty minutes the bishops ask these days." He took the last slice of cheddar and then asked, "Perhaps a bit more ham?"

Leave it to you to be more Catholic than the Pope, thought Matt. Perhaps he hadn't heard him. Monsignor Jamais always had selective hearing, far more in love with his own words than anyone else's. Father Matt waited until he was hidden by the refrigerator door to roll his eyes and whisper a sincere imprecation under his breath. When he returned to the table with more meat and cheese — this time on two plates — he found Monsignor Jamais looking at his watch again.

"Nearly nine. When is Mass, Matthew? I must be sure not to break the fast."

Father Matt put the plate down with a jolt. What was going on? He looked at the watch on his own wrist. Nearly nine, indeed, back in Connecticut. Was it too early to put a call into the bishop?

***

"I can't tell you how relieved I am that he is with you." Bishop Herlihy's voice sounded just like he looked, round and outgoing. "He left without telling anyone where he was going. We knew his mind was slipping, but I had no idea it was this bad."

"It seems to come and go," Father Matt said. "At least, so far it has with me. Do you have any idea how he found me or why he got it into his mind that I offered him a place to live?"

"Actually, I do. He doesn't have much family but he does — did — have a nephew, Matthew, just like you. He was killed in a car accident a month or so ago. Anyway, just before his death, his nephew came to see me to talk about having the monsignor come to live with him or at least in a facility near him. I suspect he confused you with his nephew and decided to take you up on his kind offer. From what I can see from a picture I found on the Internet, you favor the other Matthew, though I doubt he was as tall as you are."

Father Matt wondered what picture the bishop had unearthed, but it confirmed his reputation as a shrewd, competent prelate on top of his diocese. "But how did he find me? Telluride is off the beaten path."

"You've seen his moments of lucidity. He's as sharp then as he ever was. He kept track of all his students, you know."

Probably to curry favor in case any of them rose to a bishopric or got a job in Rome, he thought to himself. "No, I didn't," was all he said.

The bishop chuckled. "It was a point of great pride to him, and he'd boast of it often. A big book, a page for each of them — of you. Several hundred by now. What diocese they serve, what parish. He spent hours updating it every June. We actually used it to supplement our own data base. Finding you was no problem. You were never really out of his sight."

"That's not a comforting thought," Father Matt replied.

"I understand. He's my man, Father Gregory. I'll send someone out to fetch him if you can keep him for a few more days. There is an excellent Alzheimer's facility not far from the chancery."

The bishop's words conjured up images of the nursing homes he had made calls in. Even in the best of them, patients could languish for lack of sufficient attention. In the worst, they were abused.

"Is that really necessary yet, Excellency? He doesn't seem that bad."

"Probably not, but we need to place him somewhere he can be cared for and where he will be safe. It is difficult to make changes with...people when they start to lose their memories. It's best to settle them in one place and let them live out their lives there, somewhere they know and are accustomed to. In due course."

"If you do that, he'll be dead in six months." Father Matt was astounded at himself, but he kept talking. "He needs people around him, people he knows, people who care about him. He needs his books and conversation. He needs other priests along. He won't have that there."

The bishop's voice turned cold. "It's the best I can do. He has no family willing to take him. You cannot fail to appreciate that, on his best day, he is difficult. And he cannot stay in the old rectory. The other priests cannot take it. It isn't fair to them. Tell me, Father," he said with a deliberate and vaguely threatening emphasis on the word, "what would you have me do?"

"Leave him with me. At least for now. Think of it as an extended vacation. Let me at least try to make it work."

"Why in the world would you want to do that? What makes you think you are qualified? I am responsible for his care."

Why, indeed? This was his chance to get rid of his querulous and demanding guest. Instead, Father Matt heard himself say, "You had him living in a rectory. He'll be in one here, too. It's a small town. He can't get too lost, and even if he does wander off, someone will bring him back home. Besides, he came here of his own free will. Can you really make him leave?" Not wanting to end on a challenge, he added hastily, "Besides, I have plenty of help, and it won't cost you anything." That last was a bit of a presumption, but one easily remedied. There was help to be had for the asking, and Jane would supply the cash-money.

There was a long silence as the bishop considered his options. "All right," he finally said. "You can give it a try. God bless you, Father. Good luck. Call me if you need me."

Dear God, what have I gotten myself into? He'd better give Jane a call. Now that he was the proud possessor of a slightly demented, former professor with a penchant for documentation and a taste for the finer things in life, she would know what to do. She always did.

CHAPTER SIX

By two o'clock Skye's sister, Summer, had joined him in the morgue. Both kids had presented with vomiting, seizures, and ultimately respiratory depression. The Medical Center had drawn toxicology, but it wasn't back. The autopsies were maddeningly unremarkable, consistent with the history of death by respiratory failure. Two beautiful, brown-haired, brown-eyed children, dead for no apparent reason. I agreed with the note that came attached to the medical records from the center. It sure read like a poisoning death to me.

I was mentally rehearsing the various agents that might cause that sort of clinical picture when Lucy called from the lab. The toxicology was done. Coniine.

Poisoning confirmed, but I was taken aback. These kids had apparently died from ingesting poison hemlock, something I might understand in midsummer, because it grew in the woods around Telluride and there were occasional cases around the country, mostly involving children or foragers who mistook it for its edible cousin, wild carrot. But in the dead of winter? Where had they gotten a hold of hemlock? And, as far as I could recall, there wasn't any commercial preparation containing coniine, so it had to be from the plant itself. My mind was a little fuzzy on the details of plant toxicology. Before I could ask Lucy about the results, she headed me off at the intellectual pass.

"Yes, I am sure. I ran it three times just to be certain. Can't believe it myself, but there it is. Coniine poisoning."

I turned the information over in my mind again. Poison. Two dead children. Most poisonings are accidental, but I was having a hard time figuring out how this one would be.

"No chance this is some related compound? Overlap on the H.P.L.C.?" I knew better. High pressure chromatography results are pretty darn accurate, and I hire my staff to be the best at what they do.

I heard a snort on the other end of the line. "No chance. Coniine it is."

"Any commercial applications? Anything they could get it from other than hemlock?"

"Not really. It used to be a treatment for strychnine poisoning, but that's about it. This is plant ingestion almost for sure."

"You aren't going to tell me it doesn't grow around here, are you?"

"No. It's all over, though there have been a lot of control efforts. Pretty hard to eliminate a roadside weed, though, and no way to control it in the back country. But whatever hemlock there is currently rests under a foot or so of snow." She paused. "These were little kids, but even so, relatively speaking, they had to ingest quite a bit of whatever it was to die from it."

I pondered that for a moment. There wasn't much in the stomachs when I had examined them, which was no surprise, given the vomiting. We'd need to talk to the parents about where the kids had been and what they had eaten. "Listen, call down to the clinic and see whether we can get the clothes those kids came in with. There might be something there that will give us a clue. Then get everyone into the office. We need to do a little investigating on this one. Meet you there in five."

"Sure thing."

I broke the connection only long enough to dial Tom Patterson. I knew his number by heart. I was hopeful that this would turn out to be just a tragic accident, but his men were the ones who fielded suspicious deaths, and I was going to need an investigator on this one.

***

Eoin Connor sighed and leaned back in his desk chair, regarding the computer screen with a scowl. His head still ached from the previous evening's drunken bout, and he was irritated at wasting half the day tagging along after Fiona, even though he had vowed to try to come to terms with her, given that Jane was no longer interested in him. He had forgotten how much time that woman could waste and how tiresome her chatter was. It all distracted him from his discipline of two thousand words a day.

His right hand was swollen and tender in the bargain. It made typing more difficult but it was good penance. Writing always ordered his life even amid pain, and there was no reason it shouldn't now.

He pushed at the tobacco in the bowl of his pipe with an ivory-handled tamper. The intricate entwined knot carved into the handle had been worn nearly smooth over the years. He scowled again at the text, highlighted a section, and dispatched it with a click of the mouse, lost forever in cyberspace. He read what remained, scowled once more, and deleted the entire section, reflecting that it was much more satisfying in the old days to yank the paper out of his Smith-Corona.   The high-pitched, mechanical protest of the platen as the offending page gave way was satisfying in a way that a single electronic blip was not. It used to stir his creative juices: that sound, an audible rending of writer's block. Or so he thought. Now he just grimaced and thought through the passage he was working on, rubbing his right hand. The cuts and bruises made it hard to type, even on a keyboard. He supposed he was glad he wasn't using a manual typewriter after all.

It might be the subject giving me trouble, he reflected. He was hip-deep in the research on the murder of John Wallace, Jane's late husband. With nothing else on his plate and the woman out of his reach, he had decided to forge ahead on the book, but it was hard going. He had long ago given up the idea that this would be an objective rendering, for he was too familiar with Jane. Now it was familiarity torn asunder. What had transpired at the Chop House managed to so upend his perspective that now he wasn't sure how even to start. Every time he began, a mental image of Jane Wallace after dinner floated between him and the screen, her eyes sad and anticipating yet another grief in what, when he looked at it with his writer's eye, was an unbearable sequence of disasters. And this time, *he* was responsible.

He sighed again and typed a few cautious words. He was glad to be interrupted, first by the vibrating of the cell in his pocket, then by the ringing of the old-fashioned — they called it retro, these days — black telephone on his desk. He always forwarded his cell number to his landline when he was in residence, preferring the heavy feel of the black resin hand-piece to the insignificance of his smartphone. It made him feel grounded and, besides, it fit his hand better. He picked it up, wincing a little as he closed his hand around it and spoke gruffly, annoyed at the artless start he had on his chapter.

"Connor here."

"Eoin! I didn't think I'd get you!" It was the cheerful voice of Ciaran Ryan, his mate from the old days, lately a well-placed monsignor in the Archdiocese of New York.

"Then why'd ye call, ye old bugger?" Connor was gladder still of the interruption. Ciaran was a good man and a good friend.

"That's a fine way to treat a man with grand news for the sorry likes of yourself." Ciaran's voice was light and teasing, just like the old days.

Connor puffed at his pipe, then laid it down and exhaled slowly. "I could use some good news. But if it has to do with the reconsideration for a decree of nullity, no need to bother. It seems the woman in question isn't interested."

There was a small silence on the other end of the phone as Msgr. Ryan digested the news. "I'm sorry to hear that, truly I am, Eoin. But I called, because it's the oddest thing. I can't find any record of your case ever coming before a tribunal. Anywhere. There's no record anywhere that you ever asked for a decree of nullity and certainly no record that one was ever denied."

This time the silence was on Eoin's end, and he kept it until he was able to answer slowly and in measured tones. "Tell me that again, Ciaran. Once more. Slowly." Ryan's words had washed over him like a cold wave and left him with an immediate, if unwelcome, sense of clarity.

"I know it makes no sense, but there isn't any record anywhere of a request for review of your marriage. I've checked. I called back home and had them check. I pulled in every favor I have, and no one, not here, not in Ireland – no one can find evidence that you ever even asked. Nothing." There was a pause, and Ryan continued. "That's good news for you. If you make a petition now, and you can provide evidence that she tricked you into marrying her, well, I can't promise, but I would hope the tribunal, any tribunal, would find the marriage invalid. Though it will take some time."

Eoin stared at the screen, unseeing, his mind back in Ireland, to the parish priest who had taken the papers from him that cold October day and who, nine months later, had come back to his mother with the news that his petition was denied. He was in Liverpool by that time, exiled, and received the news in a letter. He still had it, tucked into his old missal.

The priest was uncle to Fiona and to the mate of his he'd left with a broken jaw in a Derry back alley. The mate he'd fought against to save the skin of a poor young Protestant lad, the mate who, with his cousin, the then-decamped Fiona, had made sure all the world knew Eoin Connor was a turncoat. That priest, their uncle. Their favorite uncle.

"Eoin? Are you still there?" The voice on the phone was concerned.

"Yes...yes. Never submitted?"

"Never. Clean slate, Eoin. That's a good thing." Then,

a pause and a question. "How did you ever get the idea you'd been denied?"

Eoin considered telling him that he'd been deceived by the very man of the cloth he'd depended on to help him, but his swelling anger made it impossible to speak for a moment or two. All he could see in his mind's eye was the life that was stolen from him: wife, children, home, hearth, perhaps grandchildren by now, comfort, and meaning. Finally, he managed a brief recitation of facts. "Father Clancy. He told me. I never saw the papers. I just took him at his word. No reason not to."

He stood abruptly and strode across the rug, turning sharply as he reached the end of the telephone cord, pacing like a caged animal, too angry to think, and then sat heavily in the chair again for lack of an alternative. His right leg immediately took up jostling to dissipate the angry energy that surged through him once more. His hand rested lightly on his thigh, moving up and down in rhythm, a twinge of pain with every bounce.

Another small silence and then: "Mother of God. I am so sorry, Eoin. What a waste for you."

Eoin sat upright, his leg still, suddenly clearer of heart and mind than he had been since Fiona arrived. "No need, Ciaran. But thank you for calling." His voice was calm and hard and something in it frightened his friend.

"Eoin? Eoin! It's not something that can't be fixed. In fact, you're better off than you thought. Those days were clearer looking back than they were going forward. There has to be a reason. Perhaps Father Clancy confused you with someone else. Perhaps you just misunderstood him."

Indeed, it was a hard time, Eoin reflected. The I.R.A.

was bombing something every other day or so, and Fiona's cousin, the one he'd toppled, was a hard man, violently and bitterly opposed to the British. His uncle — the priest — was an old man, even then. Was he just as angry, wanting to punish Connor, or was he simply weak and tired and afraid of retaliation himself? It didn't matter, he decided. What was done was done.

But Connor did wonder, unkindly, if the poor man ever confessed his lie. If he'd ever done penance for ruining another man's life in the name of the Church, at a time when people in general — and he in particular — took what she said so very seriously. "I understand, Ciaran. Thank you for your help." He worked hard to keep his voice even and flat, giving no hint, he hoped, of the rage that threatened to break out of him. He wanted Ciaran off the phone, or he was likely to pull it right out of the wall. Tossing it through the plate-glass window of the study might provide satisfying relief.

"I can help you submit your petition now." Ciaran Ryan's voice was sympathetic.

Connor was suddenly still, examining the ceiling and thinking of two women. "I'll let you know, Ciaran," he finally said. "All the best."

"All the best. Take care." The voice was doubtful, but kind. The line went silent.

Eoin Connor re-cradled the receiver and sat looking at the screen, unseeing for a long time, wondering. Did Fiona know, too? Had she always? Surely she had. She was far too clever and far too manipulative to be innocent of this deceit.

He stood up abruptly, shoving the chair back from the

desk so hard that it toppled over. He headed for the spare room, the one where he stored boxes of research until he needed them, and the one in which his punching bag hung. He found it as he always did, silent and gray, ready this time to absorb his anger, pain or no pain, so that he might eventually sort this out. For now, the image of Jane Wallace vanished from his imagination, to be replaced by nothing at all except a memory of a long-ago murder in a Belfast flat that had killed more than an innocent young lad and left him broken in its aftermath.

CHAPTER SEVEN
January 11

It was difficult to retain any sense of normalcy between Eoin's bombshell and the poisoning deaths, so I did what I always do under such circumstances: I buried myself in my work. I spent the better part of the day going through reports and reviewing letters from lawyers wanting assistance from me or from the Center. I nearly always agreed to the ones asking for forensic help. I was far more particular about the requests to co-counsel. Too many of them were from plaintiffs wanting to follow in my footsteps and sue various medical corporations in the hope of getting a windfall settlement. I generally wrote a polite reply, declining on the basis of my calendar. What I really wanted to say was that that game wasn't worth the candle it took to light the field. It would have been the better part of valor for me to resign my position and move on than to challenge Hardy-Finch Labs in court. I would have been poorer but I'd still have a husband, who had been murdered as a result of the verdict and my vicious partners.

Considering the last few days, there was a surprising dearth of bodies at the moment, leaving Sadie Jackson at loose ends. She wandered up to my office, bored I supposed, and perhaps a little lonely. I know I was.

"Hi, Boss."

I laid down my work.

"I thought I'd take a late lunch. Want to come along?"

Letters could wait. One nice thing about my line of work is that nobody's going to die if I'm a day or two late in getting something done. I wasn't accomplishing much, anyway. "Sure. Where to?"

"How about Amanda's?" She named a new bistro in Mountain Village, which required a trip on the gondola over the top of the mountain. Why not?

The ski lines were long, but we were able to cut ahead as foot passengers. The ride up was bright and beautiful. Sadie commented about my decision to hire her. It was meant to be conversation, maybe even flattering. I didn't receive it that way. It felt like she was buttering me up, and I was suspicious.

"I really am glad that you are spontaneous. I love being here. I really didn't think you'd hire me when I barged into your office that day."

"It's nice to have some help." I refrained from telling her that spontaneity was not exactly my long suit. The silence broadened. I hadn't done much to get to know Sadie; perhaps that was the source of my unease. *No time like the present,* I thought. "Tell me about where you grew up, Sadie." Question number one in the Southern Belle handbook, guaranteed to prod even reluctant conversationalists into chatter. People usually like talking about themselves, and Sadie was no exception.

"Mom and dad were archaeologists. Technically, I suppose, I was raised in Illinois where they taught, but really I was raised at their digs: Morocco, Brazil, Indonesia, Africa. I suppose it's why I can't settle down."

"It must have been interesting. I've never travelled

outside the U.S. "

Sadie was astonished. "No way! Why not?"

"Medical school, kids, jobs, that sort of thing. It was too hard. John and I planned to travel when the kids were grown, but we never got the chance." I banished the incipient sadness. That was over and done with. "I have a passport, though, so I'm ready."

"I loved it. Traveling, I mean. Some of the places weren't so great, and I liked getting back home to the States every fall. Every couple of years, we'd move onto a different spot. Mom and Dad were never academically famous but they kept their jobs, and I guess that's all they wanted. That, and to dig up stuff. I guess that's why I became a forensic pathologist."

"Are your parents still alive?"

Sadie shook her head. "They died in a small plane crash on the way to their dig about a year ago."

"I'm sorry."

"It's okay. They didn't suffer." Her words were so matter-of-fact that they stunned me. "I think that's the worst. I hate to see people suffer. If I had realized that is what medicine was about, I would have stuck to archaeology."

I was taken aback. "What did you think medicine was?" What did she think forensic pathology was, for that matter? There was no lack of suffering in our work, even though it was vested in the survivors. Our patients were past pain by the time we got to them.

"A good way to make a living. I like science, and my advisors suggested I go into medicine. It was a perfect time for that. Women have an advantage these days. I just want to pay the bills and be free to do the stuff I like." Sadie's grin was genuine.

"It's certainly a different perspective than my medical cohorts and I shared," I said. "Most of us went into medicine with a high sense of purpose. Out to save the world and all that."

"Not me. I just want to earn a nice living and have enough free time to enjoy myself before I check out."

"Interesting," was all I could say.

Sadie shrugged. "What else is there?"

I debated keeping my mouth shut. This was supposed to be a light conversation on the way to lunch. No need to get all philosophical with someone who plainly did not care about very much at all. But somehow silence felt like ratification so I just said, "Lots, Sadie. There's lots more. I hope you find it."

So much for question one in the Southern Belle handbook. I'd skip over the others: who are your people, and where do you go to church? I was pretty sure the answers would unnerve me.

The noonday sun was bright, and Mountain Village was crowded.   Sadie looked around at the hotels and condos that ringed the stone plaza. "I love this place. Wish I could afford to stay up here."

I gave her a sideways glance. "These are pretty pricey. Digs at the Center not good enough for you?"

She flushed. "I didn't mean that. It's just that I've never lived in a really nice place..." Her voice tapered off, and the flush deepened. I chuckled. Whatever else, Sadie had the grace to be embarrassed at the implication that the apartments I provided as a perk of working for me were substandard. I let her off the hook.

"Those were meant to be utilitarian, not elegant. I know what you mean. There are some pretty snazzy condos up here. But I must say, I would be a little apprehensive. It's been a long time since I lived so close to other people. I prefer my solitude."

"Not me. A white noise machine and I'm fine. I love being in the thick of things." She paused a moment, glancing at a balcony overhead before continuing. "I bet with what those places cost, they're pretty soundproof. I might not need the noise machine."

"I would hope so." Grateful for a neutral topic that engaged Sadie, I waxed on about cliff dwelling, John's term for apartment or condos. "I can imagine how awful it would be to live next to someone who had one of those heavy bass stereos. You know, the kind that they have in cars. You can feel them before they pull up."

Sadie laughed. "Whumpata, whumpata. Yes, I know what you mean. Maybe I should have gone into E.N.T. work. I could make a fortune on hearing assessments and hearing aids for people who have made themselves deaf with their music. Course, I'd have to wait a while, till those folks hit their fifties."

"Not a bad thought. Did you know one of the local ranchers got so annoyed at a man who was following him, playing music like that, that he shot the stereo out of the car?"

"You're kidding!"

I grinned remembering it. "Front page news the next

day. There was road construction going on. Part of the road was blocked, and the rancher was first in line for when the lane opened up again. This guy pulled up behind the rancher with the music blaring so loudly you could hear it four cars away. The rancher asked him to turn it down, and when he didn't, the rancher went back to his truck, pulled out his rifle, and shot the stereo."

"Oh, man!" Sadie was laughing now. "I've wanted to do that myself. The noise actually makes me agitated. How funny! Did they arrest him?"

"It seems that everyone hated that music. The guy reported it to the police, but he didn't have a license number — imagine that! The road crew swore they didn't see a thing, and no one came forward when the sheriff put out the call."

"Frontier justice."

"It has its uses." We had reached Amanda's; the lines weren't too long. The menu was more for snow bunnies than serious skiers, so the lunch rush didn't affect them too much. I held the door for Sadie to enter. As I turned to go in myself, a familiar figure caught my eye: Fiona, in the company of a distinguished man, not her husband — not Eoin. They were walking slowly, heads bent, deep in conversation but stopped in the center of the plaza. They embraced briefly, the hug of friends parting ways. Even accounting for Fiona's dramatic streak, it was clear from her body language that she knew this man very well.

I let the door close behind me and followed the hostess as she seated us, trying to catch the thread of Sadie's chat as I did.

***

Eoin Connor fidgeted in his overstuffed chair in the lobby of the Peaks. Fiona was supposed to meet him at four on the dot, but Fiona was always, always late. He tried to take his mind off his rising temper by looking out the big plate-glass windows, onto the snow-covered golf course and the mountains beyond. He was about to get up to pour himself a cup of cocoa from the big brass urn on the side table when Fiona walked up.

He rose, and she gave him the briefest kiss on his cheek. "Sorry, my darling. My hairdresser took longer than I thought. Of course, I wouldn't have been there today if she'd done her job properly in the first place. I do so miss good salons." She turned from him to sit down but not before inspecting the nails on her left hand.

Eoin wasted no time. "What do you want, Fiona? Why are you here?"

Fiona pouted. Her eyes were downcast but conniving, as they looked up from beneath her lashes. "I want to make amends, Eoin. I want us to be together again. I've treated you badly. I want to make up for it."

Eoin considered a moment before answering. He remembered that look, that manipulative way of hers. It worked, many years ago. Not now, and especially not after direct, unvarnished Jane Wallace came into his life. "Pack it up, Fiona. I've no interest in taking up with you again. You aren't my wife, and you never were. We both know that."

"The Church says I am, Eoin. And you know that I am. I'm willing to try again, really I am. I want to make it all up to you. I want to be with you. With all my heart. I am sorry for all the years I wasted — all my fault. I know that."

So she did know, Eoin thought. "No," was all that he said, his voice carrying a finality that could not be missed.

He was unprepared for what followed. In the past, Fiona would attack or muster up tears. Now, she sat in silence for a moment, her eyes closed as though against a sight she could not bear, every muscle rigid. When opened again, it was as though she had endured some horrible but passing pain; her left hand shook in her lap. Her blue eyes seemed out of focus, and it was a long minute before she spoke. "I'm sorry, Eoin dear, what were you saying?"

He started to give a sharp answer, but something about her bearing made him stop. Something was wrong, and he said so.

"Nonsense." Fiona looked down at her nails again, as though to dismiss him. "I am quite well, just a bit distracted." Was it his imagination or did she slur the "s" in 'distracted' ever so slightly? Had she been drinking? "Please forgive me. What were you saying?"

Eoin Connor took her hands in his. "Fiona, don't lie. Not now. If you need something, just ask. I'm not coming back to you, but I won't abandon you, either, if you need me. We have too much between us for me to do that. Just tell me, straight out. What do you want?"

The change in her demeanor was startling, even though Eoin was used to her mercurial nature. Fiona jerked her hands away, raking his palm with the bright acrylic nails. He wasn't sure it was entirely by accident. Her voice was harsh.

"You *will* come back to me, Eoin Connor. I'm your wife, and you'll come back to me."

"Perhaps once I might have done that, Fiona," he replied, as quietly as he could and still be heard, conscious now that eyes were on them because of the strident tone of her voice. Fiona always slipped back into the sounds of Falls Road when she was angry and always would. Being refused apparently still made her angry. He wondered how her cultured husbands had felt about that. Perhaps she was better at controlling her temper and her accent in Italian and German. Perhaps they hadn't cared.

"You will. You can't have that dreadful woman, that...that..." She grew exasperated and seemed to struggle for words. "That Joan Wall...ace of yours. And she can't have you. You belong to *me*."

"Fiona, listen. I'm not yours. I never was, you saw to that. But if you need me, I'm here. Just not as your husband. Not now." Silently he added to himself, *Not ever*. He stood to leave. Looking down at her, he added, "I'm going home, Fiona, to sort this all out once and for all. And I will marry Jane. This time your lies can't stop me."

He was halfway across the lobby when he heard the screech behind him. "You will never have her, Eoin Connor. I'll see to that."

He turned to look back at her. She stood by her chair, gripping it tightly. This time he was sure she had slurred her words. "Call me when you sober up, Fiona. But ring me in Ireland. I'm leaving as soon as I can get myself packed."

CHAPTER EIGHT

I needed a good retreat; neither the house nor the office suited my mood. Lunch with Sadie was pleasant enough, but seeing Fiona soured my mood. A hot cup at the Steaming Bean, and I decided I was sufficiently civil to take my place outside on the bench with the large black W painted on the back and watch town go by as I ruminated. My mother would have said I was restless as a long-tailed cat in a room full of rocking chairs. I preferred to think of it as a frustrated physical need to focus on the various crises that were afflicting me: the fact that Eoin was married and not married at the same time, the poisonings I couldn't resolve, and my general restlessness. When the kids were little, I could always predict their growth spurts by the change in their sleeping patterns; they became restless and irritable. Presumably, I had a big growth spurt coming.

I was on my second cup when Father Matt plopped down beside me. Both of us on the Group W bench, resting place for misfits. It seemed appropriate. He handed me a paper bag.

"Got something for you."

I peeked in the bag. "This is Josie's, isn't it? Where did you get it?"

Father Matt took a gulp of his own coffee before he answered. "I went back to the clinic that same day. I meant to tell you about it, but...uh...things got in the way.

I thought maybe you could test it, maybe we could find out the truth." He looked deep into the coffee cup. "She was murdered, Jane, I know it."

I sighed. "Confession time, Father. I meant to call and get this myself. I forgot. I am sorry." That was happening too often these days, and it was not like me at all. Or at least not like what I imagined myself to be. "But this will never prove it."

"I thought you could test it."

I stared up at the clear blue sky for a moment before I replied. I extracted the IV bag. Sure enough, it was Josie's. Some fluid remained in the bag, and the butterfly needle was still attached. "There's no chain of custody. Even if we found something, it wouldn't be admissible. And it's not likely we'd find anything."

Father Matt collapsed against the back of the bench himself. "I didn't think of that. I was just so mad. So mad."

I sat back myself, leaned my head against the wood, and looked up at the sky again for a long minute before I answered. "I get it. I'm mad, too. Few things — at least in my line of work — are worse than knowing…" I paused a moment for the right words before repeating myself. "…knowing who committed a murder and not being able to prove it." I turned to face him and gave him a wry look. "And in this case, much as it's a worrisome set of events, we're not even sure there was a murder."

Father Matt kept his gaze fixed upward. "It was, Jane. I just know it." He stood up abruptly, looming over me. I stayed where I was. He was silent a minute or two, then continued. "It's not just Josie that worries me, Jane. It's

Proserpine. It's just Proserpine," he repeated.

I shrugged. "I get it. Let me see what I can do." I stood up myself. "I understand — at least a little — where they are coming from. It's hard to watch someone suffer." At least I had been spared that with John's death. Then again, I had also been spared the chance to say goodbye. "It's human nature to try to avoid those things that hurt. We all do it."

Father Matt looked at me, clearly unhappy with my reply. Then his face cleared. He seemed to have resolved something in his mind. "Good!" I could almost feel Father Matt relax; he had my answer, and we had a plan. Together we watched passersby for a few minutes, companionable in our silence.

Father Matt was the one to break it. "It isn't that I don't understand, Jane. I do. I understand what it's like to want to end suffering. I watched my kid brother die by inches with leukemia and my parents' marriage along with him. It was awful. I wanted it to end. It took so long."

"So what's your beef, then? Josie was terribly sick. Dying by inches. Half-inches. Millimeters, even." Four years is a long time to be terminal, and that's just about how long Josie had lived after her diagnosis.

He leaned forward, forearms on his legs. He cocked his head in a gesture of dismissal. "Most people would say because mercy killing ignores the dignity of the one we kill. I suppose it does, but only in our eyes. Human dignity is a precious thing, and the way we preserve it in ourselves is to see it and preserve it in others. Whoever killed that little girl killed something in himself — or herself — too." He turned again to look at me. "Jane, I don't know. Part of me knows the relief that death brought those parents. But a bigger part of me…I just have to know, and if I can, make it right." I recognized the conflict in his face. Head and heart opposed to each other. Heart wins every time. His heart told him to joust at windmills for Josie. Just like mine told me to joust at windmills for Eoin. Probably to the same effect. The difference was, of course, that Father Matt was actually jousting. I was sitting this one out.

The medical examiner's credo, I thought to myself. *Must know, must follow the facts wherever they go.* Except, of course, no matter how many facts we have, we never know it all, never know enough, never really know much of anything apart from a few hard facts. We just make things fit some pattern in our own minds and make the best of it. The last few weeks had proved to me that life — mine, anyway — was a journey in the dark. At least I was growing accustomed to it. I knew from experience that Father Matt's journey would end where all of mine had, the place where it was just beginning, on a bench, watching the world go by and wondering how to make sense of things that made no sense.

I wanted to tell him to give it up for a bad business. Instead, I gave him Lucy's direct line. "Tell her I told you to drop it by. Tell her to test the contents and the line segments separately." The latter was superfluous; Lucy knew exactly what to do.

***

The main dining room at the Peaks was crowded. Jacob Baladin, founder and moving force behind Proserpine, stood in the doorway for a long moment, scanning the crowd until the hostess approached to offer help. She took too long to turn away from her conversation with a server for Baladin's taste. He didn't wait for her to speak first.

"I am here to meet the countess," he said.

The hostess looked puzzled. Baladin sighed an exaggerated sigh. "She is a very beautiful woman. Auburn hair, blue eyes. Quite elegant."

The hostess gave him a dismissive look. "This way." She led him to a banquette table in the back corner. Fiona was already there, a glass of moscato in her hand, the rim stained by the red of her lipstick. She replaced it delicately on the table and extended her hand. Baladin, no fool, raised it to his lips.

"You are so kind to meet me," Fiona said.

"My pleasure, Countess." He turned to the server, ordered himself a glass of wine, and waved him off before turning his attention back to the woman in front of him. She had chosen the side that put her back to the wall; the better to survey the crowd, he supposed. It was his habit, too, but he was happy to give up the seat if it meant a chance at some European millions for Proserpine.

And himself, of course. The director of such a cutting edge and necessary non-profit needed to maintain a certain lifestyle to be able to entice rich benefactors. Just now, that was getting hard to do, with the expenses of the move to Telluride. Still, he thought, it was a good choice: a community as receptive to Proserpine as any in the country and one that saw a steady stream of rich and famous people, most of whom were more than happy to become part of a cause if it meant publicity.

Proserpine always got publicity. *Our specialty,* he

thought. "I am honored that you would consider us worthy of your interest, Countess," he said.

Fiona smiled a distant smile, one that made Baladin worry he had overplayed his hand. That was the trouble with these European aristocrats. Half of them were so infernally pompous, you practically had to drag your forelock to get anywhere with them. The other half forgot completely who they were and were bowling-alley chummy until you crossed some unseen line of affront and they cut you off. Surely he hadn't committed the unforgiveable social sin this soon. He waited, unsure whether to try to paper over a mistake he wasn't sure he made, or carry on. He decided silence was best.

He was rewarded after a moment or two of discomfort. "I am most interested in your work, Dr. Baladin. It must be a great thing to help in the elimination of human suffering."

He relaxed a bit and gave one of his stock answers. "Indeed it is. We have come so far in medicine, able to do so much. But too often the price of better care at the beginning is worse suffering at the end. Proserpine is at the forefront of moving us toward kinder, more compassionate end-of-life care." He leaned aside to let the server place his glass of wine on the table, sipped it, and nodded approval.

"I've read some of your materials. But, please. You tell me about the work you do." He watched her assume the posture of the entitled: head tilted, eyes engaging his but dropped just enough to indicate sincere appreciation, leaning enough forward to convey engagement without implying familiarity. He mentally sifted through his alternate presentations and settled on the one he thought would fit best.

"Proserpine really evolved out of a tragic case I was a part of years ago. A young woman was severely injured in a car accident, and despite everything, was comatose — vegetative, really — after all was said and done. For years, her husband held out hope against hope that somehow she might recover. She didn't, of course. He made the very painful decision to remove life support from her."

"He must have been considerably consoled by the presence of his new wife. As I recall, she was quite lovely." She took a languid sip from her glass.

Baladin looked startled in spite of himself. Surely she wasn't a plant from one of those reactionary religious groups. He considered for a moment. She was Catholic; with a name like Idoni, she could be no other. He remembered with a bit of relief that she had sported several husbands; probably she had no serious opposition to progressive ideas like his. Still, it would pay to be cautious.

He ducked his head just the least bit, deferential but not really obsequious. His time was valuable. If she wasn't going to help him out, he wanted to know as soon as possible, wind this up as charitably as he could, and get out. There was always other work to do. "We do not get to choose our clients, Countess. They choose us, because they are in distress and they need help. I don't condone what he did in remarrying so soon after her death, but I understand the pain of a man watching his wife slowly die. Worse yet, see her all but dead and kept alive by a hospital afraid of a lawsuit and parents who were estranged until she was injured and then couldn't let go of her out of guilt."

No response. Baladin squirmed a bit. He soldiered on. "At any rate, it made me realize how often this happens. Most cases just don't get noticed, and most people are bullied by a system that is weighted against the patient and in favor of the institution. We acknowledge that people should have control over their lives, that patients are at the center of it all and should have a say." He paused, assessing Fiona's reaction.

She shifted slightly and took another sip from her glass. "Tell me more." Another sip, and her eyes lifted to engage his.

It was enough. Baladin continued. "It's time to give people control over their deaths instead of paying homage to some archaic notion of the sanctity of life and the state's interest in its citizens. That is why Proserpine was founded. You know the legend?"

"Of course." Fiona's look was pitying and she continued, "Proserpine was the daughter of Ceres. She was abducted by Pluto to the underworld. When Jupiter sent Mercury to bring her home, he found she had eaten pomegranate seeds. Anyone who eats the food of the dead must remain with the dead. Proserpine was permitted to come back to earth for only six months, because she had eaten six seeds."

"Exactly. What most people don't understand is that according to one version of the myth, she ate the seeds of her own free will. She chose the life and death she wanted. What could be more important? It is Proserpine's mission to remove the barriers that the state and the churches have put in the way of people freely deciding how to live and how to die." He paused.

"You don't strike me as a man with particular interest in his fellow man," Fiona said.

Baladin took an instant to size her up and then took a gamble. "For the most part, I am not. I do believe in what Proserpine does, whether or not I do it out of altruism. It has provided me interesting work and a comfortable living."

Fiona looked at his well-cut clothes, the kind only custom tailoring produces. "So I see."

Baladin was long past being shamed for what he did. He reiterated. "It is an interesting and comfortable living. I intend to see that Proserpine's vision prevails. You see, when my time comes, I want to be in control, and I'll do everything I can to see that that happens." He was surprised at his own candor.

Fiona reached into her bag and took out a fountain pen and began to fill in a check with dramatic, purple stroke. "That is reassuring. I have always been willing to pay what it takes to keep those things that are precious to me. When the life I have is no longer precious to me, when it's no longer worth living, I will want a kind friend to help me. Or if not a kind one, one self-serving enough to know when my interests and his intersect."

She tore off the check and handed it to him. "Insurance," she said.

Baladin blanched at the figure; it was twice what he had hoped and four times what he expected.

He folded it and slid it into his wallet. "I'll see that a

counselor calls tomorrow. It's always best to plan ahead." He lifted his glass. "To your very good health."

Fiona returned the gesture. "Indeed."

CHAPTER NINE

I was sitting at the one-off corner table at the Chop House again, this time with Father Matt, but waiting for Eoin Connor. Father Matt was chewing on a breadstick; I was nursing a cup of Earl Grey. It had taken all of Father Matt's persuasive skills to get me here. As it was, I wasn't sure why I had said yes, except to shut him up. My stomach lurched at the thought of seeing Eoin again, especially here. I grabbed a miniscule sweet roll from the breadbasket and dipped it in my tea.

Father Matt looked at his watch for the fifth time since we had been seated. "He said he'd be here."

"If he said he would come, he will." I returned to my tea and sticky bun, and we fell back into silence. Father Matt was on his third breadstick when he suddenly stood up.

"Eoin!" Father Matt's voice was too loud and jovial. It made me suspicious, but Eoin was at the table before I had the chance to hiss a question at him.

Eoin said nothing as he pulled out the side chair and sat himself down, Father Matt to his right and I to his left. "Thank you, Jane, for meeting me." His voice was serious. He waved the waiter over and ordered his customary glass of whiskey. Early in the day for that. It worried me a bit. I wasn't exactly disappointed that he did not lean over to brush my cheek with a kiss, but I had to admit that I missed it.

We made small talk until the whiskey was delivered, along with a new pot of hot water for my tea and another basket of breads. As soon as the waiter was out of earshot, Eoin took a swig of the whiskey, placed his hands carefully on the smooth, white tablecloth, and announced, "I am heading to Ireland tomorrow. I'd like for you to come. It's important to me that you do."

Both men looked expectantly at me. When I refused to speak and instead reached for another sweet roll, Father Matt took up the cause with the obvious question. "Why?"

"I got a call from an old friend, Monsignor Ciaran Ryan — formerly of the Archdiocese of Armagh but currently in New York. It seems that not only did the Church never deny my petition for a decree of nullity, they never got it. I'm heading back to set that right. But I could use help. I'm not even sure who is still around after all these years, let alone who will talk to me. But I'm going to put this to rest, once and for all." He pulled a folded paper out of the inside pocket of his brown corduroy jacket. "I've already made the reservations."

"That was foolish," I said. "What makes you think I would want to go?"

"Because you love me, and you want to clear this up as much as I do."

"You are awfully sure of yourself." My words were sharp.

"Irish trait." So were his.

"Back the truck up a block or so," Father Matt said, looking from Eoin to me and back. "What do you mean, the petition was never filed?"

"There is no record of it. I suspect the priest threw it away and lied to me. He was Fiona's godfather," he said, in a tone that implied that explained everything.

In a way, I supposed it did. I didn't know much about Eoin's wife — ex-wife? I wondered for a moment how I should think about her, and settled on Fiona out of simplicity and a desire to spare my poor mind any more contortions.

Ignoring Father Matt, Eoin took my hands in his, first the one closest to him and gesturing with a wave of his fingers until I offered the other. He looked at them and then at me, raising them slowly and kissing them the same way he had once before. It still took my breath away, but even as it did I recalled the bat and the door. Correction, doors. I tugged on my hands to free them. He let them go, but continued to look at me. "Will you come, Jane Wallace? If you won't fight for me, will you help me fight for us?"

He didn't give me time to answer, and I wasn't entirely sure what the answer would be, anyway. This put everything in a new light. I let myself imagine for just an instant that Eoin might, after all, be free to marry me and just as quickly pushed the thought aside. I was not ready for another disappointment. Losing a man once was bad enough. I wasn't sure I wanted to risk it a second time.

"This is ridiculous." I found my voice. "Absurd. I can't just go to Ireland at the drop of a hat. And you shouldn't assume I can."

"Why not? You hired Sadie to cover for you. So you could have more free time."

"Not that it is any of your business, but yes, I did. I've

been thinking about it for a while. With a grandchild on the way, I want more time to be able to travel."

Father Matt gave an ungentlemanly snort, and I shot him a look that bought his silence. He ducked his head, suddenly interested in his napkin.

"Perfect. You can start with Ireland." Eoin paused for a moment, worried. "You do have a passport, don't you?" He hesitated for a fraction of a second too long.

There it was, my perfect excuse: deny I have a passport. Except, of course, that it would require a lie, and Father Matt wasn't above calling me on it. "Of course." I'd gotten it a few weeks before John was killed. His murder made the trip to Italy we had planned an impossibility. The pristine blue booklet had lain unused in my desk drawer ever since.

"Then it's settled. You will come, Jane." His words were confident, but there was pleading in them all the same.

I was silent for a long moment, weighing the situation. "No, Eoin, I can't," I finally answered. "This is something I can't help you with."

An equal silence on his side. "It isn't? It's not something I can ask the woman I love to help me with?"

How to explain? I desperately wanted Eoin to be free to marry, but I just as desperately wanted to avoid the pain of trying to work it out and being hurt again. Wounded solitude had been my retreat after John died, and it was familiar even if it wasn't my preference anymore. Risking disappointment in the pursuit of happiness was just not something I was able to do. I was being a coward and I knew it.

"I'll leave you to dinner," I said as I stood up. "Safe journey, Eoin, and safe home again, here, to Telluride." *To me*, I added in the silence of my heart. "I wish you the best of luck, really and truly I do. But I'm not coming along. I can't. I just can't."

***

The concierge of the Malmaison in Belfast picked up his extension on the first ring. A familiar, imperious voice greeted him.

"Good morning, Charles. Can you have my usual suite available in two days? I am coming back to Belfast for a while."

"Of course, Madam."

"Excellent. I shall require some arrangements. Several important appointments that must be made."

"Of course, Madam." Charles Bowman picked up his pen, found a fresh pad of paper, and signaled his readiness to serve. "Yes, Madam?"

Ten minutes later, he had filled two pages. He sighed. The countess always tipped well, but she made him work for every penny. Might as well start on the list. He ran a manicured finger down the paper. The usual flowers, bell of Ireland and Calla lilies, red and dark purple, pricey but available; wine, Italian; Stilton cheese, prosciutto, biscotti fig jam and walnuts; and chocolate for the suite. The food was on hand, not a problem. The wine he could order, and it would be here in the morning.

Two prescriptions to be collected from the local Boots. He recognized the one name as that of a sleeping pill she customarily used, the other was unfamiliar. A fax was to follow with the necessary forms for filling a foreign prescription in the U.K. He'd drop them by later in the day and call to make sure they were both in before sending Paul around. Her usual order to feed her nicotine habit. The shop was just around the corner from Boots; Paul could pick up both packages on the same run.

Reservations at her two favorite restaurants — easy enough — dinner for two each time. Tickets to the new show at the Lyric — harder, but still possible. Her usual list of demands.

But the last few requests were strange. A car to take her to some godforsaken town to the north, one of those tourist places on the sea. An appointment with a specialist he did not recognize at the Independent Clinic of Belfast, a pricey place that catered to the rich and famous. She always stayed there as she recovered from her various nips and tucks. It was a bit soon after the last one, but it was his experience that the time between procedures got shorter and shorter as the patients got older. And an additional room on the countess' tab. He'd never known her to foot the bill for anyone else's room or even her own if she could get someone else to pay for it. She specified that it was to be the adjacent suite.

Must be an important visitor, he concluded.

CHAPTER TEN

After my abortive lunch and the little ambush Eoin and Father Matt engineered, I took the long way back to the Center, window-shopping along the way. In one of them, a shop that specialized in custom hats and boots, a poster with a pomegranate logo caught my eye. Proserpine was having an open house this very evening. I decided to take advantage of that to do a little reconnaissance. I walked the last few blocks to the Center with a lighter step and a clearer mind.

I made short work of the pile on my desk, dashed off a few letters to consultants in response to inquiries, and even made some headway on organizing my office. It was nearly sunset when I left, the alpenglow rosy on the peaks. Just a few minutes after the Proserpine open house was due to begin. I was still reeling from the recent referendum that legalized physician-assisted suicide in Colorado. That promised to make my life a whole lot harder. This was as good a time as any to beard the lion in his den, and besides, I had some concerns about my cases and my staff that Proserpine might just have a part in.

It wasn't hard to find their office. It occupied the entire first and second floors of a three-story brick building around the corner from an eclectic store that offered everything from furniture to beading supplies. Even if I hadn't known where the office was, the steady stream of people converging on a building that had once served as headquarters to some of the town's lawyers, less than a block from the main street of town, covered by late afternoon shadows and nestled among drifted hedges, would have tipped me off. The building had been recently and expensively renovated. Its former mud-brown exterior was now pale and tasteful, the result of an army of workmen who cleaned the façade, one brick at a time, with plumber's torches and scrapers. The windowsills and shutters were painted gold. The same gilt paint covered the pomegranate on the sign, the calligraphic P of the name tucked into the right edge of the fruit. The letters of the name were stark black.

How apt! Green to black, life to death. It amazes me how, with enough money, you can find someone to shill for anything. What kind of advertiser — marketing maven? — got his jollies and his bread and cheese from making killing look attractive to already sick, frightened, often lonely folks?

The day had turned warm for winter, almost forty degrees, and the air was still, which permitted the use of the small back porch to enlarge the area for guests. People milled about, drinks in their hands, chatting amiably, wait staff in heavy gold and maroon sweaters bearing the logo I had seen on the sign circulating among them with drinks and hors d'oeuvres. Paper lanterns decorated the porch and provided light, no doubt from LED bulbs rather than the traditional tea candles.

I scanned the crowd for familiar faces and found one right away. A man who towers over the great percentage of the human population can only go unremarked in a crowd for so long, shorter still when he arrives on the scene wearing a black cassock. I caught his eye just as the chatter went quiet. Most faces reflected only curiosity of one degree or another, but a few were hostile. Father Matt gave a polite "thank you" to the young man with a shaved head and tattooed neck as he accepted a champagne flute and made his way to me, his face as impassive as he could make it. The beard helped.

On the porch was a gray-haired man, movie-star-handsome, holding court. He looked familiar, but I could not quite place him. "Jacob Baladin," Father Matt whispered to me when he arrived, seeing the furrow of my brow. He scanned the crowd. "Mara, his wife, is nowhere to be seen."

We were on the other side from where the man stood, perhaps ten feet away. Jacob Baladin wore a maroon down jacket; on the narrow collar was a small, gold pin, the Proserpine pomegranate. A formerly obscure philosophy professor from a backwater college, he found a better and more lucrative market for his ideas when he turned them in the service of what he called "patient advocacy." Judging by the cut of the coat and the fact that he could afford real estate in downtown Telluride, I judged he'd done rather well for himself. The third floor of the building was his private apartment. I strained a bit to listen over the hiss of the heater, by which Father Matt and I stood uncomfortably close.

"That's a very interesting question, Yvette. Very astute." Baladin's voice carried over the crowd now that they were paying rapt attention to him. I noticed that a disproportionate percentage of the crowd was made up of young women, not a demographic I would ordinarily have associated with concern for the dying. Still, there were more than a few gray-heads in the crowd, too: women with hair chopped short or long and twisted into elegant braids or buns. But still, many more women than men were crowded onto the porch. That, at least, was familiar; when it came to affairs of the heart — and dying was certainly that — women were more passionate than men, and the women were far more likely to be interested.

"No, I don't think that a baby born without a brain is human in any real sense of the word," Baladin continued. "It's our personhood that makes us human, the ability to act and interact and reason. Without that, you cannot be a human, really. And human care belongs properly only to humans. Humans only owe responsibility to other humans. When we lose those things that make us human, we have already died, even if our hearts keep beating."

I saw Father Matt smile a wry smile at that one, and I followed suit. Baladin should learn his audience better. He was among folks who were inclined to feel that humans owed Mother Earth and dumb animals more in the way of relationship than they do each other. But he was selling his snake oil in a smooth, well-trained, salesman's voice. I still couldn't place where I had seen him, and it bothered me. Perhaps I just recognized him from his face, smiling out of those posters all over town.

"But cases like that don't really pose much of a problem for society. Few of these babies are born, and they die on their own very quickly if you just leave them alone, though it probably would be a kindness to end the parent's misery, if not the child's. The greater problem is the drain on scarce and precious medical resources that babies born with other defects — ones that aren't fatal — pose to society. Or those people who are old and tired and whose life is a burden and who can contribute nothing to society. You see, medical care isn't an endless right. We can't compromise the care of the vast number of relatively healthy people by squandering resources on a small number of people whose lives will be miserable, whose care is expensive, and whose humanity is doubtful. With a medical care system that would try to resuscitate a telephone pole if doctors got paid for trying, providing compassionate end-of-life care and counseling people that they can take charge of — plan and control — their own deaths is one of the great remaining social missions of our day."

Father Matt straightened himself in sheer astonishment at what he heard, forgetting his proximity to the heater, knocking his head and singeing a few hairs in the process. The pain and the smell brought him to an abrupt halt, but before Jacob Baladin had a chance to respond, I heard an oddly familiar voice break in.

Rubbing his head, Father Matt whispered to me, "That's Monsignor Jamais! What is he doing here?" I saw a rotund little man emerge from the crowd to stand very nearly toe to toe with Baladin. The little man looked rather like Hollywood's version of a mobster in his long, black overcoat, black scarf and fedora, even a red flower in his lapel, if Hollywood mobsters stood only a bit over five-and-a-half feet tall.

"Who?"

"An old professor from seminary. He showed up on my doorstep unannounced and...well, he's staying with me now. For a while." He paused, then whispered again, "Where'd that rose come from? There were no flowers in the rectory. At least, not when I left."

I raised an eyebrow. The rectory was small, and I had

trouble imagining Father Matt sharing it. I was pondering that when the diminutive professor got my attention again.

"Really, Dr. Baladin, if you wish to produce a sound argument, it's best to begin from sound principles. Aside from the breathtaking ignorance of even the most basic forms of moral philosophy and no knowledge whatsoever of theology, you make the assumption that medical care is scarce and thereby must be expensive and rationed according to merit rather than need. Your premise needs examination, dear sir, in a country that spends as much on sodas and useless vitamins and supplements every year as it does on cancer care. Not to mention movies, cable television, and pornography. Health care is expensive, because we have made it so. We can remake it so it is not."

He paused for a breath. Father Matt leaned over with a grin. "That's his full professorial mode in action. Hear that supercilious tone of voice and see those eyebrows arched behind those glasses? There'll be no stopping him now." Father Matt was clearly enjoying the spectacle. I wasn't so sure I was.

Baladin squared up and opened his mouth, but he delayed too long. Jamais' resumption of his thought caused Baladin to shut his mouth and listen. I thought professors only had that effect on people within their sway and under their thumbs. This little man was impressive. Apparently his skill was greater than that. Ordinary mortals seemed to be susceptible, too.

I was impressed, too, at the cogency of his thought. As if in confirmation, Father Matt leaned over to whisper a running commentary. He was clearly enjoying this. "God bless him, moral theology is his bread and meat, and rhetoric the sauce he dressed them with. Monsignor might not remember what he had for breakfast, but he can still slice an opponent to ribbons. Watch."

I did, and Father Matt was right.

"As for your assessment of what is human, it is so woefully lacking in substance as to be not worth responding to. But I will pose you the question: how can that child be anything but human?" Jamais paused, providing the opening the gray-haired man wanted. Part of me wanted to warn him that this was not a good time to take Monsignor's rhetorical bait; the rest of me wanted to watch. The rest of me won.

"It cannot be human, because it does not do what humans do: think, relate, experience. Anything," Baladin emphasized the second syllable, "that cannot do those things cannot be human." A small wave of approval rippled through the crowd.

"Really, Doctor, you do yourself an injustice if that is the best argument you can muster. I can think now; tomorrow I may not be able to. Does that make me less than human? Can it change me from something I was into some other kind of creature entirely? Nonsense. A tree cannot become not a tree, and an oak always looks like an acorn at the beginning. Whatever we are we have always been and will always be; we can be nothing else. And that child you describe — the one without a brain — I believe the proper term is anencephalic — he may not think and experience as you and I do, but that is of no consequence. We are more than the sum of our thoughts, Descartes notwithstanding."

Monsignor paused for a moment, looking lost in

thought for just an instant. I felt, rather than saw, the fear in him as his hold of the thought he must have wanted slipped for an instant, and then the relief when he grasped it firmly again and went on, no one the wiser. "I should think the resolution to the question of what is human is rather easy to resolve. If anything," Jamais, too, emphasized the second syllable, "comes forth from human sex, it is human, whether or not you are intelligent enough to recognize that fact. And if human, then a person." He spoke the word particularly clearly and with great relish. "That person deserves our care and respect until his last natural breath. He certainly does not need us to dispatch his soul into the next life on our whim because he is inconvenient to us." Monsignor Jamais took off his glasses and rubbed them against his jacket in a gesture even I recognized as closing the argument.

The crowd erupted then, conversations going back and forth among the attendees who were now hotly debating this or the other point made in that brief verbal jousting match. Several young women, clad in bright, puffy, down jackets, were engaging Baladin; their attention made him turn away from Monsignor Jamais, though he cast one last, poisonous look in his direction before nodding forcefully in the direction of the door.

A burly man made his way toward Monsignor Jamais with a determined look in his eyes. Jamais was sparring with a thin, young man sporting a neatly trimmed black goatee. From the looks of it, Jamais was getting the better of him, too. The man's gestures broadened, and his voice rose with each sentence. Father Matt saw it, too, and grinned in spite of himself.

"'Lower the volume, polish the argument,' that's what

Monsignor always taught," he said to me. "This is quite a display of lucidity in a man who only yesterday couldn't remember that he'd had breakfast, let alone what he ate."

"And if looks do not deceive, he is having a roaring good time at it, too," I observed.

"I suppose it's because this is in his very bones," Father Matt said. "It's like the old immigrant who loses his command of his second language, but never his native tongue. Arguing — that's Monsignor's first language."

The big man, clearly a bouncer of sorts, took Jamais by the elbow. "Come on, old man. You've worn out your welcome here. This is a private party." His words boomed.

Matt started to surge forward to protect him but paused when he saw Jamais shake off the hand and wave it away almost airily. "This is no such thing, young man; it's an open house advertised to the public, though I do admit I am not particularly welcome here. No need to stay." He started through the crowd, which parted for him out of relief, respect, or both. As he passed a waiter, he grabbed a glass of champagne.

"Come along, Matthew," he said as he pressed past us. "These people weary me. So incredibly dull and shallow, and besides, I am rather hungry. After all, I haven't eaten at all today. Really, Matthew, I know that you are young enough to manage on one meal a day, but those of us of more mature years need to eat regularly. Please do try to do better." At this, he snagged a pig-in-a-blanket from another waiter and stuffed it in his mouth. He paused, saw me, and gulped. "And who is this?"

"A friend. Jane Wallace. Doctor Wallace. Actually doctor and lawyer Jane Wallace." Matt knew how much I disliked titles outside the office. I suspected he was using them to gain some cachet with Monsignor Jamais.

"Delighted to meet you, Doctor Wallace."

I extended a hand, which he bent over rather than shook. "It is my pleasure, Monsignor."

Father Matt sighed and cast an exasperated look in my direction. "Let's go for some dinner," he said. "There's nothing at the house. How about Mexican? Join us, Jane?"

"I really can't," I said, a statement which earned me a poisonous look from Father Matt. I'd hear about my treason later.

I watched them disappear and followed behind. I had found out all that I needed to know. And I remembered where I had seen Baladin before. In the plaza at Mountain Village when Sadie and I went to lunch.

***

Hearing no disapproval of his suggestion, probably because the monsignor had grabbed another hors d'oeuvre and his mouth was full, Father Matt shepherded Monsignor Jamais out of the house and down the street to Tres Amigos and settled him into a booth. They ordered food and beer and staved off hunger with chips and salsa until it arrived. Father Matt never ceased to be astonished at how much Monsignor could eat.

The server, a pert, dark-haired girl, was particularly attentive. "You remind me of my grandfather," she said to the monsignor, and she doted on him through the meal, even bringing him a plate of churros with chocolate sauce on the house. It was nearly eight when they finished and headed back to the church.

"Let me lock up downstairs, Monsignor. You go on up to the apartment; I'll be there in a minute." Matt was glad that he'd put lights on timers months ago. He hated to come home to a dark apartment. For Monsignor, still unfamiliar with the apartment, it would have been dangerous.

Father Matt entered the church by the back entrance, walking down the hall past the offices and coming in by the altar. He always left dim lights on; the church had a tendency to be dark even in daylight, and he liked to leave it open in the early hours of evening, though few people stopped in to pray.

He paused to genuflect before the tabernacle and to let his eyes adjust to the dimness, and to examine his conscience and offer a prayer or two for the day. He made the Sign of the Cross, genuflected again, and started toward the main door. A movement in the shadows by the door made him stop in his tracks. A woman was by the votive rack, lighting a candle. He debated saying something and decided against it, slipping aside and sitting quietly in a pew in to watch. Luckily, it wasn't one of the creaky ones.

She made the Sign of the Cross and stood motionless for a moment. Then she blessed herself again, stuffed a bill into the offering slot, and opened the door to leave.

In the light of the streetlamp, Father Matt saw her face. What was Fiona doing here so late at night?

He waited until she left. There was one candle left unlit in the votive rack. He lit it and prayed as he always did, for the intentions of those who had prayed there during the day. He mentioned Fiona by name.

CHAPTER ELEVEN
January 12

I smiled at the pristine, unbroken doors that now greeted me as I walked into the Center. Eoin had left for Ireland, and the doors had been replaced on the same day. I wondered whether that was an omen portending a clear path for me ahead. I sure hoped so. My heart ached a bit knowing that Eoin was gone, but in a strange way it was also lighter. I was so weary of crises in my life. Having some of them fly out of the country was a relief, whether I wanted it or not.

Tim greeted me with his usual smile and handed me a sheaf of papers, including a clipping from the local news. The funeral of the two children was featured, photos of the mourners included. It reminded me I had made no progress at all in figuring out how they died. I shook my head. "So sad."

Tim agreed. "Worse because grandma died the day before. That family has a lot to bear."

Some sixth sense made me ask about Granny. A cluster of two deaths was pretty bad; a cluster of three in one family within a few days pretty much unthinkable. Either these folks had the luck of Job, or there was something going on.

"Yeah," Tim said. "She was that old woman they found dead at home. Elva...Ellery..." He struggled with the name.

"Elsie. Elsie Teague." Sadie's sign-out case. I skimmed the article, but there was no mention of Elsie. "How do you know that?"

"I went to the funeral."

I hoped my face didn't reveal my shock, but either it or my stunned silence prompted Tim to elaborate. "Two little kids. I'd want people there if my kids died. Just to show they were sorry, too. The dad talked about it in his..." he searched for the word.

"Eulogy," I supplied.

"Eulogy. Anyway, he said that the grandmother died a day or two before and now this. He was pretty torn up. It was his mother."

"I'm sure he was. I would be." I considered this information for a moment, thanked Tim, and headed up to Lucy Cho's office. Then I thought the better of it and went the other way to Sadie's office digs.

I knocked on the doorframe to signal my presence. Sadie turned around, and I negotiated my way into the office past the same pile of papers, not noticeably more orderly than before except for the fact that the envelope from Proserpine wasn't on top anymore. I made a mental note to follow up on that before the end of the day. "Sadie, I just got some very interesting news. You remember that woman you signed out, Elsie Teague?"

"The F.D...the one they found at home? Tox negative?"

"That one. Turns out she was related to those two kids." I waited to see if Sadie would make the connection.

Like a shot. "Oh, man! I wonder if she died of the same thing."

"Give the lady a cigar," I said. "You only ran a drugs-of-abuse screen, right?" That particular screen was narrow and specific and would not have picked up that poison.

"Right. I thought that would be enough," she added a bit defensively.

"It was a good choice at the time, but not now. More information. How about seeing whether there's a little coniine mixed in there?"

"On it!" Sadie turned back to her computer to sign out, and I threaded my way back out of the room, heading for my office.

My desk held my own version of Sadie's pile. On the top of it was a tattered, gray file with one of Tim's stickies on the front. John Potter was up for parole again. I'd deal with that later.

My fingers threaded through the pile until I found the green folder — green was this year's color — that held the information on Skye and Summer Gleason and called down to Tim to bring me the file on Elsie Teague. I glanced at the contents, ran my hand over my face in frustration, and went for a cup of coffee. The pot was empty, so I used the few minutes it took to brew a new one to look out the big glass windows at the slopes beyond. I envied the skiers who were coming down Telluride Trail. Ski lessons really ought to be on my list of things to do, but who has time?

Thirty minutes and two cups of caffeine later, I had a list of things I knew, one of which was that Elsie Teague had died of coniine poisoning, too. Lucy was quick, and this time she knew exactly what to test for.

Apart from that, the list was pretty short. The

investigative reports were complete but brief. The children had been healthy apart from a bad head cold over the past few days. Mom and Dad left them with a sitter and went to a movie. The sitter did not have much to add. She fed them, put them to bed, and didn't think much about it until they both started vomiting and wouldn't stop. Then the younger one started having seizures, and she called 911. The medical records were unrevealing, apart from Lucy's tox. We'd gotten the clothes they had been wearing, and the vomitus contained coniine, no surprise. The police report indicated they had eaten canned beef stew for dinner. Nothing to go on.

Coniine poisoning really ought not be that hard to pin down. Some folks took hemlock intentionally to commit suicide; not the case here. Most other cases, my review of the literature had confirmed, were accidental cases: foragers who failed to note the difference between poison hemlock and its harmless and less colorful cousin, wild carrot. I might have had a source if the stew had been homemade, prepared by a forager who wasn't capable of spotting the telltale purple on the stems of hemlock, or even if this were the middle of summer instead of the dead of winter. But it was winter, and as far as I knew, Dinty Moore hadn't recalled any stew because of hemlock contamination, and besides, who knew whether Grandma had eaten any? I was stymied.

Somehow I needed to find a source for the coniine. There had to be one, and it almost certainly had to be an accident. It was time to visit the parents. I figured it was a teachable moment for Sadie and buzzed her office to invite her along.

The Gleasons lived in one of the new Victorian-style

houses that stood cheek by jowl at the end of town. The front yard was miniscule. An abstract metal sculpture poked through the snow. The porch still held a molded, plastic toy car, faded from the summer sun, and a deflated soccer ball. A pair of tiny ice skates hung on a nail jutting from the porch rail. I glanced at Sadie to see her reaction. She was looking across the street at Town Park. Sadie might've been great in the morgue, but it seemed her ability to learn about a case from its surroundings was limited.

A thin woman with straight blond hair answered the door. She wore jeans and a designer sweater but no makeup. Good thing, because her eyes were red-rimmed from crying. "Sally Gleason?" I asked, recalling the name from the file.

She nodded.

"I'm Dr. Wallace. The medical examiner. I am so sorry about Skye and Summer. I wish I could help, and perhaps I might be able to. But I have a few questions first. May I come in?"

She nodded and stepped aside. The living room was small but clean and trendy; I saw a short woman disappear around the corner. The maid, probably. I know I wasn't up to cleaning in the days after John's death.

We talked for a few minutes, Sadie shifting in her seat the whole time, eyes roaming the room. Sally Gleason had nothing much to add to what I already knew. The children were recovering from a cold, in the coughing stage. They'd used a humidifier and that helped. Yes, the children had visited their grandmother a few days before. They loved going there. No, neither she nor her husband

foraged.   Elsie did, but they never ate food Elsie made
from her expeditions; they were too afraid she might make
a mistake and besides, it tasted awful.   Elsie didn't have
too many problems apart from asthma and getting older.
The babysitter was an old friend. Yes, we could look at the
bedrooms; they had not been touched. She couldn't bear
it.

The whole conversation took about five minutes, Sally
responding in a flat voice. The maid — I had been right —
hovered in the background. When I was finished asking
questions, I sat for a moment, at loose ends. I had, over the
years, learned how to do this, but I never am comfortable.
Sadie was still surveying the room, anything to keep from
focusing on the woman in front of her.   I had some
sympathy for her, but she'd be writing up this report just
as an object lesson.

I'd look at the room, but first I extended my hand and
laid it over Sally Gleason's. It was clenched tightly in her
lap; I remembered the pose myself. I left my hand there
for a full minute by the clock, which seemed like an
eternity to me. The fist did not relax, but when I rose and
said softly, "I'll go look at those rooms now. I am so
sorry." She looked up and met my eyes. Best I could hope
for; more than I could take. Sadie leapt out of her chair,
anxious to be off.

The maid showed us two tiny rooms, one decorated in a
fantasy woodland style, the other in a circus theme. The
beds were rumpled, and toys were scattered everywhere. I
started photographing the scene with my smartphone.
Once that was done, I moved methodically through the
rooms, just as I would move methodically across the span
of a slide under the microscope, relaxing my mind and

focusing my attention in hopes of finding something out of place. What, I did not know.

Two hours later, Sadie and I left, carrying a plastic bag containing a top sheet and a face cloth, both of which were stained with an odd-smelling, yellowish residue. It was probably nothing, but I needed to be sure. I handed a receipt to the maid and assured her that we would return the items as soon as possible. I was hoping Lucy could extract whatever stained them without cutting them apart. No need to add another insult to Sally Gleason's injury.

***

Sadie Jackson rankled at the assignment. After the visit to the Gleasons, Dr. Wallace sent her out in search of the family babysitter, which was turning out to be tricky. The woman didn't answer her phone, so she was forced to drop by her apartment. No one home.

As she was leaving, the door to the adjacent apartment opened. A muscular man in a ski suit came out. Sadie flashed her identification.

"I'm with the M.E.'s office. Do you know where..." She had to search in her notes for the name. "...Sherrie Miller is?"

The man shrugged. "Went home to momma after those kids died. She was real broken up about it."

"Where's home?"

"South Dakota? North Dakota? Not sure."

"I don't suppose you have a number so I could reach her?"

The man shook his head and began to edge past her. "Nope. Not that kind of friend. The only reason I know she left is that she palmed off her cat on me until she gets back."

He started down the stairs. Sadie sent a "Thanks a lot!" after him.

Dr. Wallace had given her a dressing down about her behavior on the last visit and made her write up the report. When she presented it, Dr. Wallace had torn it to shreds, adding all sorts of ridiculous details nobody cared about. She suspected that this was karmic justice, making her chase down a witness face to face, some punishment for not doing the report to Dr. Wallace's exacting specifications, whatever they were.

Sadie much preferred managing investigations by internet and email. Cleaner, easier, less…messy. The face-to-face stuff was so hard.

She turned into Leona's to grab a bite of lunch, took her usual table in the corner, ordered a hamburger, and sat facing the wall, head down, engrossed in her smartphone. She was scrolling through the feed on Facebook when she became aware of a figure standing behind the chair to her left. She looked up into the round face of a short man dressed in black.

"Liana! I was certain it was you!" The man's face lit up with delight.

Sadie looked around in confusion. He was talking to *her*. She sat up straighter and said, "You've mistaken me for someone else. I'm not Liana."

Confusion passed over the man's face, and his expression crumbled. He mumbled an apology. "I was so certain."

Something about him made Sadie call out. "Wait! I...uh...I'm not Liana, but...do you want to have lunch?" The old man reminded her of her grandfather. Besides, eating alone was so...difficult.

He brightened. "Delighted, my dear." He plopped down in the chair next to her and patted the table in front of the chair opposite him. "Sit here, my dear, so we can chat more easily."

She laughed. The man certainly had a way about him, and somehow she didn't mind doing as he said. She shifted and put away her phone, then extended her hand. "I'm Sadie Jackson."

"Monsignor Charles Jamais, my dear. A pleasure to meet you. You really do remind me of my niece. Wife of my nephew Matthew. A lovely girl. An artist. Do you draw?"

What a character! At least lunch will be entertaining. "Not unless I have to. I'm a doctor."

"A doctor! Of course there are many lady doctors these days. Do you enjoy it?"

Sadie reflected for a moment. "I suppose so. It pays the bills. And it is interesting."

"Healing is a wonderful calling."

The server appeared and Monsignor Jamais turned toward her. "Excuse me a moment," he said to Sadie and then to the server, "What is your soup today?"

"Cream of fresh mushroom."

"Excellent. A bowl, please, and a slice of good brown bread and butter. And put this young woman's meal on my tab, as well." He waved away Sadie's protest. "Now,

Sadie — that's right, isn't it?" Sadie saw a look of concern pass his face until she nodded. "What is it that had you so engaged? It must be interesting work for you to turn away from the world and be so lost in thought. Though these days you young people are always engrossed in something or other on those pocket phones of yours."

Sadie weighed the merits of telling him she had been doing exactly that, but for some reason, she wanted this charming little man to think better of her than that. "I was thinking about a problem at work," she said, which had the effect of immediately bringing the puzzle about the coniine poisonings right back into focus. "I'm trying to figure out how some children got into a poison. A rare one."

Monsignor Jamais sat back in his chair, a look of distress on his face. "Oh my, that is dreadful. Dreadful indeed. Did they recover?"

Sadie shook her head, and he made the Sign of the Cross. "Their parents must be devastated. The hardest thing in the world for a parent is to bury a child. I'm glad I never was a pastor. I've never had to deal with that."

"What did you do? I thought all priests were pastors." Sadie had at least pieced together his vocation.

"Oh, my dear, no. I taught priests. Moral Theology. Here, in the States, in Rome, in Spain. I could tell you stories..."

I bet you could, thought Sadie. She started to ask for one in the interests of sheer entertainment when he continued, back to the topic of her problem.

"And you've looked at the usual possibilities? Of course, you have," he said.

Of course, I have, Sadie thought. She was about to say so when the old man continued. Apparently, once he had a train of thought you had to talk fast to get a word in edgewise. Oddly, it did not irritate her. It was nice to have something, even the ramblings of a pleasantly offbeat old guy, fill the silence. She hadn't realized how bad her mood was. He was cheering her up, and Sadie determined to let him.

"Children, so very interesting. I never had any myself, of course, but I come from a large family. Nine brothers and sisters, countless cousins. These days people have so few children, it's a shame. I only have a few nieces and nephews — ten, I think. Eleven? No, ten, that's right."

Sadie was fascinated. It was as though the man were pulling on a thread in his mind, encountering the occasional knot, and moving on. He was clearly suffering from some kind of dementia, but he was managing pretty well. She wondered why he was out on his own. She supposed Telluride was as safe as any place to wander around, but still there was a lot of danger on the street.

"Yes, ten. Children are always going about in their own little world — fantasy, really, but so real to them. Make-believe is the mother's milk of the young, you know. Every day is the chance to make up a new story. One day, a fireman, one day, a soldier. One day, a princess, another, a maid." He looked at her with a clarity of expression that she had not yet seen. "Perhaps your answer lies in that world, not ours."

It was a good thing the server arrived with their drinks at that moment. It gave Sadie a chance to recover from her astonishment.

CHAPTER TWELVE
January 13

Sadie was uncharacteristically late coming to work. I buzzed Tim to alert him that I wanted to see her as soon as she appeared. Although everyone lived on premises, I required they clock in at the front desk every morning. It kept things clean, dividing free time from work time. I was scrupulous about paystubs and overtime.

In the meantime, I reviewed her report from the day before. No luck getting the babysitter, so it was brief and businesslike. Better, though, than the report she wrote after our visit to the Gleason home. Probably because there wasn't much to say. I tossed it aside. It wasn't the quality of her reports that bothered me; it was Sadie herself.

Yesterday had been devoted to doing a little digging. Sadie, I found out, was a regular at Proserpine, on a first-name basis with the girl at the front desk who was a font of knowledge, after I bought her a cappuccino at the Bean and complimented her on her jewelry. What troubled me was that she had referred a number of people to talk to Sadie as a doctor. Medical examiners have few patients that need care, but Jack Kevorkian had blazed a trail as a pathologist that I was all but convinced Sadie was following. Referrals from Proserpine were highly suspect in my book.

Sadie, as it turns out, and according to my voluble

contact, was also good friends with the nurse Father Matt was so concerned about at the clinic, something Tim had confirmed as he handed me the report on the results from the IV bag Father Matt snagged. When I finally looked at the report, sure enough, the bag, the drip chamber, and the tubing all held regular saline. The injection port, down near the end, where one would push potassium chloride in to cause a sudden death, held a higher concentration of potassium, consistent with just such a push being given through the port. The police report from that day said that the nurse had just given Josie some medicine to help calm her stomach when she died. No wonder her father was upset.

I was now all but certain that she had been killed, but there was no way to prove that the line had not been tampered with. Once again, I cursed well-meaning do-gooders — even Father Matt — who managed to foul up my investigations. It wasn't like me to miss things like that, and I had failed to ask for that bag when Father Matt first came in. I'd dismissed him. We'd never prove it now, but if I hadn't been so caught up in my own misery, I might have. And even though Sadie wasn't involved in that, she was close enough that I wanted her gone.

After I learned about the Proserpine referrals, I ran a pharmacy audit on Sadie. It was not entirely kosher, but I could shoehorn it into the investigation of Josie's death if push came to shove, which it wouldn't. Most medical examiners didn't keep a prescribing number for narcotics, but Sadie did. During the months before she showed up on my doorstep, there were regular prescriptions for small amounts of the barbiturate to four or five patients. I was willing to bet that they were Proserpine staff or supporters and that those meds ended up in the hands of their "counselors." Colorado only recently passed a right-to-die law that would have permitted her to prescribe it outright. It had to be done under the radar before then, and these prescriptions antedated the law.

The prescriptions were not so frequent or so large as to raise suspicion of narcotics investigators, but they sure raised mine. I was willing to bet that Sadie couldn't produce a chart proving that she was treating those folks for anything, let alone something that called for barbiturates. Still, that would get her, at best, a sanction from the medical board. I wanted her and Proserpine as far away from the Center as I could get them.

I had just finished rehashing the data one more time when Sadie walked in the room with a bright smile and a cup from the Bean. "Tim said you wanted to see me?"

I experienced a twinge of guilt, but only a twinge. Sadie had no idea what was coming. No sense delaying. Always best to get to the heart of the matter, and I did. "Pack your stuff, Sadie. You're fired."

Sadie looked up at me with an expression somewhere between perplexed and anguished. "What do you mean, fired? What have I done?"

"You haven't done anything. You are still in your trial period. I can let you go for any reason or for no reason. I am letting you go. Pack your stuff. I want you out of here. I have a locum arriving today, tomorrow at the latest. Old buddy of mine from medical school. Made a fortune in the stock market and retired. He does M.E. work for kicks. We've worked together before."

She leaned over my desk, face flushed, every freckle

standing out. "You can't do this!" She tried very hard to be fierce and intimidating, but it's hard when you're several inches shorter than your adversary who has a good deal more experience in being nasty. "I'll sue."

"Go right ahead. You'll lose, and then I'll sue for abuse of process. I am clearly within my rights." *By only a few days,* I thought. But a few days is enough. "Look, I know this is short notice, and you didn't expect it. Too bad. I'll give you a decent recommendation. Not a great one, but you'll be able to get another job. And the contract provides for 90 days severance in this situation. Not a bad deal." I had put that in over my lawyer's objections that 30 days was plenty, given a trial of two months. I've found that a little generosity goes a long way in fending off bothersome litigation.

She said nothing; there was nothing to say.

"Quick will be by with some boxes. He'll help you pack." I tossed the formal letter, already faxed upstairs to her home machine, on her desk.

"I just want to know what I did wrong." Sadie sounded genuinely hurt, and she probably was. Overachieving medical types do not take well to the idea of being told they are found wanting.

"Sadie, I don't need to give you a reason. I'm not going to," I said. I stood up to show her the door. "The subject is closed. Pack up your office and your apartment. Let Quick know what you need, and he'll help you out. I've reserved a one-bedroom condo for you at the Stenmark in Mountain Village. It's paid up for the next six weeks." My offer wasn't entirely altruistic. I was not above good, old-fashioned bribery if it cleared this particular annoyance out of my life. "If it is at all possible, you need to be out by end of business tomorrow. Please give me the keys to the Center, and when you are done clearing out your place, give the apartment keys to Quick."

Sadie left without another word, and I went back to my desk. There was work to do. Sometimes it felt like all I did was piece together stories in my head, making things fit when maybe they didn't. But it's what I had to do, and I'd made them fit like I always did. I took the facts, put them together, and Sadie was gone; I had to act on what I knew, and that was that. Until, of course, some other set of troublesome facts arose to remind me that there are not really any answers, just more questions. I wondered what the next ones might be.

***

Eoin stood at the Ballycastle Harbor, watching the ferry approach from Rathlin Island. Over his head, the steel images of swans in flight reflected the early morning sun. He nursed a cup of tea from the hotel in a foam carry cup emblazoned with its logo: a stone castle in a crashing wave. Seeing the ferry bang its way across the rough inlet, he was glad he decided to forgo the included full breakfast and opt for tea and toast. Crossings to Rathlin were always a bit rough, but in winter, rough took on a new meaning. And today was an especially raw day, windy and damp-cold, in spite of the fact that the clouds were few and the day would clear.

He was also glad he had opted for the ferry rather than taking Terry up on his offer to come across in his Zodiac. The ferry might be slower and it would certainly be a thumping ride, but at least it stood taller than the waves.

And if his stomach settled once he was on the other side, he'd enjoy one of his sister Molly's good farm breakfasts.

He sat on a bench in the sheltered part of the boat, away from the spray and the diesel fumes. There were only a few passengers, in part because it was the first ferry over and in part because it was winter. Rathlin's two-hundred-some-odd residents parted ways with the island around October, heading for more hospitable climes. Few tourists made their way across in the dark months, and so the island was left to a few hearty souls: farmers, mostly, or hermits. Those who couldn't leave and those who wanted to stay, because it was the only time they had peace and quiet.

His brothers and sisters took turns watching the family place over the winter, caring for the livestock and looking after repairs to the homestead. They did it, he supposed, out of loyalty to him, for they all had lives on the mainland: kith, kin, and kindred. Rathlin had once been their home, but they had moved on. Only he remained really attached to it and was glad that they made it possible for him to keep that attachment. Though, he supposed, if they wanted to give it all up, he could find a tenant well enough. He could take lodging in a spare room, even then. Or take a room at one of the new hotels on the bay.

The trip was shorter than he remembered but just as difficult. He sat as near the middle of the salon as possible, which helped with the forward motion but not the swing from side to side. He watched the spray wash over the deck and splash against the windows, scored and salt-sodden from so many passages. He remembered the time his brother lost a gas can overboard to a particularly bad wave and smiled. *You really did have to want to get to Rathlin Island,* he thought.

The sun was full out from the scanty clouds when the ferry docked. He slung his pack over his shoulder and started out for the farm. Nothing on Rathlin was very far from anything else, and it took little time to hike the distance to the far end of Ballycarry Townland where the Connor cottage stood on the northeast corner of the island, close enough to Scotland to spit. After so much time in Colorado, the climb up the crest of the island bothered him not in the least. He took his time, enjoying the wild desolation of the island now that only the most tenacious of the inhabitants were in residence. He loved Ireland when it was caught in the chains of winter, not so much green as umber, showing the melancholy side of the Irish spirit. A melancholy that, today, fit his own.

He walked up the path to the cottage door, his boots splashing mud from the rains of the last few days. He'd no sooner opened the door than he heard Molly's voice. "Eoin Connor, scrape those boots! I just mopped the floor!"

He smiled, glad to be home again, doffed his boots and went in stocking feet to the kitchen for a cup of tea and some consolation.

Breakfast lasted more than an hour, between Molly's good food and catching up on what was happening with the farm. He enjoyed a pipe before going out to walk the grounds. Terry, as usual, had everything well under control. The farm was making quite a bit of profit these days, thanks to his good stewardship and the fact that Molly rented out one of the rooms during the summers.

"So how is it all working, with this new bed and breakfast idea?" Eoin asked as he and Terry approached the old byre that had served as a storage shed for years. The Connor farm kept no cows. Sheep were enough of a problem.

"It was booked nearly solid between her cooking and the fact that we sit overlooking the sea on one side and the East Lighthouse on the other. Fits the tourist's desire for the exotic to look at." Terry was manipulating his own pipe, hoping to coax it back into operation. He finally succeeded. A plume of smoke drifted up, tentative at first, then strong and blue-gray. He puffed once or twice to be sure, then took the pipe in hand as he added, "There's always a stream of hikers up this way looking for Robert Bruce's cave."

Eoin laughed. The cave was only accessible by boat, something he knew all the island literature mentioned, and he said as much.

"Ah, but who pays attention to that? Anyway, Molly's thinking of putting up a sign and offering tea and sweets to passersby. But you didn't come here to talk about the farm, Eoin. What's on your mind?"

As briefly as he could, he outlined his predicament. "I need help, Terry. I need to run down all the witnesses who might help me. I mean to marry Jane Wallace. I assume you'll speak for me."

"Of course, yes. I never could understand why you weren't granted that petition in the first place. I suppose I am glad it was not filed, rather than the Church doing wrong by you."

"I need to connect with some of our old mates,

especially those who knew Fiona before I did. Have you kept up with any of them?"

"A few. Morris, Paddy, Declan. I'll give you their information. Declan and Morris are still in Belfast. Paddy moved to the Republic a few years ago. Somewhere near Limerick, I think."

"Thanks." Eoin surveyed the dim interior of the byre. The shelves held a variety of bottles, jars, cans, and boxes, all containing odd bits that once might have been useful in repairs but had long since passed their utility. Eoin picked up a jar of nails, rusted and bent. He laughed and shook it at Terry.

"Remember how Da always had us foraging nails and straightening them? We used them for practice." His mind went back to his childhood days, when his father patiently taught him to measure, saw and join wood so well that the joints held fast, and the resulting structure was safe against North Sea gales. Learning to make them beautiful, as well, had been Eoin's own touch and had ultimately landed him a job in Belfast when both Da and the farm were but a recent and painful memory. "Hard to believe this survived."

"I suppose. They didn't do much with the farm apart from leasing the pastures out. There's a lot here left from when we were young. Remember this?" He held up a yellow box.

"Wound powder. I do indeed. That and black salve was about all either Ma or Da needed to cure anything in man or beast." Eoin took the box from his brother's hands. "Sure looks like the same stuff. Remarkable." He handed it back. "Then again, I ought to know that. All the times

I've been here working, and yet I never noticed."

"Not like you, Eoin."

"Not like me at all." He picked up a bottle from the far end of the shelf, tall, with a label bearing the skull and crossbones. "I guess they didn't touch anything here. This stuff has been off the shelves for years. Nasty stuff, but it worked for the garden." He put the bottle back and wiped a smear of dark, smelly liquid onto his handkerchief and put it in his coat pocket.

"I remember. Molly still uses it from time to time. It still works. Black Leaf 40 did a good job for us. Still does. Probably always will, at least until we run out."

Eoin tapped his pipe out onto the dirt floor of the byre and stepped on it for good measure. "I think I'll take a bit of a walk, Terry. I've some things to mull over. If you'll get those names for me, I think I will head back to Belfast on the first ferry tomorrow."

He watched his brother's back until he disappeared around the corner. Then Eoin Conner walked the gravel road to the East Lighthouse and a bit beyond until he stood on the bluff that he knew was just over the cave in which Robert the Bruce watched a spider toil over and over to spin his web. Bruce found inspiration in that and made another attempt to return to Scotland, ultimately freeing it from English rule.

Eoin took heart at that and started back to confer once more with Terry and to plot out his travels to see who was still around to help him win his own freedom. He stuck his hands in his pockets and tipped his head back, whistling in the wind for the first time in a long, long time.

CHAPTER THIRTEEN

January 14

The sky was darkening by the time I returned from lunch across the street at Baked in Telluride. With the colder weather, they served an amazing chili, and this was shaping up to be a chili kind of day. I just hoped Sadie's temporary replacement arrived before the storm that was moving in hit. The Telluride airport occupied the top of a mesa and with the landing strip ending at the steep drop-off. It didn't take a lot of snow to shut it down.

I started clearing my desk. At the top of the everlasting pile was a pad with the notes I had made regarding Sadie. I debated the merits of keeping them as opposed to throwing them away. I elected to split the difference and send them to my own lawyer as pertaining to a possible lawsuit. I hoped it wouldn't come to that, and I had done everything possible to forestall it. Sadie was hurt, but I'd treated her well. I hoped it was enough. If some judge decided to rewrite my contract to require reasonable cause even though it was drafted otherwise, I'd be in trouble, but I could deal with that later.

I had to admit, I had gotten used to a little free time and some peer-society in the office. I was glad Mike Delatorre took me up on my offer and surprised me when he walked into my office just before two.

"Mike! You're early — so good to see you!" I came out

from behind the desk to give him the requisite welcoming hug. He looked just the same as always: medium height, slim build, a closely trimmed black beard, dark brown eyes and eyelashes any woman would kill for.

"I didn't want to get stuck in an airport because of the storm. I decided to leave a day early, spent the night in Denver. Nice place."

"I assume there was a change fee. Leave it with Tim, and we will take care of it."

"No worries." Mike dropped a well-stuffed pack from his shoulder. He always traveled lightly. "You have digs for me?"

"The Sheraton for the next night or two. Then you can stay at the Center in one of the apartments, if you'd like. It will be free by then."

Mike raised a ruddy eyebrow. "So what was the emergency? Not that I mind being in the Rockies during ski season."

I debated how much to tell him and settled on the unvarnished truth, realizing that it would undo all my careful, legal toe-dancing if Sadie brought push to shove. "I just couldn't have her here, Mike. Especially since I am not at all sure we don't have a problem with assisted deaths here in town, hard as that is to believe."

Mike shrugged as he pulled off his down coat and tossed it on top of the pack. "Not so hard to believe, but not your problem anymore, either. It's legal."

"It's legal under some circumstances. Gotta be competent and gotta be over 18."

I had his interest. His watch cap joined the jacket and

revealed that his hairline was receding. "Say more."

"A case I just can't get out of my mind. A kid died in the local clinic. She had a terminal illness, and I suppose it wasn't outside the realm of possibility that she just reached the end. But I tested the IV she had in her, and there was potassium in the injection port."

"Sounds pretty straightforward. How did you sign it out?"

"Undetermined. No good chain of evidence, though I probably could gin one up. The person who brought it to me is pretty trustworthy, and he'd stand up under questioning. I can't bring myself to sign it as a natural death." I shifted positions. "I am really glad you are here. By big city standards, there's usually not all that much work here, even with overseeing the remote sites. I just got used to having a colleague here, and to be honest, I want to be able to take a little time off. I have had a rough patch lately."

I didn't add that I missed having male companionship, and Mike was no threat to Eoin. His tastes ran in other directions. He and Simon had been together since medical school. "Really, Mike, put on your thinking cap. Or ask Simon. He's a screenwriter. Maybe he'd have some ideas." Forensic science and law were turning out to be not much help.

"There's another one, too. Not a problem exactly; it's an accidental death, three of them actually, but I can't connect all the dots." I briefed him on the coniine deaths.

"For a small town, there's a lot happening here."

I laughed. "I moved here thinking it would be quiet, too, but it hasn't been. At least, not since I got here.

Maybe it's me. Maybe I am the Typhoid Mary of Forensic Pathology."

Mike laughed out loud, one of those infectious laughs that cheer the soul. "Come on, then, Mary. Show me the ropes."

***

It was nearly a blizzard when Father Matt finally headed home from a pastoral call in Placerville. He hated driving the road into town in bad weather. Although the plow had been through and the road was decently gritted, snow was sticking to the roadway again, and a thick sheet of ice was beginning to form. He had set the car in four-wheel low when he pulled out of the drive near the turnoff to Woods Lake, and so far he had not lost traction. But the snow was increasing, making it more difficult to see. The white flakes against the windshield and the dark of the sky made him feel like he was in some sort of movie special effect — the sort of thing he was used to seeing as portrayed flashing through time and space by a wormhole or some other such imaginary space accessory. But the visibility and the ice slowed him to not much more than a crawl, even though his mind was sure he was rocketing along. He kept focusing on the road, with only the occasional short prayer present in his mind — *Dear Lord, let me get home safely; Saint Frances of Rome, intercede for me!* He'd always liked the saint who swept the path with light for the traveler.

The fact that a miscalculation could send him hurling down a precipice to land on a road below, or worse yet, into the San Miguel River, increased his anxiety. Although he was a native to Colorado, he'd grown up in the flat part of the state. Lots of snow, but easy driving compared to here. He felt his shoulders tense as he hunched forward to peer into the darkness, looking for taillights ahead and snow poles alongside. He recited the prayer for motorists he had learned as a child, then brought his mind back to the road. Just now his concentration on driving would have to serve as devotion.

The snowplow passed him going away from town at a curve he recognized in the combined glow of the headlights as the last big one before the climb into town. He permitted himself to relax a bit and to think about a warm apartment, a glass of wine, and the last of the green chile stew that Pilar had brought by a day or two ago. He rolled his shoulders in an effort to relieve the sharp pain between his shoulder blades. It didn't work. He tensed again as he felt the Jeep slip sideways a bit before it caught on some grit and stabilized.

He glanced at the clock on the dash as he passed Society Turn, and relief washed over him as the lights of Telluride came dimly into view through the blowing snow. Nearly eight o'clock. Almost an hour to drive a mere ten miles. He rolled his shoulders again; the pain in his back had intensified, and now his forearms ached, as well. He realized he held the steering wheel in a death grip. As soon as he passed through the roundabout, he freed first one hand, then the other, to shake out the stiffness.

Light shone from the apartment window that faced the parking area beside the church. Father Matt saw a short figure pass, glass in hand. Monsignor Jamais was still up. Unusual. He headed to bed almost as soon as the sun went down, though he woke in the middle of the night and had taken to wandering about the small apartment.

More often than not, turning on the living room light to wake Matt from his uncomfortable slumbers on the couch. Father Matt switched off the car, gave thanks for a safe arrival, and unfolded himself from the Jeep. He slid once on the sidewalk but didn't fall.   The warmth of the stairway to the apartment was welcome indeed.

Father Matt hung his coat on the hook by the downstairs door and kicked off his snow boots, hurrying upstairs in his stocking feet. He found Monsignor Jamais settled in the big easy chair, a glass of scotch in his hand. Unusual. He rarely drank.

"Matthew!"   There was real pleasure in Monsignor Jamais' voice.

"Hello, Monsignor. I'm surprised to see you up."

"Couldn't sleep, dear boy. Couldn't sleep."

Not for the first time did Father Matt wonder when he has ceased to be Mister Gregory, delivered in caustic tones, and become Dear Boy. He stretched his neck and rolled his shoulders. It did nothing to relieve the pain. "I'm sorry to hear that."

"I believe it comes with getting older. I thought a bit of scotch might help."

It comes from sleeping so much every night and napping twice a day for the last week, he thought unkindly, then reproved himself.   It was the fatigue and the hunger. Aloud, he replied, "Probably will," distracted as he reached down a bowl for the stew and pulled some cornbread from the plastic container on the counter. His mouth was already watering. He was about to turn to the fridge to get out the stew when he noticed a bowl in the sink, the remains of chile stew stuck to the sides and bottom. He gripped the sides of the sink, his knuckles turning white. It only made his shoulders hurt worse. The muscles in his forearms twitched as he fought an irrational desire to scream and throw things. He tried breathing deeply to calm himself, but it had been a long day. Too long.

"I am not sure it isn't my dinner. I am not sure that spicy food really agrees with me. Please, Matthew, could you arrange for something less exotic for me? Perhaps some good pasta?"

"If you didn't like it, why did you eat it? I'm cold, I'm tired, I'm hungry, I ache all over from sleeping on a couch, and all I wanted was a nice bowl of stew!" Father Matt ran his hand across his forehead in exasperation. "Why don't you just take over the apartment? I'll move out. I'll camp out in Town Park if that's what it takes to get some peace and my own space. I'll have Jane send someone in to look after you. I can't do this anymore. What are you doing here in the first place?" Father Matt listened with horror as the words spilled out, unintended and shameful. He clenched his teeth, afraid that if he did not, more awful words would come out. *Sweet Jesus, what have I done?*

Monsignor Jamais' face kaleidoscoped from disbelief to understanding to fear. His mouth worked, but nothing came out. And his lip trembled. He nearly dropped the glass in his hand.

Father Matt shook his head to dispel the images, hoping to shed the disgrace he felt building even as his frustration flared again. "I'm going to get something to eat," he said as kindly and as calmly as he could. "Don't wait up." He ducked his head to avoid seeing that round, confused face and made sure not to slam the door behind him, the only gesture of reconciliation he could muster.

The snow had let up some by the time he got bundled up again. The drifts came to the middle of his calf, and it was hard going. He paused at the edge of the street, deciding where to go to eat. There were only a few hardy souls out, and he suspected that the restaurants were closing early. *I need company*, he thought. *Real company*. A coherent conversation. He missed the comfortable presence of Eoin Connor and breathed a prayer that Eoin's quixotic trip to Ireland would yield something to allow him to marry again. Good friends, he was finding, were hard to find, and right now he was experiencing a sudden dearth of them.

The memory of the green chile stew surfaced again as his stomach growled. "Pilar!" He thought. Smiling, he turned his steps toward the big green house. He could see it through the last diminishing snowfall and quickened his steps.

Pilar answered the door when he knocked. Her smile wrinkled the corners of her eyes.

"Padre! Bienvenidos!" She paused a minute to switch linguistic gears, then added, "Come in! It is cold, come in!" She stood aside.

Father Matt hesitated. He saw the snow shovel by the door and remembered that, although there were plenty of adults in the house these days, all of them were women. "In a minute, Pilar. I came to beg some food. Monsignor ate my stew and I'm hungry. Will you feed me if I shovel your walk?"

Pilar clucked her tongue and shook her head, but she

was smiling. "Si! Thank you. I will make something nice." She flicked a switch to illuminate the big porches that surrounded the house and disappeared.

Shoveling snow made the ache in his forearms worse, but it dispelled his irritation at Monsignor Jamais. He carried on an internal conversation with each swish of the shovel, cascading arguments over each other as he tossed the snow aside. By the time he was finished, he was sweating underneath his coat, the pain in his shoulders was gone, and he was ashamed of himself, even as he knew that something had to change in his living arrangements. *I guess it isn't enough to want to do something noble*, he thought to himself. *I just can't do this anymore. I'll call Bishop Herlihy in the morning.* The thought of having to go back on his word churned his stomach and made him toss the last shovel of snow into the wind, so that it blew back onto the porch.

I'll come again in the morning, he thought, as he watched the snow blur the sharp edges of his work. He leaned the shovel against the door, knocked the snow off his boots, and went into the warm house.

He knew his way to the kitchen. The sitting room was empty but strewn with toys instead of books as it had been when Jane was in residence with the rest of them. He could hear the sounds of a television from the den in the back of the house. The children, he supposed, were asleep. He was intruding into the only quiet time this house ever saw. *I won't stay long*, he promised himself.

Pilar led him to one of the chairs around the granite island and placed a heaping plate of rice, beans, and shredded beef in front of him. "Ropa vieja," she told him.

"Because we cook the meat so long, it falls apart, like old clothes." She handed him a fork, and he dug in without remembering to grace the food. A small plate of hot flour tortillas materialized at his right side and a cold beer on his left. Pilar sat with him as he ate his fill in silence. When he was done, he prayed thanksgiving for a good meal. He looked up to find Pilar signing herself even as he did.

"Amen!" she said. "So the small priest, he ate your food?"

Father Matt felt his cheeks flush. "He did. I got angry and left him there alone. I should get back. He isn't well."

Pilar smiled at him. "No. He is not. My husband was like that before he died. Forgetful, demanding. Like a child again, only not a child, so it was much harder. He would not learn to get better, only worse. It made me very angry." She cocked her head and regarded Farther Matt for a long moment, then reached across to brush a stray curl off his forehead. The intimacy of the gesture shocked him, and he drew back.

"Hijo," she said. "You cannot help being angry. But he cannot help who he is, either. He is just a man, now becoming a small boy again. Soon he will be no more than a baby, and then he will be gone." She stood up and reached across the expanse of granite to clear the dishes. From the sink, her back to him, she added, "You are always welcome here. So is he. Desgracia compartida, menos sentida. You understand?"

"Sorrow shared is halved. Yes, I do," he answered. "Thank you, Pilar. I had better get back to check on Monsignor. I'll come by to do the walk again in the morning. It will need it."

"Muchas gracias," she said, turning from the sink and pushing a stray gray hair away with the back of her hand. "Come for breakfast. Bring the priest. I will feed you both."

Pilar turned back to the sink to finish the dishes. Father Matt let himself out.

The walk back was easier in part because the plow had come by and cleared the street, in part because the meal had mended his bad temper for the time being. He would apologize to Monsignor Jamais in the morning, but he'd call the bishop all the same. No one would blame him, least of all, the bishop. He had tried. God knew, he had tried.

He glanced at his watch as he mounted the stairs, surprised at how late it was. It was almost ten. Dinner had not taken so long; shoveling snow had made him lose track of time. The kitchen light was on, and he could see a gleam from the bedroom.

"Good, he's still awake. I don't have to wait until morning." He knocked softly on the door. "Monsignor?"

No reply. He knocked again, louder and raised his voice. "Monsignor?" Still no reply. He eased the door open and drew in a sharp breath.

Monsignor Jamais was slumped in the easy chair in the corner of the room. The glass that had held the scotch was tipped over on the side table alongside an open pill bottle, the contents of which were strewn across the table and onto the floor. He picked it up, some sort of sleeping pill, prescribed by a Dr. Brownmiller.

Father Matt covered the distance in two long strides, dialing 911 as he went.

***

It took only three paces to cover the length of the waiting room at the clinic. Father Matt lost count of the times he stepped off the distance, to and fro, as he fingered the beads of his rosary, waiting for some word about Monsignor Jamais. He rounded the beads over and over for his health and healing, even as his mind was a jumble of thoughts.

He had the presence of mind to collect the pills and bring them along. It was a prescription for sleeping pills, from the expensive clinic at the end of town. He recognized the name of the doctor, Jennie Brownmiller. The name of the drug sent a chill down his back. It was one prominently mentioned in the Proserpine literature as an effective means of a quiet death. He wondered how the Monsignor had gotten the prescription in the first place. What on earth had been going on? He felt a pain of guilt as sharp as the pain between his shoulder blades. An old, demented man needed care, not just a bed.

And it's probably my fault, he thought. *Please God, don't let him die because of me.* Not even a beat of his heart before the unwelcome thought surfaced in the wake of concern. *But it would make life so much easier if he did.* He increased his pace and fingered his beads with a vengeance.

CHAPTER FOURTEEN
January 15

"Father Matt!" I shook his shoulder gently, and his brown eyes struggled open.

He was draped across a green chair in the waiting room of the clinic, his long legs sprawled out before him and his head tipped back at an impossible angle, snoring. He must have been exhausted.

He sat up rubbing the back of his neck; it had to be sore. "Jane? What are you doing here?"

"I heard Monsignor was sick." I refrained from explaining that I heard from my office staff; I had gone home after settling Mike at the Center, still in a sour mood from my discoveries about Sadie and in no mood for company, not even the children who were the usual antidote to my bad temper. I ate a solitary dinner in the kitchen and retreated to my study with apologies to all. I was into my fourth hour of cooking competition shows — having temporarily given up on the idea of sleep as a bad business — when I got a text from Lucy to meet her at the office. Given the hour, a few minutes before midnight, I figured it must be important. She met me at the door with the news that they had a drug screen from the Center, positive for barbiturates, prescribed by Dr. Brownmiller according to the submission slip. The patient was one Augustine Jamais.

It was a clear violation of privacy laws that could cost me and my staff a great deal of money and aggravation should any of the local A.C.L.U. types with an attitude get wind of it, which is why she told me in person. Lucy knows when and how to play fast and loose with the rules, especially mine. It was what I expected from my staff. Medicine — even the forensic kind — runs on the fuel of judicious gossip. As, I suppose, does life.

It also concerned me that he had taken the same sort of pill found in Proserpine's literature and prescribed by a physician I had seen at the Proserpine open house. Just too odd to be mere coincidence, though I rationalized it by reminding myself that an unsettling percentage of my medical colleagues supported what they called "assistance in dying." And given that there were so few physicians in Telluride, was it really that surprising to see one at Proserpine? And that didn't necessarily mean support for their program; after all, Father Matt and I had been there, too.

My mental contortions left me reeling, but in spite of them, I supposed that the same sense that told Lucy that Monsignor's overdose wasn't what it appeared to be made me worry it wasn't so simple, either.

Father Matt's face contorted. "I think he overdosed on sleeping pills. It's my fault, Jane." I watched him will himself out of his sleepiness to speak. "It was my fault," he repeated.

I doubted that but said nothing.

"I lost it with him, Jane. He's just so impossible. I came home and he'd eaten my dinner, and I..." He paused again. "I yelled at him. I told him I was moving out, that he was..." Father Matt swallowed. "Anyway, I left in a huff. When I came back, he was passed out. He'd had scotch and took a mess of pills."

I'd seen the numbers. A couple or three, not a mess. Perfectly understandable in a man who couldn't remember from one minute to the next what he had done. Still, especially with his age, it was no laughing matter. Both barbiturates and alcohol depressed the central nervous system, and the combination could be deadly, even in relatively small doses. Many a bored wife in the sixties died accidentally from taking the same sort of medication with martini chasers. When we were out of earshot of the clinic staff, I'd tell Father Matt so. For the meantime, I just took his hand in mine and asked, "Any word?"

He shook his head and then looked at his watch. "It's been five hours. I guess it's a good sign."

"Very," I answered. "Only one glass of scotch?"

Father Matt looked at me as though I had lost my mind. "As far as I know," he answered. "But it was a stiff one. I guess he likes scotch, though I have no idea where it came from. I only keep bourbon. No idea about the pills, either." His voice was glum.

It sounded like the good monsignor had been wandering. The scotch was easy enough; there was a liquor store in town. The sleeping pills with Jennie Brownmiller's name on the prescription meant he must have been seen at the Regent Clinic at the edge of town, a long walk but not beyond his capacity. I could follow up on that later, but it was typical of the alternating confusion and capacity of Alzheimer's in the early days. I recalled an old uncle who could not remember much of anything on a regular basis but could find the local bar if you dropped him blindfolded in the middle of Alaska in a snowstorm at midnight.

I did a quick mental calculation. Assuming the good monsignor didn't have any serious health problems — he looked healthy as a horse, except for being pleasantly balmy from time to time — he was probably just sleeping it off with the added benefit of a pumped stomach, a little nasal oxygen, and an IV. I was about to say as much when Clive Rivers, the newest addition to the local primary care practice, came through the swinging doors that led to the treatment rooms. He greeted me with a smile. "Hi, Jane! What brings you here?"

"Just keeping a friend company," I nodded in Father Matt's direction. I knew from the relaxed look on Clive's boyish face that the news was good, but Father Matt was too tired and distracted to connect the dots. He stood up quickly, anxiety in his very bearing.

"Is he going to be okay?" He blurted out the words.

Clive smiled. "Sure. He was never in much danger, really. The drug levels weren't too high and neither was the alcohol. You got him here fast, good for you. He's out cold, sure enough, but he'll be fine as soon as he sleeps it off. Which," he added, "will be a while. We came out to tell you earlier, but you were sound asleep yourself. The nurse didn't want to wake you. Then we got busy with another case — figured you could use the sleep if you were snoozing on those chairs." Clive paused, expecting a reply, but Father Matt just stood there, eyes closed, fists clenched, for a long minute. Prayer, I suspected. Thanksgiving that this was just a near miss. When he opened his eyes, he smiled one of those determined smiles that bespeaks a monumental attempt to maintain equilibrium in the face of disaster.

"Thank you, Doctor. When can I take him home?" There was an odd note in Father Matt's voice I didn't recognize.

"Why don't you go home and get some sleep? We'll keep him here for a few more hours just to be sure he is okay. It will take a while for the drugs and alcohol to pass out of his system." Clive paused. "I take it your friend has Alzheimer's?"

"Or something. He's not himself. Forgetful."

"He has trouble sleeping?"

"Some. At night. He sleeps fine during the day."

"I'm a little surprised Jenny didn't prescribe him something lighter. He's going to be okay this time, but barbiturates are not a good choice for older patients, never good for demented ones. It's too easy for them to overdose, especially when they aren't closely supervised. I'd get rid of it if I were you and ask for something less...problematic. Do you have help?"

I saw Matt flush. "I didn't think I needed any. I didn't think he was that bad. I thought he was just..." His voice trailed off. "...annoying," he finished weakly.

"Get some," Clive advised. He looked in my direction. "I expect Dr. Wallace can help you find someone appropriate." He pulled his cell phone out of his pocket and checked the time. "Still got a few hours before morning clinic. I'm going to catch some winks. I suggest you do the same. Come back in a couple of hours, and we'll have Mr. Jamais packed and ready to go." He waved a casual goodbye and walked back through the swinging doors. I suspected the winks would be grabbed in an empty exam room rather than back at his down-valley home.

I regarded Father Matt, feeling slightly guilty myself that I'd been so tied up in my own problems that I had not seen the crisis brewing at the rectory. Two men in a one-bedroom apartment with no help. It was a wonder it hadn't blown up in Father Matt's face before this.

I clapped him on his shoulder. "Let's get you home. We'll sort this all out in the morning." I stopped when I saw the look on his face.

"I can't go back there just now, Jane," he said in a quiet voice.

I shrugged. "Fair enough. The Victorian Inn always has a spare room. Let's go. My treat. You need some sleep, and so do I. I'll ask Pilar to come by and collect the monsignor. She can look after him for a while. He'll love it. You sleep until you wake up." Before he had a chance to protest, I added, "That's an order," and held his coat open for him. He slid his arms in without a word, pulled on his bright mittens, and followed me out the door.

I settled him into his room, but instead of heading home, I went to my office. I had a lot to think about. It was possible that this was just an accident, and given Monsignor's performance at the Proserpine open house, I could not imagine him taking the combination of alcohol and sleeping pills with the intent to end his life. But it bothered me that an otherwise very competent, if abrasive, physician had prescribed an unsuitable drug to an old man. Perhaps I was getting paranoid, but I couldn't help but wonder if it wasn't her attempt to set up a situation that, sooner or later, would rid the community of a troublesome old man that had marred Proserpine's debut into polite, Telluride society.

Jennie Brownmiller and I were going to have a talk as soon as the clinic opened. Until then, I could catch up on some work. I switched on the computer, but the last few days caught up with me. It wasn't long before I was asleep on the green leather couch.

***

"Tell me again, Matthew. Where are we going?"

Father Matt took Monsignor Jamais' arm to help him over a patch of ice. The storm was past, and the late afternoon sun made the snow sparkle. "To see some friends, Monsignor. Some women. You've met Jane Wallace. She is one of them. She has room in the house for you and would be honored to have you stay; she told me so this morning. I think it might be more comfortable for you than the rectory apartment. It's so small." Monsignor had been there with Matt several times but had no recollection of it. Father Matt supposed he hadn't had time to fix it in his memory.

Jane came up with the wild idea that Monsignor Jamais needed to be staying with her rather than at the rectory. A wild idea that somehow he was now trying to make happen.

"Indeed, it is small, Matthew. A priest deserves good quarters, you know. Your parish ought to provide you better."

All I would have to do is ask, thought Matt. "It's fine for me, and it's not a wealthy parish. There are so many more important needs."

Monsignor looked at him quizzically. "I never took you for a Franciscan, dear boy. There's nothing wrong with comfortable living."

"Which is why I am taking you by to see these ladies. They have a guest suite that might suit you very well." It had taken some fast talking to get the bishop to consider the idea. One of his priests residing in a house full of women? Unthinkable! Think of the scandal. He volunteered to send someone out to fetch his errant cleric back home to be cared for there. Only when Jane had intervened — God bless her for calling him — with her excellent persuasive skills, not the least of which was the fact that she would be footing the bill for his care, did the bishop relent.

"I suppose an assisted living facility is an appropriate setting at this point," he had said, closing the conversation with a demand for regular reports. Matt supposed Jane would do some fancy legal footwork to get the necessary permissions in place, sooner or later, to placate the bishop.

Why he wanted to keep Monsignor here with him, Father Matt wasn't entirely sure. He had never liked the man in seminary and truly he had been a royal pain since his arrival. But there was something engaging in him these days, as though the dementia peeled away all the artifice that he used to wield power over his seminary students. All that was left was a man with a wonderful command of the past — at least the long past — no particular worries for the future, and a surprisingly engaging personality when he wasn't harrying Father Matt for things he missed, eating his food, or misplacing his things. And a faith that was so deep he would never lose it. *I need to be around that,* Matt thought. At any rate, the desire to keep Monsignor close by and to be his friend was as strong as the call to priesthood had been. He was glad they'd found a way to make it work. The old fellow deserved to die holding the hand of a friend, not a stranger.

Pilar opened the door. She was expecting them and would hold court in Jane's absence. She wore her best black dress with a crisp white apron on over it. "Come in, come in."

"Let me introduce Monsignor Jamais," he said, as he entered the familiar hallway.

Before Monsignor could speak, Pilar took his hands and kissed the palms, an old-fashioned gesture of respect for the office that Father Matt had never witnessed. Monsignor tut-tutted, but a tear slid down his cheek. Seeing it, Father Matt felt a bit guilty for all the times he'd made fun of Monsignor in seminary.

"Dios te bendiga, Monseñor. It is an honor to have you here. Please, come in."

The whole family was there: Pilar, Lupe, Isa, the children, all in their Sunday best, lined up like a receiving line to welcome him. Cookies, finger sandwiches, and petit fours were laid out on the coffee table and a silver pot — it had to be from the previous owners, as Jane would never have one — sat on a tray with cups, cream, and sugar.

Lupe, the quietest and youngest of the women, escorted him to a chair and settled a small table at his side. The children took turns serving. Pilar directed conversation. First in English, then Spanish when she realized he was fluent. The youngest clambered onto Monsignor's lap to listen. He smiled benevolently and stroked the child's black hair as he described in great and glorious detail the time he was sent on an errand to Barcelona and ended up serving in the Sagrada Familia for three months, enjoying the life in Barcelona, cafes and music, and long walks in beautiful gardens. When his cup went dry or his plate was empty, Pilar was there to fill them again.

Father Matt sat off to the side. *Please God, let this work,* he prayed. *He deserves better than I have been able to give him.*

When Monsignor was sufficiently full that he waved away his fourth cake with apologies for not eating more, Lupe took him to see the guest suite: a large bedroom and sitting room on the main floor, the one Jane retained as guest quarters for her children when they visited. Father Matt hung back to talk to Pilar.

"It won't be easy to take care of him, you know. He can be very demanding. He's on his best behavior."

"That is only another way of saying he is a man," she retorted. Then her face became serious. "I know how hard it is. He is not afraid yet, but he will be when he understands what is happening. Then he will be angry, and he will blame us for anything that happens. He loses his pants; we stole them. He cannot find his wallet; we stole it. He will be impatient, demand too much, shout, maybe even throw things. But that will not last long. When he loses more of his memory, he will still be annoying, because he will ask the same thing over and over, but then again, everything will always be new to him. Everything beautiful. Always a surprise. So it was with my husband. I understand. They understand."

"Understanding is one thing. Living with it is something else. If it does not work, I can move him. And Jane insists that you are to be paid for taking care of him."

Pilar waved an imperious hand when he mentioned money; he'd let her fight that out with Jane, and frankly, he wasn't sure who would win that one. Then she looked at him with a gentle expression. "It will work, because we will see that it works. This good man gave up his chance to marry to be a priest, to be our father. What kind of children are we if we do not take care of him?"

Her words stung. "You'd be like me. I can't take care of him, Pilar. I can't. He drives me crazy and he makes me angry, even though I know it isn't his fault. What kind of priest does that make me? I even — God forgive me — wondered whether it might be better for him if he didn't get better from the overdose." Father Matt stopped abruptly, horrified at what he was saying, even as he was relieved for having told the truth to someone.

"You are just a man, Father. A good man, a good priest. But this is our work. It is not for you. That is why you cannot do it. There is nothing to be ashamed of. Thoughts are not acts. You brought him to the clinic, and you brought him to us. It's enough." She touched his cheek again, just as she had before. This time the intimacy was welcome, a mother comforting her son. "Leave this to us. Just pray, eh?"

It took a moment for Father Matt to be able to speak. "Dios te bendiga, Pilar," was all that he could say. Then, when he regained control of himself, he added, "Thank you."

From across the hall, in the general vicinity of the guest suite, he heard an imperious and familiar voice. "Matthew! Be sure you don't forget my breviary when you bring my things. I couldn't find it this morning. Your housekeeper must have mislaid it."

It was hard to tell who laughed more, Pilar or Father Matt.

CHAPTER FIFTEEN

January 17

I was taking my time getting into the office. Mike would be there to handle the incoming, and given the way things were going these days, I wasn't doing such a great job handling my end of the practice. I made a cup of coffee with the machine in my room and enjoyed it, along with a chapter in the book I was trying to read and a couple of cuts from Stan Kenton's Cuban Fire until I was sure that the children had finished their breakfasts and were shuttled out the door to the parish daycare. When the noise level abated, I dressed quickly and went downstairs to claim my share of whatever was left from breakfast.

Pilar frowned at me for being so late. She was already clearing the table. Monsignor Jamais was at the end of the counter, finishing a plate of chilaquiles and eggs. I looked at Pilar with hope and apology in my eyes. She mumbled something under her breath, but she dished me a plate of fried tortilla strips covered with red sauce and cheese, topped with two fried eggs. It was a measure of her displeasure that the eggs were fried. She knows I can't stand eggs unless they're scrambled. I wasn't entirely sure why she was put out with me, apart from being late to table. It would pass.

Monsignor, on the other hand, clearly enjoyed her good offices. She took his plate with a smile, refilled his teacup, and pushed a plate of fresh fruit toward him. "Even breakfast deserves dessert," she said.

"What a delightful thought," Monsignor said, as he took a couple of pineapple spears and pushed the plate in my direction. "Do you have breakfast here often?" he asked.

Clearly, the details of his current lodging were a bit unclear. "As often as I can," I said. "Are you well this morning, Monsignor?"

"Wonderful, wonderful. I'm ready for my morning constitutional. I thought I would take a walk before it's time for Mass."

The thought of Monsignor loose in town did not appeal to me, especially since I had not yet had time to solve the mystery of his sleeping pill prescription. Pilar broke into my thoughts with one of her own.

"I must go to the market today, Monseñor. Perhaps you would come with me, to help with the groceries? We can be done in time for Mass."

"Delightful. I would be happy to come. Let me get my coat and hat." He stood up, puzzled for a minute at his surroundings.

"Across the study, down the hall by the stairs, first door on the right," Pilar said.

"Of course!" He bustled off.

I smiled at Pilar, and she winked at me. I thought whatever was bothering her had clearly passed, but her expression became serious again. She refilled my coffee cup and passed me the morning paper. "Cuidado. Bad news."

I wondered what that might be, but I wasn't prepared

for what I saw on the front page. There, above the picture of Eoin Connor, was the headline: *Irish Author Arrested for Murder.*

It was the same time-stands-still feeling I had when they told me John was dead. This time it was Pilar instead of Quick who caught me, holding me in her strong, brown arms. She stroked my head like I was a child and crooned something, I know not what. My heart heard it, though, and eventually I began to breathe again. And some time after that, my mind returned to its space between my ears, back from the walkabout it took in the land of the living dead when I saw the paper.

The local rag is not the best source of international news, and it generally runs about twenty-four hours behind the rest of the world on that count. Not surprising for a small town paper, and to be fair, this would not have been news here at all, had Eoin not been in residence these past six months. Pilar watched as I read through the article with increasing disbelief. When I put it down, she looked straight at me.

"Is it true?"

Good question. "I cannot imagine that it is," I said, with as controlled a voice as I could muster. It couldn't be. Still, the image of a broken bat and two shattered doors kept insisting that it could be.

Pilar sniffed. "I thought he was a good man. Perhaps I was wrong."

The lawyer in me snapped to attention. "Don't jump to conclusions. There's more to this than what's in the papers." There had to be. I fought back tears, feeling the same sort of punch-in-the-gut pain I had felt when John was murdered, the same sort of betrayal. I wanted to cry, to throw things, to take a bat to the door of my office, if need be. But I had to be calm and reasonable. It cost me almost more than I was willing to pay, but pay it I did.

One black eyebrow cocked. Pilar was not convinced.

I got up from the table without a word, measuring each movement as though the pain were physical and not emotional. Pilar cautiously hugged me, put a smile on her face, and decided in her own mind that Eoin was innocent. "No man who loves you would do such a thing as this," she said with finality. For her, it was as simple as that, bat or no bat.

It wasn't so simple for me. I hid myself in my study for the rest of the morning, scanning the various European news feeds, watching the B.B.C., and just generally trying to figure out what was going on between uncontrollable bouts of crying. It was simply too much, and I did not want to face it, even though I knew I had to, that there was no choice in the matter.

By noon I had cried myself out and gleaned that Fiona and Eoin had been staying in the same hotel in Belfast. They had a loud and very public argument in the hotel bar the night before she was found dead, and Eoin was seen leaving her room only a short while before her body was discovered by an unnamed assistant. Eoin's fingerprints were found on the poison container, an outdated pesticide called Black Leaf 40, a concentrated solution of nicotine. And I knew that he had a dandy motive for murder. Several, in fact. If I were a cop, I would have arrested him, too.

By noon, the reports were repeating themselves, and I

had researched the finer points of nicotine poisoning. I asked Pilar to pack a bag, notified Mike that he was the one-and-only until further notice, and checked into the cost of a trip to Ireland. The charter jet was expensive, but it was available; the airport was open, and it would have me in Belfast by morning. At least now I knew what the next question was. Was I going to go?

I sighed and headed out to my office. I had a few things on my desk to finish sorting there, and it might help me sort my mind, as well. I had not been there more than a few minutes when Father Matt materialized in front of me, dispatched, no doubt, by Pilar.

"What are you going to do, William?" he asked, using his nickname for my warrior persona. William Wallace, wielder of broadsword and pursuer of justice.

I paused in my sorting, measuring my words carefully.

"Do you know what it's like, Father, to be a medical examiner all your life? To be privy to such terrible things, and have to live them and relive them over and over while the rest of the world gets on with life? Even the families can get past it; they have to. We just have to keep dealing with it." I wasn't sure whether Ireland was my ultimate destination, but I was determined to leave the Center, at least for the time being. The packed bag would not go to waste. I would work out the details. Right now I just wanted to flee. Anywhere. Not very much like William Wallace.

A tattered, gray folder lay on top of one of the shelves; my bad habit of stacking things in odd places. I remembered it well and tossed it at Father Matt. It landed on the couch next to him with a minor thud and slid, spilling a few faded color photographs out onto the rug.

Father Matt leaned over to pick them up and then stopped, images in hand, as he realized what they showed. He sat back up slowly and opened the folder to put them back in their place quickly, as though they burned his hands, and closed the gray cover with finality before he looked up at me. His face was pale under the brown of his beard. "What was that?" he finally asked.

I shrugged, matter-of-fact. I had seen those pictures so many times that they had lost much of their power over me, though the smell of rotting potatoes would always bring the scene back to my mind. My first brush with a serial killer. "What's left of a little girl. She was raped and strangled and stabbed and left in the woods for a hunter to find six months later. We carried what was left of her back to the morgue in a garbage bag."

I remembered reassembling the remains on the cold steel of the morgue table. It took most of the day. At the end of it all, I could announce from the remains that it had been a girl of six or seven, fifty inches tall or so. The missing girl — April — had been abducted from a friend's seventh birthday party, and at her last doctor visit had been square in the middle of the growth chart: 51 inches tall.

Some of the bones were missing. Most of the rest had marks on them, evidence of scavengers at work. I'd been lucky enough to find the tip of a blade embedded in a rib, evidence of the cause of death, and enough to link the girl to her murderer who still carried the clasp-knife in his pocket on the day he was arrested. Fifteen years later, he was still alive, but April was still dead, and I was still giving testimony at his periodic bail hearings. Her parents had divorced — the father remarried, the mother a drunk. The story had been on some true crime television show last year. When they called, I declined to give an interview.

"You hear the sins, Father Matt; I see them. In all their lurid detail, and then I have to talk about them over and over. To the cops. To the D.A. To the defense attorney. To the judge. Sometimes to the loved ones and sometimes to the press. It never goes away. I know all about the dark side of life." I took a long drink from the overly large glass of water on the shelf and continued pulling books and files out and packing them into boxes. "It's what I do. Now I have to decide whether the man I...." I paused, sitting back on my haunches to look at Father Matt again, hesitating to say the word. I decided I could not. "Whether Eoin Connor is one of those monsters that I've worked to put away all my life."

Father Matt took a deep breath, as though bringing in enough air might cleanse him from what he had seen. I knew from experience it wouldn't, but he'd discover that soon enough. "I can't say I blame you for how you feel," he finally said. "But must you give up on Eoin, too? Isn't he worth your doubt, unless something is proved against him?"

I took my glass in hand and folded myself onto the floor, looking up at him, my packing forgotten for the moment. "I'm just acknowledging what is. He was married, and he kept that from me. His wife showed up, and that's that. He destroyed my doors with a ball bat. Now he's in jail as a suspect in a murder. He's wealthy enough to afford a first-class lawyer. Nothing there for me to do." I paused. "I might be able to find a way to love a man who lied to me. I can't love a murderer."

"You know he didn't do it."

I tended to my shelves and answered over my shoulder. I didn't trust myself if I were to look into those brown eyes. "No, Father, I don't. He's more than capable. I saw that myself."

Father Matt was customarily direct. "You already love him, Jane."

"Perhaps. I thought so, at least."

"He came to see me that night, you know."

"I was down at the police station. Of course, I know."

Father Matt shook his head, as though to clear it. His expression was impatient. "He came to tell me about you. And Fiona. He was going to ask you to marry him, Jane, to wait for him while the marriage was sorted out. He had no idea she was in town. He was devastated. You were married. You had a wonderful life. Eoin was denied that, but he got to see a glimmer of what might be — in you and your own family. Imagine how he must feel, wanting that kind of intimacy and being denied it because of someone else's selfishness. Most people don't think that matters to men, but believe me, Jane, it does. It matters deeply, and the more passionate the man, the more it matters. Just when he thought he might have that — finally, with you — along came Fiona to yank the rug out from under his feet again. "

"Congratulations, Father. You've just outlined a pretty good motive for murder."

"He gave me this." Father Matt changed tactics and passed over a slip of lace. I unfolded it and a plain, gold ring dropped out. "His mother's ring, some of her lace. He had them with him to give to you that night."

I turned the lace over in my hands, then sat up long enough to place it, folded again, on the shelf, with the ring atop it. When I confronted my pastor again, my eyes were hard, and I could feel the flush rising on my neck. "Do you know why I loved John so much, Father Matt?"

No answer. I didn't really expect one. Father Matt didn't budge, still leaning expectantly towards me.

"John was my complete other half. He was as gentle as I am cantankerous. As believing as I am cynical. He was gentle and kind and patient, and he never once raised so much as a finger to me in all the years we were married. He couldn't even set a mousetrap; that was my job." I drained the last of the water in one swallow, wishing it were something else. "Eoin Connor came after me with a baseball bat. Tell me, Father, how am I supposed to love a man like that?" The fact was, I did love him, or had, and it was frightening. How could I have been so wrong about the man who had been so careful of me as we kept company over the last few months? I stood as still as I could, but done with the conversation, with Father Matt and with myself.

Father Matt stood, too. "Eoin Connor is a working man. He came from a rough life, Jane; he was a dockworker: tough, hard, not like John. He opened up for the first time in thirty years to let you in only to have Fiona walk in and toss the applecart from him. He was drunk, Jane, and in great pain, and he didn't come after you. He came after a door. Yours and mine, too — nice, safe, inanimate objects to take out his anger on. And I'll tell you,

I've never — never — seen a man in such pain. Never. He loves you, Jane, and the thought of losing you sent him over the edge. Can't you understand that?"

"I understand that at first it's doors and then it's faces, Father. I understand that men who hit things hit people. That's what violent men do, Father. I understand that I can't live with that." I folded my arms across my chest for emphasis. "I can't love that."

Father Matt took a step back and regarded me, and he suddenly smiled. Not his usual radiant smile, something softer and unsettling, as though he understood something for the first time and was not going to share it with me. "Perhaps," he finally said. "But you do, Jane Wallace, you do. And if he's not cleared of this murder, really cleared, you'll never be able to marry him."

"Father, if he is convicted, I wouldn't marry him, anyway."

"That's not what I mean. All it takes for a not-guilty verdict is a bit of doubt. The tribunal is not likely to see things that generously."

"Fiona's dead. Eoin is free to marry. Why would the tribunal get involved?"

Mistake. He knew he'd pricked my interest in spite of myself. Damn my curiosity. I didn't really care. I reminded myself to keep repeating that from time to time.

"This is pretty high profile: murder of a man's wife — in the eyes of the Church — presumably because the offended husband wants to be free to wed again. Crimen — the obstacle of crime, which is, in this case, the murder of a spouse — is an obstacle to marriage."

"No worries. I won't even think of marrying him if he is convicted. If he's not, then he's not guilty."

"He has to be innocent, Jane. That is different than not guilty, and you know it. The tribunal represents a law — well, not unto itself, but unto the Church. Different standards, often higher ones, especially in a case like this. Unless the evidence shows Eoin to be clearly innocent of the crime, he may still not be free to marry."

One of the problems with close friends is that they know your Achilles' heel. Mine is running the facts to ground wherever they lead. I can't stand loose ends, even when they don't affect me. This particular loose end, if it ever appeared, would affect me greatly. Maybe. Perhaps. Then again, maybe not. I didn't know.

Father Matt glanced sideways at me. He knew he'd won. He knew I'd never take that risk.

"I can help you book your flight," he said, with the faintest of smiles.

I shook my head. "No need. But you can drive me to the airport."

***

"I didn't kill her. God knows that I had enough reasons and sometimes, I wanted to...but I did *not* kill her." Eoin Connor regarded his defense counsel across the expanse of a metal table in an interrogation room. He supposed they all looked alike — spare, down-at-the-heels and furnished in the latest in second-hand, dented metal chic.

He saw Peter Suskind, the man in charge of defending the 'celebrated Eoin Connor,' look at him over his half-glasses. A man in his mid-forties, he had a reputation as the best in criminal defense in all of Northern Ireland. *He probably expects such a statement from his client,* thought Eoin, but if he understood lawyers, it didn't really matter to him so much the truth of the matter as much as how he would put the prosecution to the test of its own theories. The corners of Suskind's mouth turned up slightly, and he ran a well-manicured right hand, which was adorned by a signet ring in the family crest, through his brown hair before he answered.

"Never mind that. Where were you on the night Fiona died?"

"I visited her in her room, right enough. She was in the same hotel I stayed in, by design, no doubt. She never was one to take no for an answer."

"Why did you visit her?"

"She wanted to talk. She wanted to reconcile with me. She'd broached the subject several times before, and I refused. I went to make sure she understood I meant business."

"Say more."

Eoin thought back, tipping back in his chair, calling up a vision in his mind of the rooms Fiona had taken as suites in the Malmaison. He was sure it was for proximity rather than style; Fiona generally detested modern furniture, and the suites were done up in stark black and gray with the odd splash of golden-orange tossed about for relief. All angles and very minimalist, the opposite of Fiona's taste. He had taken a seat in an overstuffed club chair — gray — next to the gas fire, deliberately so that she could not sidle up to him and sit close. He wanted distance between them, real distance in space as there was in his heart.

Fiona had sighed and took her place in a chair of the same style opposite his. She had raised a languid hand to mute the television, currently tuned to some overwrought drama or another — just Fiona's style, in contrast to the furniture. He waited for her to speak first.

"Eoin, darling. I admit I've behaved badly, dreadfully to you. Especially last evening in the bar. I did not mean to fight with you. But can't we put that behind us and make a new life together, in the time we have now? Can't you forgive me? For the fight and for the past?"

Forgive you? he had thought to himself. *Yes, I can forgive you, but I'm damned sure not going to give you the chance to hurt me again.*

"She wanted to reconcile. I told her no."

"Just like that?"

"More or less."

"Why did you initially part ways?" Suskind was fishing.

"She ran off with another man."

"How did you take that?" Baiting the hook now.

"Given that I was on the lam myself, I didn't give it much thought at the time."

The solicitor sighed and leaned forward to rest his arms on the table and pass a hand over his forehead. "For a storyteller, you are certainly parsimonious with details. What did you think about it later?"

Eoin's mind wandered back again to the suite. The gas fire had been a good one, with the flames playing along ceramic logs enough like the real thing to pass. He had stared at them for a long time as Fiona talked.

"Why did you lie?" he had asked.

"Lie?" She had been all innocence. For a moment, he thought it was genuine until he saw the telltale duck of her chin. Fiona always did that when she had something to hide.

"Wasn't it bad enough to leave me? Did you also have to steal any chance I might have at happiness later on?" Remembering it, he felt the anger rising just as it had that evening. "How did you convince Father Clancy to lie and tell me my petition had been submitted, let alone denied?" Her face blanched, and for an instant, she lost control of her face; the horror of being found out played across it. In an instant, he knew.

"Holding me in reserve, weren't you — for when you were too old and faded to find another fancy husband." He saw her eyes widen, and he pressed it home. "Understand me once and for all, Fiona. I am not your husband and never was. I was willing to have you once, but you tossed that away. I am not willing to let you back in my life now. I'm filing that petition with the tribunal now, and I've no doubt it will be approved. Live alone and die alone, I don't care. You've done enough damage to me and mine. I am marrying Jane Wallace, count on it. I am going to make the life for me that I've missed out on all these years because of you." He recalled the sheer force of will it took for him to maintain a veneer of calm. It still did.

Eoin looked up at Suskind. "I thought she was a vindictive bitch and was glad to be shed of her. It didn't bother me too much until recently. Somehow she arranged for the local parish priest to lie about a decree of nullity I asked for.   I found out about it when I went to reapply, because I want to marry Jane Wallace. I have a motive. A good one."

"But you didn't kill her."

"I did not."

"How did your fingerprints get on her glass?"

"She asked me to fix her a drink. I did. Campari and soda. One of her affectations. I had scotch."

Eoin watched Suskind relax and his posture telegraphed his approval of the details.   Eoin chuckled inwardly. *I'm getting positively voluble. Good.*

"Do you know anything about Black Leaf 40?" Suskind asked.

This time Eoin Connor laughed out loud. "As much as any farmhand would. We used to use it. Awful stuff — thick and dark and poisonous as hell but a good insecticide."

"So you knew it was poison?"

"I did."   A pause, then, "I can't imagine sneaking that into a drink. It's dark, and it stinks. It would never pass."

"The autopsy shows she died of nicotine poisoning. There were traces of nicotine in the glass, and it had only your fingerprints and hers on it. And there was a bottle of Black Leaf 40 in the trash in the suite. Your fingerprints were on it."

Eoin laughed again. "That ought to prove my innocence right there. After writing about so many crimes, do you think I'd be daft enough to leave the poison there, complete with my fingerprints on it? Or use one so crude? There are so many better ways to off someone with poison.

Cyanide. Strychnine. Ricin.   But remember, poison is a woman's weapon.   Had I actually killed Fiona, I would have broken that pretty little neck of hers.   But I didn't. And I didn't poison her, either."   He paused for a long moment of thought, casting his mind back to the byre and all the old bottles and jars in there.   The only way a bottle of Black Leaf 40 with his fingerprints got into that room was because it came from the farm.   He wondered how. More importantly, he wondered why.

Setting aside that unpleasant line of thought, he continued.   "More information from my stash of true crime investigation.   Nicotine deaths are rare.   And they are ugly. Nausea, vomiting, sweating, seizures.   I don't care what the coroner says.   Nothing could have induced Fiona McLaughlin to drink enough Black Leaf 40 to die.   And if she did, she did it after I left."

"Reports don't lie."

"Then there is more to it. And I did not kill her."

"How did your fingerprints get on the container?"

"No idea."

"Who else might have a motive? Or access? How did that Black Leaf 40 get in Fiona's suite if you didn't take it there?"

The last few minutes of that night suddenly became clear in Eoin's memory. His last, harsh words to Fiona had faded when she looked at him with an expression somewhere between regret and anger. "Don't count on marrying your precious Jane just yet, Eoin. There's still a matter of the tribunal. She won't marry you if there is a cloud on your title."

Just like you to equate marriage with a real estate transaction, Eoin had thought as he rose to leave. All he said was "Fiona. It's over. Whatever we had — and it wasn't much — it's gone now."

She had remained motionless in the club chair, reaching for her glass of Campari and soda. *Such an awful drink, so bitter,* he thought, and then with a wry smile to himself thought it fitting. *A bitter drink for a bitter woman.*

He had let himself out into the hall. The doors to the tiny, dark elevator opened and a short, plump woman had pressed by him, her head down and her face almost obscured by the scarf wound around her neck. She gave him a brief, upward glance, all eyes and cheeks between the scarf and the hat pulled low on her forehead. Her face was vaguely familiar, but he couldn't place it, quite. It was as though he knew her in her youth, though, and she had been important.

As he reconsidered that moment and regarded Suskind with a level gaze, it came to him why he knew that woman, who she was, and what she meant. Could it have been Deirdre? Poor, bewitched, abandoned Deirdre? He wasn't sure.

Suskind repeated his question. "Is there anyone else who had motive and access, Eoin?"

Eoin Conner shook his head. "Can't think of a soul," he said, and made it clear to his QC that the interview was over.

CHAPTER SIXTEEN

January 19

The nice thing about flying charter is that the seats are comfortable, it's easy to sleep, and the food is good. I spent most of the flight dozing intermittently and thinking about the past few days. All of my children had called me when they heard about Eoin's arrest, alerted, no doubt, by Ben, my ginger-haired youngest, away at Georgia Tech, learning even more mysterious ways with computers. Only he, Luke (my carpenter son), and Adam (my daredevil seminarian) had actually met Eoin. My daughters, pregnant Zoe and med student Elizabeth, and Adam's twin, Seth, studying for the priesthood in Rome, knew him only second-hand. But they all called. I suppose they were worried that I might collapse under the strain as I had when their father was killed. Truth be known, I considered it, but I'm made of sterner stuff these days.

I arrived in Belfast early in the morning, my first trip off American soil. I was sad that I was not making it in the company of John, and I had fantasized about making it with Eoin, but here I was, clearing customs in Northern Ireland all by myself, with a pristine passport and no real idea how to manage myself in a foreign place. *At least they speak English,* I thought.

Once I approached the glass cubicle, I wasn't so sure. The uniformed man with the florid face had to ask me three times what the purpose of my visit was before I understood him. "Pleasure," I lied.

I assumed the next question was about duration, and I replied, "Two, three weeks," which seemed to satisfy him. He stamped my book and waved me on. I gathered my bag, anticipating a stop in customs, but strolled right through with no problems. I sighed with relief. Airports were airports pretty much anywhere. I flagged a taxi and climbed in.

"Where to?" The driver's accent sounded much like Eoin's at his best. I was relieved. I fished my smartphone out of my purse and consulted my notes.

"The Malmaison. Victoria Street."

"Know it well. We're off. First time to Belfast?"

"Yes, it is."

"Ah, well then, shall we take the scenic route? Bit of a tour?"

I considered the proposition. It was early, and my room would hardly be ready. I appreciated his straightforward suggestion. Might as well get a little sightseeing in. Learning something about the city might help me in the long run.

"The Blue Plate Special, please," I replied.

The tables turned. "Beg pardon?"

I smiled. "Yes, please. The best tour you can. I am in no rush, and I have never been to Ireland before."

"Yes, ma'am." He smiled at me in the mirror and touched the brim of his cap. For the next two hours, he drove me all over Belfast, giving me a running commentary of life in the still-divided city. On the one hand, he drove me past Victoria Square — right across from my hotel, he pointed out — and the Titanic Quarter and the shipyards, the place that Eoin worked so many years ago. The waterfront near downtown was clean and inviting, though I wondered a bit about the huge sculpture of a woman perched on a large sphere and holding a giant ring. On the other, the segregated Protestant and Catholic communities made me uneasy with their political murals, the remains of ruined houses, the Peace Wall, and the gates that still closed at night to keep the two groups apart from each other.

My simple grasp of Irish history, supplemented by some of Eoin's stories, led me to believe that most of the conflict was behind as of the mid-1990s. That was hard to believe when I passed a house with a hooded sniper painted on the side, taking aim at anyone who passed. It was one of those paintings that seemed to follow the viewer no matter his perspective, and it made my blood run cold. To my mind, the Catholic sectors looked a bit more prosperous: the dooryards were cleaner, with fewer ruined lots. I supposed that impression might be the selective presentation of my driver, whose name was, of course, Paddy, and who sported a miraculous medal around his neck. But there were murals there, as well, celebrating martyrs to the cause, and showing solidarity with political prisoners near and far, including one for imprisoned Basques. There was even one expressing welcome for Middle Eastern refugees. I had not quite appreciated how deeply the English occupation affected Irish life, and as a result, how strong was the identification with the downtrodden. It gave me pause to see support for causes not quite so well-known, and certainly not so popular, in the States.

By ten, we were headed back to my hotel, passing the murals on Falls Road. The Troubles weren't ancient history; they were supposedly past, but still very much alive on Falls Road and the Shankill. The Irish had long memories and short tempers, or so it was said about them. It proved true in my own beloved South, still scarred by a war nearly a hundred-and-a-half years ago. I hoped it would not prove true of Eoin.

The Malmaison was housed in a dun-colored, Victorian building. From the outside, it looked very conventional, all arches and windows. The inside was a different story.

I felt as though I had fallen through Alice's rabbit hole. The lobby was decorated in black and shades of purple, with a checkerboard carpet and a chair that looked for all the world like the Queen of Hearts would be arriving any moment to hold court. A gigantic wooden box camera stood to one side, near the elevator. I chose the hotel because it was where Fiona died, the better to nose around. I was perplexed. From what I knew of Fiona, this was anything but her style.

The woman at the desk was pleasant and helpful, dressed in the requisite black dress, her hair in an asymmetrical geometric cut. Her accent and her name tag indicated she hailed from London, and my ears were thankful.

"Your room is ready, if you'd like to go on up," she said as she returned my credit card to me. "I suspected you might be tired from your long trip; Americans always arrive early in the morning, and they are always tired." She handed me a plastic key card and motioned for a young man standing nearby. "Paul will take you up to your room and Charles, the Head Concierge, can help you with any arrangements you need to make during your visit." I glanced in the direction she gestured. A dignified man with russet hair sat behind an oak table. The lavender square peeking out of his gray suit matched the color of one of the carpet squares. He nodded almost imperceptibly in my direction, all the while keeping one eye on his computer screen. Beside him, a young man in black slacks and white shirt, open at the collar, stood. He winked. I suspected that the man at the desk would have disapproved. I winked back.

Paul picked up my suitcase and led me to the elevator: a tiny, dark, mirrored thing that rattled its way to the third floor. I stepped out into the hallway, incongruously decorated with religious art, and followed him through a French door to my room at the end of the hall.

It was modern to the extreme, with two bottles of wine and two glasses on the counter and a flat-screen television on the wall. There was a tiny fridge, and the bed was queen-sized, with a bright, white duvet and five overstuffed pillows. Paul left my bag on the luggage rack. I tipped him and saw him out.

A minute later, the lights went out in the room.

Great. I called down to the desk.

"Front desk. Elizabeth. How may I help you, Mrs. Wallace?"

I drew in a sharp breath. I was Dr. Wallace these days. No one called me Mrs. Wallace since John's death. I recovered and explained my predicament.

Elizabeth laughed, a pleasant sound, not at all derisive.

"It's the key. You have to put it in the slot by the door for the lights to work. Paul should have shown you. I'll have a word with him. It saves on electricity. It's actually quite common here."

I was glad I hadn't gone downstairs. My face was flushed with embarrassment. "Please don't say anything. I wasn't really paying attention; I'm sure he did, and I missed it. Thanks. Sorry to bother you." That wink of Paul's paid off, I suppose.

I flopped on the bed, which was softer than I would have liked but would serve at least for a few days, and dropped into a restless sleep for a couple of hours. At length, I sat up again and got the number Ben had found me for Eoin's brother, Terry. It was time I started my investigation.

***

"You're here?" Terry Connor's voice held a note of incredulity. "You want to meet with me about Fiona?" His sister, sitting across from him at the breakfast table of the family farm, a half-eaten plate of sausages and eggs in front of her, cocked her head in query. Terry shrugged his shoulders and held up a cautionary finger as he continued to listen. "Right. Very well, then. I'll meet you at The Hammersley. It's a small pub about a block from your hotel. Meet me in the snug at five. It's quiet there, and we can talk." He paused again, nodding his head. "Yes, yes, of, course, nothing to it. I'll see you then."

Terry touched the screen of his smartphone and replaced it in his breast pocket, then picked up his knife and fork, going after his over-easy eggs with vengeance. Not for the first time did he think the Americans had cutlery right as he struggled to get the runny yolk to adhere to the slick egg white, rounded by the tines. Across the table, his sister, who could have been his twin with the same straight graying brown hair and blue eyes, waited impatiently for him to finish chewing.

"Well?" she asked as he washed down his bit of egg with a sip of hot, strong, dark, sweet tea.

"That was Jane. Eoin's Jane. She's in Belfast."

"What?" Molly Connor set her own mug down with a start. "Belfast? Why?"

"Seems she thinks that she can find something here to clear Eoin."

Two fine lines, a perfect little eleven not treated to Botox (like those of so many of her friends), appeared between Molly's light brown brows. "Eoin's prints are on the bottle of Black Leaf. It had to come from the farm. He was just here, before Fiona was killed. As much as I love our brother, it seems pretty grim for him."

"True enough. It seems all the evidence points to Eoin. And God knows, he had motive."

It was Molly's turn to postpone her response with a bit of food, and a bit of sausage and toast wiped through the remains of the yolk on her plate. "He's reason enough, that is certain. Does Jane know about everything Fiona's done to him?"

"I doubt it. You know how Eoin is. Rather a stoic. I'd have drowned the woman long ago." Terry thought back to their time in Dublin when Eoin worked in the shipyards to keep the rest of them on bread and cheese. When he'd married Fiona, he'd had to take on extra shifts, so free was she with his money. "I've never believed that Fiona miscarried. I think she was afraid that if she told Eoin she lied about being pregnant to get him to marry her, he'd have petitioned for that decree of nullity right then and there."

"She didn't know him very well, did she? Once he made a promise, he kept it." She glanced up at the Infant of Prague over the doorway, a pound note just peeking out from under its base. "He always took the Church so seriously. I always wondered why our big brother never took the cloth."

"I'm guessing in large part because he was married."

"Point taken."

Terry reached across for the jar of marmalade, nearly empty, and spooned out the last of it, golden and just bitter enough to be interesting. He'd never developed a taste for sweet jams. A few toast particles clung to the spoon as he returned it, clattering, to the jar. "She told me she's sure he couldn't have done it. But she didn't sound as though she believed it herself."

"Eoin could have. I could have," Molly stated firmly.

Terry looked at his sister and she gave him a sympathetic glance before she continued. "You could have, and you know it. Eoin is not the only Connor with a motive for murder. Given half a chance of getting away with it, sure, and I could. She's been a curse to the Connors since the day Eoin met her. And a blessing," Molly reminded him. "Had she not set Seamus Devlin after me, Eoin would not have been forced to take a runner to England. Never would have been a famous writer, none of that. We'd still be poor and living in a council house in

Belfast, or worse." She reached around to the Aga for the teapot, freshened the leaves, and filled the waiting pot again.

"It didn't seem so good at the time." Terry remembered the incident with a familiar stab of anguish in his gut — part fear, part shame. Seamus Devlin, an all-around rounder and darling of the local I.R.A., had taken a shining to Molly. Eoin had been the only one with enough worry and courage to do anything about it. He'd tipped the R.U.C. to a meeting going on in one of the council flats, a meeting at which would be one Seamus Devlin, considered a prime catch. It was Eoin's personal tragedy that the R.U.C. got the wrong flat and killed an innocent boy, Tam Murphy, in the bargain.

As if reading his mind, Molly broke in. "Bad enough Tam died, but that wasn't the end of it."

Terry nodded. "I remember that day like it was yesterday." Tam's father had stirred up a mob from the pub to go after a young Protestant dockworker, new to Belfast from England, unfamiliar with the Troubles and all they brought, who'd trailed Eoin to the Catholic part of Dublin and had struck up an acquaintance with a Catholic girl. "Poor love-struck sod," he said aloud with no need to clarify who he meant, for Molly's face told him she was standing beside him in that long-ago time, looking on the scene, though at the time she'd been home and heard only second-hand about the fight and Eoin's flight. "He had no idea that it might be a death sentence for him and the girl in those days. We're just lucky that it wasn't Eoin who got killed."

He saw Molly's face cloud slightly. "Will you tell

Jane?" He knew she had a sister's tender heart for the men in her life, especially quiet, passionate Eoin, the one who a sister's love had glossed over many sins, large and small. Eoin was not perfect in her eyes, but by the same token, there was nothing she'd change. "I'm not sure she loves him enough."

"Who knows? If I need to tell her everything about him, I will." Terry felt the familiar stab of admiration tempered by jealousy at Molly's words. She was a second mother to all her brothers, even the older ones. Too bad she'd never had a family of her own. He wondered if she'd have had a favorite among them like she did among her brothers? It still galled him that he wasn't the one.

"Perhaps she needs a dose of reality about Eoin, the saint," he said.

Molly smiled as she checked the tea for steeping. "Terrance Michael Thomas Connor, you should be ashamed," she said. "If she's known our brother very long at all, she'll know he's no saint. Unlike you."

He smiled at her genuine affection and teasing and he let her refill his cup, the dark tea making leather out of the milky residue. "It's time you quit being envious. Eoin's not worth your own poor soul, you know. He's had great successes and great tragedies, and this is just another. Who knows how this will end, but Jane's the one to ride it out, not us." She set the teapot down and passed the sugar bowl, full of small brown cubes. "I prefer the quiet life to the heroic one, don't you?"

Terry took a deep breath and then let it out, long and loud. Molly always had the knack of bringing him about. "I do, indeed," he answered. He took three small cubes and dropped them into his tea with the worn and tarnished tongs that had been the pride of his mother's table.

CHAPTER SEVENTEEN
January 19

The Hammersly was a block-and-a-half down from the hotel, its bright red façade announcing the name in gilt letters over the door, gas lights with frosted gloves in the shape of flames glowing in the windows. I pulled my overcoat snug against the dreary weather, turning the collar up against the damp wind. The sun had already set, and with the gathering dark, the wind had picked up and the soft rain was becoming icy. I found myself missing the more congenial cold of Colorado as I quickened my steps, dodging a yellow taxi as I crossed the street and opened the door.

The pub was crowded with an end-of-the-day custom: workmen three deep at the bar. I watched the man behind the bar pull pints for a moment or two, partly filling glasses, setting them down to rest, and coming back to top them off as soon as the stout settled out into two layers. I marveled at how he could keep track of the dozen or so glasses he had set out in front of him.

"Meet me in the snug," Terry Connor had said. I cast eyes around the room, looking for a likely candidate, but there were no solitary men, no one looking as though he were waiting for someone. I must have looked as perplexed as I was, for a waitress, four empty glasses in her hands, stopped and gave me a look that was half-amused, half-annoyed. I was, after all, standing right in her path to the bar.

"Lost, are you?" She raised one painted eyebrow so high it almost met her henna-red hair.

"I'm meeting someone. Terry Connor. He said to meet him in the snug." I shrugged and added, "I don't see him."

"Snug's outside."

Now I was really confused. "But he said to meet him at the Hammersly."

"Snug's outside," she said again, then pushed past me, leaving me more confused and increasingly uneasy. She muttered something that I took to be unflattering, even though I could not hear it, to a short, barrel-chested man in a dark blue sweater standing at the corner of the bar. He responded with a grin, pinched her through her tight green pants, and ducked away as she turned back with a scowl on her face.

The man made his way through the crowd. His round face was sunburned and stubbled. His brown eyes were rimmed and moist, but bright enough. "You poor wee thing," he said when he reached my side, even though I stood a head taller. "You're lost, are you? Looking for the snug?" Without waiting for an answer, he took my arm and dragged me back out the door I had just entered, around the corner from the big glass window, to a small, dark, oak entrance on the side alley. Above it was a carved sign, almost too dark with age to make out in the dim light of the street light: Hammersly.

"Years ago, ladies were not allowed in the public bar," he explained. "The snug was a place they could meet and get a pint and still maintain their dignity. If Terry said he'd meet you there, there you'll find him." He paused and regarded me with a suddenly sharp look. "Must be important for him to meet you there. And not for everyone's hearing." He opened the door for me. I slid past him, anticipating that I'd receive the same pinch the barmaid did, but it's hard to get a purchase on a greatcoat.

Apparently he figured the same, for as I passed through into the small room, I felt a pat on my rear and heard a chuckle both behind me and ahead. "Thanks, Liam," said a man sitting on an armchair upholstered with tired red leather.

"You must be Terry." I stepped forward and extended my hand. There could be no doubt. He had the same green eyes and the same open face, though he was a few inches shorter, and his hair, more brown than gray, was straight and thin.

"I am." He pulled a second chair out from the table, helped me off with my coat, and settled me in. A half-drunk pint of Guinness was on the table. "What will you have?"

I shrugged. I have no taste for stout, but I felt foolish asking for wine. I shivered a bit without my coat. There was a coal fire in the corner of the snug, but it had died down and the room was cold. I was finding Irish cold to be wet and miserable. "Could I just have some coffee? Black, please."

"Anything your heart desires." He walked to the pass-through and shouted to the barman. "Coffee, please, Seamus. Hot and black. Make a new pot if you have to, you old robber, you." I heard a guffaw from the other side, and in an instant, a heavy green mug was pushed through.

I cradled it in my hands as Terry sat down. The warmth felt good. I studied the dark liquid, trying to decide how to begin. He took advantage of the delay to shovel some coal onto the fire. It flared up. I found the smell of the coal fire oddly welcoming.

It seems Terry Connor knows how to exploit silence as well as I do. He sat down opposite me, silent as the grave, unmoving, taking the odd sip from his glass. I finally looked up.

"Tell me about Eoin and Fiona," I said.

Terry sat back, arms folded across his chest. "So that's it. What do you want to know?"

I shook my head and regarded my coffee again. "I just need to understand. You know he's been arrested for her murder. He didn't do it. He couldn't have done it." I didn't sound convincing even to myself. "I just thought if I understood more about him — her — them — I might be able to figure out who did kill Fiona and why."

Terry laughed, a short, sharp sound. "There'd be no end of candidates for that position," he said, starting with every man she's ever tangled with. "Fiona McLaughlin is — was — a conniving bitch who used every man she ever met to advance her own pocketbook. And not starting with Eoin."

It was my turn to bide my time. This time I sipped my coffee without looking at it, keeping my eyes fixed on Terry. His face was bland and unemotional, but his eyes narrowed when he spoke Fiona's name. "Her family was as poor as they come, and the Troubles did them no good at all. Her father was a drunk and a violent man, her mother, too, abusive and alcoholic. Fiona was the youngest of a bad brood, all of them dead or in jail by the time they were twenty. Fiona was different. Prettier, smarter, determined to do well any way she could."

"And the way she could was by taking advantage of men."

"Not until they had taken advantage of her. Fiona was a slut."

I've never heard that word said so matter-of-factly. Terry drained his glass and went to the pass-through to ask for another. Drawing a pint the fine art it is, it was several minutes before he returned. I nursed my coffee until he was back, then nodded in his direction. "And...?"

"She was a slut," he repeated. "Chased anything in pants and usually caught them, and she was always, always trading up, leaving the last man for one she thought could keep her better. One day she got caught — or thought she did — between men and being pregnant. She got into Eoin's bed, announced he was the father of her child, and he married her. My brother, you may have noticed, is afflicted with a serious case of morals. And loyalty."

I thought again about my door. I wasn't so sure about those morals.

Terry took another draught from the glass and set it back on the table carefully. "Only she wasn't pregnant. But now she had a fine, clean, warm place to live and a good man to look after her until she could find a better one."

It took me a moment to be able to speak. "I see." I

regarded the coffee cup again, empty now, because I was afraid to let Terry see the emotions playing on my face. "Did he love her?" I still didn't look up, but I could hear the shrug of his shoulders in his voice.

"Who knows? In his way, perhaps. He was young, and he has principles. He would have married her, love or not, because he thought the child that turned out not to be at all was his. And then he tried to make a go of it, if for no other reason than he had promised to."

I could understand that. In fact, I'd experienced it.

"She left him soon enough. Went off with some Italian play-acting at being a reporter. Eoin had troubles of his own by then."

"How so?"

Terry finished his glass in one long pull and leaned across the table toward me. "You told me Eoin didn't kill Fiona. That I believe, lass, even though I am not sure you do."

I flushed. Was I that transparent?

Terry continued. "She wasn't worth it to him anymore. But kill her, he could have. And there were times in his life when he would have cheerfully broken that long, pretty neck of hers with his bare hands, if she'd given him the chance."

"Go on." We looked at each other across the small table, unblinking.

"You know that scar of his, the one on his cheek? Did he ever tell you how he got it?"

I shook my head.

"Eoin was working as a joiner at the shipyards. One of

the few jobs a Catholic could get in Ulster in those days. The man in charge owed our da a favor. Most of our mates gave up looking for a job and left for America or took the dole, but Eoin refused to leave Ireland, and he's always needed the dignity of work. He can be stubborn." Terry slid the glass aside and played with the coaster; I could almost feel him organizing his words. "Eoin worked alone, the only Catholic among the Protestants there at the shipyard. He'd arrive earlier and work later and never gave them the flimsiest excuse to fire him. Along the way, he made friends with a young brickie — a Protestant, as friendless in his way as Eoin was in his."

"Brickie?"

"Bricklayer. That was a Protestant job in those days. Funny how those things went. Anyway, that particular day Eoin was on his way back to Falls Road to meet a few of the lads at the pub. They were already several pints into it when he got there. Eoin always nursed his one pint, waving away the extras when someone shouted a round. He's never been one to get drunk without a good reason. That night he had just stood up to leave when Tam Murphy's da staggered in." Terry paused again, then continued. "I was there, too. I've never seen such grief. Tam had been killed by accident in a R.U.C. raid a few weeks before — Eoin was there — and that night Tam's da was already drunk and rowdy, shouting that there was a f—"

I smiled at Terry's censure of himself; I've heard the word before, and even in the short time I'd been in Belfast, discovered that there was a strain of Irishman who used it like a comma in conversation. He continued, "There was a Prot up at the corner chatting up one of our girls, bold as brass." A smile crossed his lips as he continued. "Tam's da was known for his language, even amongst us, and ours was none too good. I'll never forget what he said next: 'If you had a pair of balls among you, you'd be up there teaching him a lesson for my poor Tam.' What Tam had to do with that poor, love-struck boyo, I'll never know. Grief doesn't always make sense."

Tell me about it, I thought.

"Anyway, rumblings among the others began, with hot sentiments against the Protestants rising with every word until the lot of them stood up and swarmed for the door. Eoin slid away and headed out the side door, dragging me along. The last thing I heard was someone yelling, 'Bloody coward! Are you not with us, Connor? Are you sleeping with the R.U.C. these days instead of with Fiona?'"

I broke in. "R.U.C. — Royal Ulster Constabulary, the police? I gather it was a dangerous thing, in those days, to be known as a conspirator."

He gave me a wry smile just as I had hoped he would. My sarcasm wasn't lost. It eased the mood a bit, and we both relaxed. "You could say that, and particularly bad for Eoin, because — after all — he was. He was the one who'd called the R.U.C. to that flat across from Murphy's, to rid himself, his sister, and the world of Seamus Devlin." He paused again, taking a long draught from his glass. "Devlin, to make a long story short, was an I.R.A. hoodlum. He was courting our sister. Eoin's very bad luck, and Tam's, a twitchy constable shot Tam Murphy and not Seamus."

"Bad luck, indeed. I've seen my share of similar incidents."

"So Eoin says. At any rate, he got to the corner about the time that the crowd started after the brickie. He tried to hurry to a spot of safety, but there wasn't one, not in Falls Road in Belfast during the Troubles. He turned a corner into a dead-end alley, and that mistake had cost him dearly. I remember the sight of his face when the first fist came at him."

I closed my eyes in reflex. I can look death straight in the face, but I can't hear about violence without feeling it in the very marrow of my bones. I can close my eyes to images, but to words there are no borders, no obstacles to sounds. I found the darkest place in my mind's eye, sighed, and engaged Terry Connor once again. "Go on."

"He fought well, poor lad, but he was one and they were four, and it wasn't long before he was doubled over in pain, blood pouring from his face and mouth. Eoin threw a punch or two, then tried to ghost away. It was a mistake."

"How so?"

"The meanest and drunkest of our mates grabbed him and swung at his face. Eoin, sober and stronger, landed his fist on the man's jaw, and he crumpled, spitting teeth and blood, with a broken jaw."

I thought of the baseball bat again.

"After that, Eoin was all for the brickie. He put himself between the poor brickie and the fists. He hit back at the men he'd shared life in Belfast with. Eoin's a fine boxer, you know. Our parish priest inflicted boxing lessons on us all, but Eoin took them to heart, though I never saw him start a fight. He felled a second man and a third with his bare fists. Another man got close enough to swipe a knife in his face — that's how he got the scar — and Eoin felled him, too, with a kick to his groin. That one hit his head against the wall, and he died." Terry paused and looked at me for signs of reaction. I was fighting hard to have none. "It was a kill-or-be-killed fight by then," he added.

"About that time, the constables arrived. The brickie lived, but Eoin was branded a traitor, and when he got home to pack a few things before running off to England to save his skin, Fiona had already left, spreading rumors that he was a collaborator in her wake. From that moment, he was a marked man."

I knew enough about the Troubles to know that a traitor was not destined to a long and happy life, dying contentedly in his bed of an old age, but Eoin had survived. I asked Terry how.

"With the clothes on his back, he walked to the ferry terminal and hopped a boat to Birkenhead. He signed on as a stevedore there, scribbling thoughts on spare pieces of paper whenever he had a moment, for over a year, and sending as much of his paycheck as he could afford back home to Tam Murphy's ma. At length, he had a book published, a tribute to Tam. Eventually, he was able to come back to Ireland, because he paid his debt by writing a book on the Troubles that squared him with the I.R.A. His first bestseller. What most people don't know is that he sent money to Tam's parents and to that brickie for years, until he was well enough to find a job and whole enough to keep one. I think he was even asked to stand as godfather to the man's son, though Eoin, bless his pious heart, declined."

Terry pushed back his chair and went to the pass-through. He returned with two glasses of brandy, tasting one before shoving the other across to me.

"You said you don't think Eoin could have killed Fiona. She tricked him, she exploited him, she betrayed him, and just when he found someone he wanted to share his life with, she showed up to throw a spanner in the works and reclaim him as her own. That's a lot more reason to kill a man than protecting some poor brickie from a mob thrashing. Eoin is very, very capable of killing, if the circumstances are right. The question for you, lassie, is do you have enough faith in him to figure out whether he did and live with the answer, whatever it is?"

I drained the brandy in a single gulp, thanked Terry Connor in a quiet voice, and hurried out of the snug. It was beginning to snow, and I needed to think.

***

Suskind was already sitting in one of the chairs when Eoin entered the room. He nodded to the guard, who held the door and exchanged wry smiles with him. He was finding that there was an odd camaraderie within the gaol and not just among the prisoners. He suspected gaol life took its toll on the guards as well. Perhaps another book, one day, assuming he ever got out of this place. Or whatever gaol they decided to send him to if he was convicted. At least he didn't have to worry about them stretching his neck; unlike the U.S., the U.K. had no death penalty. He supposed he was pleased about that.

He sat down opposite Suskind and extended his hand. "Progress?" he asked.

"I have some reports that I want to go over with you. And a request. An odd one."

"Start with that."

"I got an offer from the sheriff in that town you lived in..." He ruffled through his stack of papers and then added, "Telluride. Seems you are well-thought-of back there. He wants to assist. How, I have no idea. But he says that he has some folks over there that would like to look over your file to see if there is anything they see that we don't."

Eoin pondered the question for a moment. This had Jane's fingerprints all over it. "Does the report mention a Dr. Wallace?" he asked hopefully. He had not heard from her since his arrest. Granted, they had not parted on good terms, but under the circumstances, he hoped she might set that aside.

More ruffling. "No. It mentions some Center for Forensic Science. Some man named Tom Patterson. A Dr. Michael Delatorre. But not her."

It bothered Eoin that he felt such a sharp stab of regret at that piece of information. She was a stubborn woman, Jane, and if she gave up on him, it would be once and for all. Perhaps she had. "No harm in it, I suppose, but not sure what they can do. Let them have at it. Can't hurt." He leaned back in his chair. "What about those reports?"

Suskind shoved a stapled document across the table. "Autopsy report and toxicology. Nicotine poisoning. Take a look at the whole thing. Anything new in there? Anything that helps?"

It only took a few minutes to read over the report. Eoin knew what he would find. He pointed to the summary of physical findings. "It's not relevant, and it probably doesn't help. But she told me this — I probably should have gone back with her, out of simple charity. But I couldn't bear the thought of living with Fiona again. Not even for a little time. And I could not bear the thought of having to care for her after all she did to me."

Suskind took the report and read the paragraph indicated by Eoin's index finger. "The brain is sectioned at 3 mm intervals. There is a 7 mm lesion in the left temporal lobe with a hemorrhagic and necrotic center. There is a small pseudocapsule, and the surrounding parenchyma is edematous. Microscopic examination reveals glioblastoma multiforme." He looked up from the page. "Plain English, please?"

"Brain tumor. A very bad one. One that was certainly going to kill her, and relatively soon. She wanted me to be with her for those last days. I'm a selfish bastard. I said no. She even offered me the whole of her estate if I would look after her. I still said no. I've plenty of scratch on my own."

"She told you?"

"She did."

"Can you prove it?"

"No."

"Did you mention this when you were first arrested?"

"No."

"Did you tell anyone else?"

"No."

"So from the prosecution's perspective, that's just a convenient admission after the fact."

"I suppose so." Eoin Connor leaned forward. "I found

out after I got here, that night in her flat, the night she died. If I had known about it earlier, do you think I would have traveled half a world away to pursue a decree of nullity, knowing all I had to do was wait her out?" He paused. "Damn Fiona! It seems even when she is murdered, she manages to ruin my life. I was on my way to her suite to tell her I'd changed my mind, that I'd see her through this, though I wouldn't live with her, when the police arrived."

"You told no one."

"Damn it, man, who did I have to tell? I thought about calling Jane to explain, but I got arrested first."

"Did you know about this?" Suskind shoved a sheet of paper across the desk. "A copy of a note found in Fiona's desk. Rather interesting, actually. Lavender paper and florid purple ink."

"That would be Fiona." Eoin read the note and dropped the paper as if it were about to burst into flames, then picked it up again and read it slowly. "Monday: Georges and Sons, solicitors: change will to eliminate Eoin. The bastard." He put the paper down again. "Fiona was never one to leave anything unsaid, especially if it was vindictive. I knew nothing about this."

"The concierge confirms that she called that evening, quite upset, to ask him to schedule an appointment with those same solicitors. He also said that she had seen them only a few days before. And he says that hotel records show her calling your room that afternoon after the appointment, and the maid says that she saw her coming toward your room that day. Worst of all, your sister..."

"My sister? My sister! Molly?"

"Deirdre. Isn't there a Deirdre?"

Eoin nodded. "Deirdre told the investigators that Fiona returned to the suite, telling her that you refused to care for her and that she told you she was writing you out of her will."

"I did refuse. The day she died. She said nothing about the will." He was still trying to process Deirdre's role in all this. Surely, she could not still be in the sway of Fiona after all these years and after being so badly abused. But he had been correct. It *was* Deirdre he had seen when he was leaving that night.

Eoin sat back in his chair and rocked it up on its back legs. It was an old one, painted over several times, and sturdy enough to stand the strain. Not like the flimsy modern ones. "That's a tight little net they have there. Paint me as a selfish bastard — which I am — interested in Fiona's money, but not in her. Throw in a threat to write me out of the will — recompense for all those years she stole from me with that lie of hers — and I have to admit, it's a strong motive for murder. One of the best. Well done, Fiona. You can ruin my life even by getting yourself killed."

He tipped his chair back to the ground with a sharp clang. "The only problem is, I didn't do it."

CHAPTER EIGHTEEN

January 21

I spent the next morning in the newspaper morgue: a modern combination of old print, microfilm, microfiche, and computerized records, finding everything I could about Eoin, Fiona, Tam Murphy, Seamus Devlin, and the incident Terry had detailed to me. The newspaper accounts added nothing and confirmed Terry in every detail. It seems Eoin isn't the only Connor with a storyteller's mind. They did, however, provide a few more leads to follow up on. I jotted down names and retired to my hotel for room service lunch and extended computer time, trying to get current addresses. Of the four names, only one still lived in Belfast; two were dead, and one I just couldn't trace. I would forward that to Ben to work his internet magic; he might be able to find out more than I did.

Sheila Fogarty had worked with Fiona in the bank and had been a flat-mate before Fiona married Eoin. One of the follow-up stories reported on Eoin's flight and the fact that his wife, too, had disappeared, casting journalistic aspersions on the absent man, insinuating that he had something to do with it. In that context, Sheila had been interviewed. She cast little light on the mystery at the time, made a few vaguely complimentary comments about Eoin's character and not about Fiona's. I gave a silent prayer of thanks for such local color padding needed to fill column-inches in the old days; there was surely no other reason to have included her at all, but there she was.

Her current address was not far from the Cathedral of St. Peter, in the section of Belfast that would have been strongly Catholic in the days of the Troubles, and if my driver was correct, still was. The Cathedral was about a mile away, and though the day was cold and dreary, there was no wind or snow or rain, so I elected to walk. It was midday by then. Traffic along Victoria Street bustled, and there were a fair number of people on the sidewalks, though that thinned as I got farther from the commercial section and closer to the residential areas around the Cathedral. I passed the apartment building Paddy had pointed out as the headquarters of the English forces during the Troubles: tall, dull, unimaginative, and with a flat roof that allowed helicopter landings. It also, as I recalled, meant I was nearing my destination.

I turned the corner into the square, across from the murals that kept the Troubles so present and vivid and had the distinct sense that eyes were following me, despite the fact that it was just past midday, and the only person I saw was a stooped, older woman entering a newsagent's shop on the corner.

Sheila Fogarty — now Carney and widowed — lived in a first-floor flat with a small dooryard garden gone to seed for the winter, a riot of overgrown brown twigs with broken, lacy tops. A crushed beer can lay next to the wall, its label faded by the sun. Yard maintenance did not seem to be Sheila's forte. She answered the door at my knock; the bell was dangling and useless. No man about to fix it, I supposed.

"Yes?" Sheila spoke through a crack in the door, wide

enough to see who was there, but not open enough to be inviting. The tidy room I saw beyond her stood in contrast to the outside but squared with the small, bright, tidy woman in the doorway. She looked to be a few years older than I, but like me, had done as little to repair the march of time as she had to repair the peeling paint on the metal door she stood behind. Her hair was red gone largely to gray, and her face was plain, freckled, and completely devoid of makeup. I liked her instantly.

"Sheila Fogarty?"

"Yes." Her response was cautious. She didn't open the door any further, but she didn't close it on me, either. I took that as a good sign and hurried to explain myself.

"I'm a friend of Eoin Connor. And Fiona." A minor lie, but I could be forgiven that, under the circumstances. It reminded me why I hate this kind of investigation so much; it requires me to be too cautious of my thoughts and speech in order to draw something out of an unwilling interviewee. "Fiona died. Rather tragically, really, and Eoin is suspected in her death. I need to talk to you, please, if I may."

A long pause. "I haven't seen Fiona for years. Not since she left Ireland. Eoin, either. I can't help you." She started to close the door, but I put one of my size tens on the threshold. "I know. I just need to find out some things about her life here. Really, it's important, and I won't take much of your time."

"Move your foot." Sheila's hazel eyes flashed, and I could see red creeping up her neck.

"Just a few questions. You were her flat-mate. You knew her, and you knew Eoin, didn't you?"

Sheila Carney nee Fogarty, now widowed, brought her heel down sharply on my instep. So much for first impressions. I yelped in pain and moved it, but I heard her answer before she slammed the door in my face. "Yes." Damn the woman, did she know no other word? There's another reason I'm not called on to do face-to-face interviews very often: no sixth sense about when I am about to get into trouble. Tom Patterson would have sweet-talked his way in and would be sitting in that little drawing room having tea and cakes.

I stood on the doorstep with not much to show for my efforts but a throbbing foot and a heart currently residing on the ground somewhere near it. Just like at home. A poor few facts for Eoin, so many against him. It reminded me why I like morgue work so well. It's much more concrete. If it's knowable at all, I can figure out a way to know it. And demonstrate it. Trial work — and, as it was turning out, criminal investigation — was not to my liking. Much more a matter of questions than answers, less about being sure than about being willing to work with what is at hand and take the consequences. I like finding the facts and leaving the arguments to someone else.

"Thank you!" I yelled at the door, certain that Sheila could not hear me and would not respond if she could, but equally sure that her upstairs neighbor could. I glanced up to see a face disappear from sight and the lace edge of a curtain fall back into place. I toyed with the idea of walking — limping, really; Sheila had planted her heel ferociously — up the stairs to have a go at the neighbor, but before I could leave, the door to the upstairs flat, next to the one that had just slammed in my face, opened and a disheveled woman with canny eyes and a soiled dress beckoned me in. "No sense talking to that one, it's biscuits to a bear," she said. "Known her all my life, I have, and Eoin and Fiona, too." Before I could wonder about how she knew the subject of my inquiry, she added, "Not earwigging; the window was open a bit to air the place, and I was cleaning the bedroom."

I looked around at a cluttered hall and a sitting room so overrun with papers and magazines that the woman had to clear a seat for both of us. It occurred to me that perhaps the dooryard wasn't Sheila's province after all. I started to sit in a threadbare wing chair, but the woman shooed me off. "That one's a bit banjaxed. You sit here." She indicated a wooden ladderback chair, and I sat down.

"I'll be back in a sec," she said and disappeared into an adjoining room. *The kitchen,* I thought to myself, and began working up plausible excuses for refusing food and drink, given the condition of the room. I might have made my way into a living room to pursue my inquiry, Tom Patterson style, but I needed to work on the details. I'd been in barns that were tidier than this sitting room.

The woman returned with a tray containing a pot, cups, and cookies in a tin, for which I gave silent thanks. She handed me a chipped cup full of steaming tea, hot enough, I noted, to sterilize anything that might have remained in the cup, and proffered the cookies. I took a chocolate-covered one.

"M'name's Moira Haggerty. I've known Eoin Connor all my life. Fiona ever since he has. What are you wanting to know?" She sipped from her cup, but her eyes never left my face.

What did I want to know? It suddenly occurred to me

that I'd started this inquiry with not the least idea of what I wanted out of it. And it occurred to me that it might be just as well to say so. "I'm not certain. I just need to know whether Eoin Connor is guilty of killing Fiona or not. Everything — well, almost everything — I've found out seems to indicate that he did, but I have a sense that I am missing something, something important."

"But you're hoping you know it when you hear it, is that it?" Those canny eyes twinkled. "Tell me, why the interest? Are you Connor's mot? Girlfriend?"

I was glad for the translation. In the few minutes I'd been in this woman's presence, my capacity for contextual interpretation had been given a workout, and I was not sure I was keeping up. I pondered my answer. "I suppose I am, or at least, he thinks I am." I hoped that would suffice.

"That will do. I can understand wanting to know, then. The advances of a murderer would not be so welcome now, would they?" Another sip, eyes still focused but understanding. I was warming to this woman.

I smiled in agreement. "They would not. Tell me what you know about Eoin and Fiona. Everything."

"Ah, now that will take some time," she replied. "I've known them for donkey's years."

I stretched out my legs, even though the chair would not let me lean back. She chuckled outright and started to talk.

Two hours, three pots of tea, most of a tin of cookies, and a visit to the cleanest bathroom I have ever seen in any house, I had a little more to work with. Moira was a fount of information with the Irish knack of telling a story.

Fiona's indiscretions, it seems, were common knowledge in Belfast, but Eoin, fresh from the family farm, would not have known. According to Moira, at least, he had been angry over Fiona's deception, and there had been angry words between the two in public more than once. It was not a happy match, though back then, there was no way out of it.

Divorce in Northern Ireland was a difficult matter then, granted mostly for adultery, and as wanton as Fiona was, Eoin could not prove her adultery with the Italian she'd been seen about town with until she decamped with him, and by that time, he was on the lam, as well. As for the Church, Moira confirmed that it was also common knowledge that the Church had held the marriage valid, though there was grumbling in the ranks at the injustice of it all. All old news to me, but it was nice to have it validated. But she did have one bit that came as quite a surprise to me. Fiona, Moira told me, was pregnant, this time for certain, when she ran off with her lover, by which time Eoin, too, was gone. She wasn't sure he had ever heard about it. Given that Fiona was supposedly bedding two different men at the time, there was some question whose child it was. The locals were betting on Eoin, for no particular reason, she admitted, other than Fiona was one to hold her favors until she'd gotten what she wanted. And until she ran off with the Italian, one Enrico Rossi, she had not gotten what she wanted: escape from Northern Ireland. And another bit of information that was a surprise to me: she'd been accompanied by another Connor, Eoin's sister, Deirdre. A sister Eoin had never mentioned but one who was enchanted with Fiona and who had followed her in pursuit of the good life, far away from Ireland. Moreover, Moira had heard rumors that Deirdre was back in Belfast these days, once again in the company of Fiona but this time as minion and not friend. If, indeed, she had ever been.

In all the research I had done, there was no mention of a child and no mention of Deirdre Connor, if, indeed, that was still her name. Moira's last words to me played over and over in my mind as I walked back toward my hotel in the gathering dusk: "Eoin was over and done with Fiona and Deirdre, as well. But if he knew she'd deprived him all these years of a child, God help her." A full day's work and all I had to show for it was a bruised instep and another motive for murder.

***

Tom Patterson, Mike Delatorre, and Father Matt sat in Patterson's office, poring over the fax that had just come in from Belfast. Twenty-five pages. Investigative reports from the Police Service of Northern Ireland, an autopsy report, toxicology, photographs, and news clippings.

"Nice to know it's the same drill everywhere," Mike said. He was reading the autopsy report, marking notes in the margin.

"Anything interesting?"

"She was dying of a brain tumor."

Father Matt put down the clippings he was sorting through.

"What did you say?"

"She had a pretty well-advanced brain tumor. A bad one. It would have killed her. I'm surprised she didn't have symptoms."

"It's a good bet that Eoin Connor didn't know that. No need to kill a dying woman," said Tom Patterson. "The police report says that she was poisoned with a pesticide. Eoin Connor's prints were on the bottle, and it was found at the scene."

"Let me see that." Mike scanned the report. "Not just a pesticide. An old-fashioned one. Not sure where you'd get it these days. It's banned just about everywhere."

Father Matt chimed in. "That makes no sense. Eoin is a crime writer. He'd never be that stupid, to leave the bottle there for the police to trace."

Patterson smiled as he took the report back and passed it to Father Matt. "I rely on stupid criminals all the time. And the brighter they are in one way, the dumber they are in others. What's bad about this is that poisoning like this means premeditation. There's no death penalty in Ireland, but murder means mandatory life sentence. Premeditation would be a solid argument against early release. Eoin Connor may not see the light of day as a free man again."

"You sound like you've convicted him."

"The evidence is pretty strong. He was seen leaving her rooms shortly before her assistant found her dead. They had an argument the day before, loud and public. He left here fit to be tied and there wasn't much love lost here, either. Motive, means, opportunity — and no other suspects mentioned in the reports."

"Maybe they didn't look for any," Father Matt said.

He was rewarded by pitying looks from both Tom Patterson and Mike Delatorre. It was the latter who gave voice to the reason. "Maybe they didn't have to."

"Well," said Father Matt, "maybe they should have. Look, what about this assistant? This Dee Matthews. What about her? She found the body. She took care of Fiona. Maybe she had a grudge."

Mike Delatorre stabbed his forefinger at the page in his hand. "No good. She also told the investigators that Fiona was ready to write Eoin Connor out of her will. Another motive for murder."

He handed the papers over to Father Matt, who looked at them a long minute, a puzzled look on his face. "Wait a minute. Going to write him out of her will? Why would Eoin care? He's rich enough. How would he even know about the will? And why in the world would Fiona leave her estate to Eoin? She hadn't seen him for years."

There was another long minute of silence as the professionals in the room digested this observation. Then a grin split Tom Patterson's face. "Well, I'll be damned! Out of the mouths of babes. You're right! Why would she leave money to a man who wanted nothing to do with her? Maybe our Irish colleagues gave up too soon." He turned his attention to Mike Delatorre. "How are your research skills?"

"Have internet, will travel. Maybe we ought to start with this Deirdre Matthews? I wonder, when was that will changed, and who was in it before?"

"I wonder, too," Tom Patterson said. "And I wonder if there's any way to get a hold of that information. I would think that it ought to be available to the defense attorney."

"If he thought of it," said Father Matt. "From that report, maybe he didn't."

Patterson nodded in agreement and looked at his

watch. "Too early to call over there just yet." He disconnected a laptop from his monitor and handed it over to Father Matt. "Here's portable internet. What say we go get a pizza and a beer and start a little nosing around of our own? There just might be more to this than meets the eye." There was just a fraction of a second's pause before he added, with more emotion than he wanted to show, "I sure would like that hard-headed Irishman to be innocent."

CHAPTER NINETEEN
January 22

At six straight up, I got out of bed, accompanied by a splitting headache, the product of an incipient cold and a restless night, punctuated by dreams of Eoin Connor. Eoin battering my door. Eoin breaking a man's jaw with a punch. Eoin discovering he had a child. Eoin's hand holding a decrepit bottle with a red-and-black label. Eoin's face the first time I met him and the last time I saw him. My energies were getting me nothing, apart from a growing conviction that the man I loved — I had to admit it now — was quite possibly a murderer. Shaking my head to dispel the thought and immediately regretting it, I pulled on some clothes, ran a brush through my hair, pulled it back in a bandeau, and headed downstairs for breakfast.

Irish breakfast will cure what ails you, and my server, recognizing me as being a bit under the weather, promptly brought me a pot of dark tea and a plate of assorted breads. I lightened the tea with cream so rich it was almost yellow and sweetened it with two small cubes of raw sugar. It warmed me all the way down, and I followed it with some wheaten bread studded with soft, yellow raisins. As I chewed, I thought.

Perhaps I was using the wrong side of my brain. I was used to following cases as a medical examiner, with all the ultimate facts in hand, having only to cast about among the possible solutions to find the one that fit. Now I was without any of the information — or any of the tools — I was accustomed to having. All I knew is that Fiona McLaughlin had died of a dose of Black Leaf 40 that had come from the Connor family farm.

Maybe I needed to think like a lawyer instead. Law was the second, and less preferred, of my professions. Lawyers deal too much in possibilities, and the system rewards those that can best massage facts into compliance with an outcome they — not necessarily the situation — determine. On the other hand, I was beginning to see the merit in the "reasonable doubt" approach to things. Given that I did not like the certainty my current venue of investigation was creating, a change in tactics seemed appropriate. I could revisit the God's-honest-truth of the matter when I had more to work with. Maybe I needed to concentrate on who else might have had a motive to kill Fiona — that number seemed legion — and also had access to an out-of-date, banned pesticide.

In the meantime, I needed to throw a bone to my medical side. Come hell or high water, I had to get a copy of the investigative file on Fiona's death and Eoin Connor. It was too early to call home and rustle up the reserves, but I could start on a list of possible suspects. The last few days had proved anyone who spent much time in Fiona's orbit was likely to end up with a reason to dislike her; her current list of contacts seemed as good a place to start as any. I pulled out my ever-present notebook, cadged a pen from the waiter as he passed, and started the list.

By the time my server returned with a plate of scrambled eggs, sausages, streaky bacon, beans, potato bread cut in quarters, and black pudding, I had a respectable place to start. I said grace, refreshed my tea, nudged the black pudding off to the side, and began to look over the list, adding notes between bites. By the last bite of egg, I had a decent starting point, though little idea of motive or access to the troublesome bottle of poison with Eoin's fingerprints on it. But it was a start.

On the way back to my room, my mood evaporated. The poison. I'd forgotten to figure that in. Whoever killed Fiona needed access to that poison. Not only access, he'd need to know it even existed. That narrowed the list of people with means considerably, at least at first blush. And all of a sudden, the helpful and congenial Terry was at the top of the list. I wondered who else had been to the Connor family farm in the last few weeks as I opened the door to my room.

There was only one way to find out. I sorted through the file on my desk once more to find out where the farm was located: Rathlin Island, a place I'd never even heard of. I called down to the desk to speak with the ever-helpful Charles to help me figure out how to get there.

"Certainly, Madam," he said. "I'll arrange for a car for you, if you'd like. A driver, too, if you don't want to try managing on your own."

I considered this for a moment. "Is Rathlin Island a common destination? I have no idea where it is."

"It's just off the northern coast. Two hours' drive. A desolate spot this time of year, but a nice destination in the summer, though the crossing can be rough."

"I think I'll go on my own," I said. "Can you have a car delivered here?"

"Of course, Madam. The first ferry over to Rathlin is at half past eight in the morning this time of year, and the last one back to Ballycastle at half past four in the afternoon. With the short days, I think you may prefer to take lodgings in Ballycastle rather than drive in the dark?"

"I would. You certainty know the timetables. I suppose it's all part of the job."

I could hear him tapping his keyboard in the background, probably making reservations for my car, and distracted. Otherwise, he'd never have let go the tidbit of information he did. "Quite so, Madam, though I just arranged a similar trip for the Countess last week. There. Your car will be here at a quarter to eight in the morning. You can catch the ferry at half past ten and be back to Ballycastle by five in the evening. I will arrange rooms for you at the Bushmills, quite a nice place. Shall we hold your room here, as well?"

"Of course. Thank you, Charles."

"Paul will be up with your confirmations shortly. May I use the credit card?"

"Please." I wasn't usually in the habit of paying for a room I didn't occupy, but considering the nugget I'd gleaned in the process, it was well worth it. So Fiona had gone to Rathlin in the days before she died. I wondered why. Perhaps Terry Connor hadn't been as forthcoming with me as I thought. After all, it seems every man who knew Fiona had a reason to despise her. Why should Eoin's brother be any different?

***

Sadie stomped the snow off her boots as she pushed through the door of the Steaming Bean. The Bean was usually crowded during the day during ski season, but today there were only a few people enjoying the warmth and the coffee. Sadie put it down to the fact that there was nearly half a foot of fresh powder on the slopes, and the snow was still coming down, hard and steady. The hotdogs were out on the slope, and the bunnies slept in.

As she pulled off her damp gloves and unwound the scarf from her neck, she took her place in line behind a tall man in a black ski suit, his heavy orange boots unlatched to permit him some semblance of mobility off the slopes. She recognized them as the hot ticket item from several seasons ago and concluded the man was not only a serious skier but probably a local. Even she had noticed that the visitors often, if not usually, made the ski shop their first stop. *Ah well, I suppose skiwear is as good a souvenir as any,* she thought as the man moved on, and she took her place at the counter to order.

"Hi, Sadie." The slight woman with the brown dreadlocks tossed a smile in Sadie's direction before turning to call out. "Soymilk vanilla latte, two shots, to go."

"What would you do it I decided I wanted something different, Gretchen? Maybe a whole milk mocha," Sadie teased.

Gretchen turned back, grabbing the second half of Sadie's usual order, an almond croissant with chocolate filling, as she did. She pushed it across the counter with one hand and received Sadie's credit card with the other. "Drink it myself, I guess. Sorry to hear about your job."

Sadie shrugged. "It happens. I kind of liked it here, though. And for the life of me, I can't think what I did to piss Dr. Wallace off." A frown passed over her face. As much as she did not like to admit it, the firing rankled, even though she had applied for the job on the spur of the moment with no real intention of making it permanent. In the short time she had been in Telluride, the town had settled comfortably into her heart, and she would miss it. Besides, firing hurt her ego in places she hadn't even known she had. And, as much as it pained her more, she'd miss the Center and Dr. Wallace, too, even though she was still trying to figure out how both of them operated. So different from the hectic, impersonal, big-city morgue she trained in. Moving out of the Center felt a lot like losing a home.

"Still, sorry. Are you going to stay around?"

"Probably through ski season." It was the reason she came in the first place, and there was more than enough in the checking account to see her through the winter, job or not, and Dr. Wallace included rent in a condo over one of the fancier restaurants in Mountain Village for three months in the severance package. "More time for the slopes."

It was Gretchen's turn to shrug as she put down the latte. Sadie took her pastry in one hand, the coffee in the other, and searched the room for a seat.

She found one in the back, an unoccupied overstuffed chair next to the steps that led to the near-legendary bathrooms, with their murals of space aliens and rainforests. Sadie shed her coat and snow boots and sat down, curling her legs under her and reaching for her drink and the morning paper. She was halfway through the opinion page — this one discussing with great vigor the proposal to create overflow parking at the edge of town — when she heard a familiar voice and looked up to see Lucy Cho standing over her.

"Mind if I join you?" Lucy gestured toward the mate of Sadie's chair, now empty and just enough cater-corner from Sadie not to be beside her.

"Sure! I'd like the company." Telluride had proved a difficult town for Sadie to make friends. She and Lucy hit it off from the first day she was in the office. Lucy was one person Sadie really missed. Her apartment on the third floor of the Center was next door to Sadie's, and they had often shared meals, drinks, and conversation late into the night.

"I thought you might keep in touch after you left. I thought we had a pretty good friendship going," Lucy said with no preamble and her customary directness. "Why haven't you been by?"

Sadie shrugged. "Uncomfortable, I guess. I've never been fired before. And I still have no idea why I was. Hurt pride, maybe?" A pause, and then, "I'm sorry. Friends again?"

"Friends again. I can see that hurt pride thing. It's weird. For what it's worth, none of us had the least idea, either." Lucy deftly pre-empted Sadie's next question; the woman had an uncanny sixth sense that way. "Anyway, I miss you. Glad you aren't mad at me. What's up?"

"Not much. Licking my wounds. Sending out resumes. Something will turn up. And Dr. Wallace gave me a nice letter. Shouldn't be too hard to find something."

"As well she should." Lucy's eyes flashed a bit. "Bad enough she fires you, but then she takes off for kingdom come and leaves us in the lurch." Lucy unwrapped an elaborate pastry with cream and cheese filling, topped with bright, glazed fruit.

"I see you are still smuggling in sweets. There's nothing like that here." Sadie smiled.

"We have an agreement, the Bean and I. I'll buy food here when it's up to my standards." She took a bite, wiped a bit of cream from her lips, and continued. "We sure could use you at the Center."

Another shrug. "I know Dr. Wallace brought in a locum. No good?"

"Good enough. Not you. You're better."

"Thanks." It was nice to know someone appreciated her abilities.

"Take those kids and that old lady that died."

"You mean Skye and Summer Gleason and Elsie Teague?" Sadie sat back a bit, surprised that she'd so easily internalized Dr. Wallace's habit of referring to the dead by their names. "What's up? Investigation stalled?"

Lucy nodded, still chewing. She swallowed, took a gulp of coffee and added, "It irritates me to no end that we know what killed them, but not how they died. Dr. Wallace was pretty sure it was an accident, but we can't prove it and it's bothering all of us." Lucy's expression darkened. "And there's that other kid, too, the one that had some lipid disease. Dr. Wallace is pretty sure she was murdered, and I found potassium in the IV injection port. But we can't prove it. I don't like loose ends."

Sadie smiled. That particular characteristic, along with unusual excellence in their chosen fields, was probably the thread that tied the very different personalities of the Center together. Like their boss, they wanted to know, down to the last details, and to solve the puzzle of unexpected death.

"Wish I could help."

The corner of Lucy's mouth turned up. "Who says you can't? You must be going crazy with nothing much to do."

"Dr. Wallace would skin you alive." Sadie had to admit the idea was appealing. Skiing was fun. Forensic medicine was her lifeblood.

"Dr. Wallace doesn't need to know. What say we make this our office? I'll come back by this afternoon with a CD of the files. Bring your laptop, and we'll go over what we've got. If we figure this out, Dr. Wallace will be..." Lucy seemed to struggle for words. Her boss expected perfection, so providing answers was nothing special. She regrouped. "Let's just say, I don't want to be around if we don't figure this out. And might not be," she added.

Sadie considered the possibility. It was a risk. It violated all manner of confidentialities. But Lucy was right. Sadie was bored, and it bothered her more than she wanted to admit that she had missed one poisoning and then been tossed out before she could redeem herself by solving all three. And this other one, this death-maybe-murder of yet another child intrigued her. And as much as she didn't want to admit it to herself, the death of kids, any kids, bothered her. A lot.

She thought a moment more and asked cautiously, "Do you have authority to engage consultants?"

"Never tried. But I have pretty free rein in my area. So yes, I guess so. Nobody here to say no, anyway."

"Well, then meet your new consultant. See you back here at — say, two-thirty?"

Lucy Cho smiled and raised the remains of her pastry in salute.

CHAPTER TWENTY

My bags were packed for my jaunt northward in the morning. Dinner in the hotel restaurant was excellent. I was well fed and should be getting well rested, but I decided to look over the information I had on Eoin one more time. There must be something I missed. Something. Anything. Anything to provide reasonable doubt that Eoin Connor killed Fiona.

I'd long since given up on exoneration. Reasonable doubt would do. I was appalled at myself, but I kept working. I who had been so indignant at Tough Tommy Berton's lawyers' attempts to raise doubts about his murder of my husband. Here I was hoping to do the same thing for Eoin Connor. I would worry about the implications of that for my immortal soul and my personal view of morality later. Right now I had work to do.

The newspaper reports were so familiar to me that, by now, I could practically recite them by heart. I decided to tackle them in a different way, reading them backwards, hoping that seeing the words in a new way would show me something I missed. Old proofreader's trick — the way to turn up something odd is to remove it from context.

Reading backwards was slow going. Midway through the sheaf of papers, I tossed my glasses on the desk. My eyes were beginning to hurt, and I rubbed them and then swept my hand across my face. Time to take a break. I stood up, stretched my back, and crossed the room to pour myself a glass of Malmaison plonk. I smiled, remembering how I had asked the concierge about the strange name on the bottle of wine that greeted me on my arrival and where I might get more. He'd laughed, saying he'd send some more up whenever I wanted it, but that I'd do best not to ask for plonk in the local pub. Turns out "plonk" means cheap wine, and I can guarantee by taste and by the bill that the stuff I was swirling about in the bowl of the glass as I looked out over the darkening city of Belfast was anything but cheap. If nothing else, I was getting a course in Irish slang as a result of this expedition.

I stood there for a long while as the lights came on and people hurried by on the sidewalk below, heading to dinner or a bit of last-minute shopping. I liked Belfast, in spite of its size. I would be sad to leave it, sadder still if I left in defeat. I watched a girl wearing a bright pink coat cross the street at the corner that I knew to be by the Albert Memorial clock tower. She hurried across, hugging her arms against the cold. A few snowflakes were beginning to fall. Time to get back to work.

It was after midnight when I finished. Nothing had jumped out at me in the midst of the pages and pages of narrative. I still had the tox reports, the pictures, and the background clippings to go through.

I decided to start with the clippings. Ben had done his usual overachieving job in putting together information about Fiona and about the murder. I decided to work backwards once again, taking the oldest clippings first. Bless his heart, Ben had printed them out for me, though I knew he would have preferred sending me a disc with all of them on it. *He'd be a great one for a clipping service*, I thought to myself, and wondered whether they still called them that in this day of electronics and bits and bytes.

And there were plenty of clippings. I wondered how my son had found articles from various European newspapers, wondered again how he got them translated so quickly. Fiona had certainly gotten around, and a lot. And she loved the limelight. And more's the curse — Eoin was right. She had been exceptionally beautiful.

There were images of her from all over Europe, usually in elegant evening clothes and jewels. I noticed several photographs of her smoking a cigarette in a long, old-fashioned, but clearly expensive, holder. I wondered if she was consciously emulating Audrey Hepburn, as her pose was so similar to the iconic Breakfast at Tiffany's image. *Nasty habit,* I thought, glossing over the fact that Eoin smoked a pipe.

I was despairing of ever finding something worthwhile until I came across one story, filed from Amsterdam some five years prior. It had to do with the loss of some jewelry, which at the time had been in the care of her companion, one Deirdre Connor. The sister Moira Haggarty had mentioned, who left trailing in the wake of Fiona when she ran off with her Italian journalist.

The famous and elusive Deirdre! The article said little about her. She still carried the Connor name, at least at that time, so I gathered that her marital fortunes were less than her employer's. I could not imagine Fiona's taking the loss of gems with any degree of equanimity. My guess was that she would have made short work of Deirdre. Time to set Ben on to a little more computer sleuthing.

It was still early afternoon back home, and I caught Ben

between classes. I told him what I needed, and he was back to me within the hour.

"Deirdre Connor served two years in prison for the theft of jewelry from Fiona, Mom. And about six months after she was released, the jewelry was found by one of Fiona's maids in a suitcase she was packing. Fiona apologized to Deirdre, but that's not the best part. She had to repay insurance money she got when the stuff was stolen, with interest. She almost got prosecuted for insurance fraud herself. And, as far as I can tell, Deirdre Connor dropped off the face of the earth. Last known information was in London, and after that, no trace of her anywhere."

I mulled this bit of news over in my mind. "Do you think she's dead?"

"I can't find any record of it. More like she's just on the fringe of things. You have to be pretty mainstream — or a criminal — to have a cyber footprint. Maybe she is just obscure."

Obscure she might be, but she sure enough had a motive to kill Fiona. Maybe motives for murder ran in the Connor family.

***

Sadie pulled up the files from Lucy's jump drive in the quiet and solitude of her condo. She was still sensitive enough about her position, and just frightened enough of Dr. Wallace, that she didn't want to risk looking at the information anywhere she was likely to be interrupted. Besides, the condo was comfortable beyond her wildest expectations. And posh, a far cry from the digs at the Center and worlds away from the intermittent clapboard home she had shared with her decidedly middle-class parents. Everything new, everything modern, clean, uncluttered, and upscale. She settled herself into the corner of the chaise that made up the end of the pale-gray, velvet sectional and arranged a gold pillow behind the small of her back. She canted her knees just enough to give her a good view of the screen, turned on the wall-mounted flat screen television for some background noise, and took a sip of wine from the glass on the side table before she began clicking through the information.

That those children died of coniine poisoning, she knew, and there wasn't much else to see in the reports, not even the one she had typed up for Dr. Wallace just before she was fired. She pulled up some information about hemlock on the internet, and it added nothing. She didn't expect it to, but sometimes retracing steps helped her to find the missing ones. Not this time. It was a simple enough problem. Find the source of the poison, and it had to be in common between the kids and their grandmother. And it certainly wasn't a commercial source. For one thing, there would be no way that poison hemlock would make its way into commercial food, and for another, this, as far as she could tell, was the extent of the cluster. Not even a search of poison control centers revealed any more recent cases of coniine poisoning.

Ergo, the source had to be within the family, and with the history that Elsie Teague was a forager, odds are it came from her. That little tidbit she hadn't known before; Dr. Wallace had made a note in the file, the day they had interviewed Sally Gleason. She hadn't told Sadie, though. It wasn't like Dr. Wallace to hold back information. Then again, Sadie hadn't had a chance to see the file since she left. No harm, no foul, but it was good to know.

Because there was no reason to suspect poisoning at first, thanks to her signing out the case, the police report on Elsie Teague was limited. By the time they got to check out her condo, her son was already cleaning it up and getting it ready for sale. It was a perfunctory report, not long on detail. But there were some photographs. They showed a cramped but tidy place, modest enough by ordinary standards, but one that would fetch half a million dollars. Not much there, just a couch and a couple of chairs, a rumpled bed, probably where they had found her dead. It was one of those Danish modern platform beds, with the side tables attached and a bookshelf in the headboard. The shelf was crammed with books, and the table held a glass, what looked like a few crumpled tissues and a square bottle alongside a spoon. Sadie frowned a bit. That was the detritus of a cold. No one had given her that information when she fielded the case. Then she shrugged. It would not have mattered. Nothing to worry about in an old lady. She would have done the same thing, but she was beginning to appreciate Dr. Wallace's attention to procedure. Even so, nothing much helpful here.

There was another case, the other kid. Dr. Wallace had taken that one, so Sadie knew nothing about it. She read the report: not a spare word and not a detail missing. And not much to show why the child died, though with a history of vomiting and a fragile child with lipid disease, nothing to worry about. Except for that report of Lucy's. There was no reason to find that much potassium in an injection port, and the report said the child received something through her IV just before she died.

Sadie flipped to the medical records. No mention of adding potassium to the IV. No mention of medication administered, either. That was strange, but not unheard of. And if she recalled, the father had wigged out and held the nurse hostage until the local priest talked him down. That was front page news the next day. The article was in the file, too. She skimmed it and came to an abrupt halt midway through the first paragraph. The nurse held hostage was Mavis Butler. She knew Mavis. She was a regular at Proserpine. She and Mavis had even shared a celebratory glass of champagne the day that the referendum on assisted suicide passed.

Suddenly, the potassium in the injection port was more than worrisome. Sadie closed the laptop, drained her wine glass, and got up from the sofa. It was still early in the evening, the night was clear, and the Gondola was running. A walk around town in Telluride sounded good to her, and maybe she'd stop by Proserpine just for good measure. The offices should be open until nine tonight.

CHAPTER TWENTY-ONE

January 23

The car arrived right on time, seven forty-five. It wasn't full light yet, but it wasn't dark, either. I punched directions into my phone, set it into the holder conveniently provided by the rental company and Charles, remembered how to manage a stick shift, and took note of the sticker on the dash that reminded me to drive on the left side of the road. There were a few jerky moments, and I got a couple of honks before I got onto the motorway, but by the time I was out of Belfast, I was at home behind the wheel. Well, if not at home, at least not on probation.

The drive up the coast was beautiful in the early morning light. The road to Ballycastle tracked the north Antrim coast. There were enough clouds in the sky to make the lingering sunrise interesting, but the weather was better than it had been since I arrived. Still cold, but not nearly so dank. And Charles was right: I pulled into the lot next to the Ballycastle pier at a few minutes before ten.

The ride over was much better than the literature that Paul had led me to believe. The channel was behaving itself, and the most that the ferry had to manage was the customary heave forward through gentle swells. She docked without incident, and I soon found myself on the Rathlin Island pier. I looked about to take my bearings.

There was a long crescent cove, along which stood a cluster of buildings extending out to the far point. I knew from the maps that the bay was at the flex of the island, the longer leg extending to the west and the shorter to the south. An old stone church stood to my left, the Anglican one, I supposed. Civilization clearly lay to my right. I headed down the asphalt road in that direction.

I had underestimated the cut of the wind off the water. By the time I reached the far end of the bay, I was shivering, despite my jacket, and wishing I had remembered my cap and scarf. I passed several shops that bespoke the island's summer clientele, arts, souvenirs, and snacks, but they were all shuttered. Apart from the crew at the pier, I saw not a soul on my walk. From the ferry, I saw a long, low building with Good Food emblazoned on the roof. I was hoping they were not gone for the winter, too.

Luckily, as I approached, I saw a short, wiry man standing on a ladder, scraping paint from the side of the building. He was more sensible than I, bundled in a dark watch cap and loosely knitted scarf in a riot of colors. It reminded me of Pilar's mittens.

He turned from his work as I approached, warned perhaps by the crunch of my shoes on the gravel of the driveway. He waved in greeting and backed down the ladder.

In typical Irish fashion, he greeted me like long-lost kin. "You poor wee thing! What brings you to Rathlin this time of year?"

Wee, I reflected, must have a different definition in Ireland than at home. That was twice since arriving I'd been called "wee," and I towered over this man. Moreover, his question made me realize I had not thought this trip through at all. Somehow, I suspected that some key to this whole mess with Eoin lay in Rathlin, but I had not stopped to think what it might be or how I might go about discovering it. Like a fool, I just rushed off. I finally settled on a response. "I'm looking for some information about a friend of mine, Eoin Connor. And his family. Do you know them?"

"Ah, Eoin. He's in the slammer, you know."

I shifted from foot to foot and hugged myself tighter. "I know. That's why I am here."

He regarded me cannily for a second, then waved in the direction of the door. "Come in, lass. Let's have a drink and talk a bit. You must be freezing."

He noticed. I entered the restaurant, a modern room with simple tables and booths and the inevitable bar. Posters and tee shirts advertised Rathlin Red, something I supposed to be a local beer. The man shuffled me onto a barstool and began to unwind himself from his clothes. Once all the layers were shed, a man about Eoin's age stood before me, his face lined and tanned by salt and sun, bright blue eyes, curly gray hair, and a close-cropped beard. He extended a hand. "Devon Burke, at your service. Coffee?"

"Jane Wallace. Yes, please." I emphasized the last word. "I didn't think it would be so cold."

"It's the wind off the sea," he said. "It'll be a few minutes before the coffee is done. Do you want a dram to warm you while you wait?"

I looked at my watch. It was after eleven, and I was still

chilled. I pulled off my gloves, laid them on the bar, and smiled. "Please. Brandy?"

"Done."

I dug in my pocket and pushed a five-pound note across the bar.

"No need," he said. I smiled and shrugged, so he slid it in the drawer, anyway, and poured me a generous measure. It burned and warmed all the way down.

"What is it that you need to know?"

Honesty is always best. "I have no idea. Everything I have found out so far tells me Eoin is guilty, but I don't believe it. The poison came from the farm." I paused. "I guess I'm just here to see what I can see." I took another sip of the brandy. "What do you think?"

Devon passed a damp cloth over the counter, even though there was nothing to clean. Barkeep's habit. "I don't know Eoin all that well," he admitted. "I'm not from here. Moved here after I retired, from Belfast. Tired of the rat race. I was a barrister."

"That's quite a change."

"I always wanted to run a pub. A restaurant is a bit more than I bargained for, but I like it well enough."

"Eoin," I prompted.

"The family keeps a farm up near the lighthouse. I gather it's the old family farm, sold when the family fell on hard times. I gather Eoin bought it back, and his brothers and sisters keep it."

"Year round? This place is pretty well shut down now. Do they stay?"

"Some of them do. The brother next to Eoin, Terry, really loves the place. I am not so sure Molly does, but she keeps with him. Mick and Joe come in during the summer and winter for a couple of weeks to give them a spell off. Eoin comes when he can."

I pondered that information for a minute. Not much there, but I followed the only odd piece I heard.

"What would Molly and Terrance do if it weren't for the farm? Is it something they feel obligated to do for Eoin?" I could imagine Eoin's passion for the old place overtaking his sibs, who might not relish life on a remote Irish island as much as he did.

"Terry was a joiner, like Eoin. I suppose he could take that up again. Mick's a plumber, making a good living in the Republic. Joe owns a hardware store in Enniskillen. Molly never worked apart from the house, taking care of the parents, then of Terry. When the farm was lost, she and her parents were on the dole. The boys helped out when they could. When Eoin made something of himself, he took care of his parents and Molly. I think the farm is sentiment for him."

I mulled that over for a moment. I'd seen too many instances where well-meaning altruism became a despised trap for the recipients. As long as I was casting about for alternative motives, Eoin's family seemed as good a place to start as any. And bartenders are a reliable source of community gossip.

"So everything isn't necessarily well and good in the Connor family?" I pushed the thought out and hoped Devon would rise to the bait. He turned to pour me a cup of coffee before he answered, setting a blue mug in front of me, along with a sugar bowl and a tiny pot of cream. It looked so rich, that for once, I poured some in the coffee and added a spoonful of sugar for good measure.

"You're asking whether anyone had a reason to be angry with Eoin. What does that have to do with the death of his tart?"

So Fiona's reputation preceded her even here. "Reasonable doubt. The Black Leaf 40 had to come from the farm. Maybe killing Fiona and framing Eoin served someone's purposes."

I listened in the silence to the tick of the clock, one for each second as the thin, red hand made a complete circuit of the face before Devon answered. "I've heard nothing from Terry, mind you," he said. "But people talk. And it wasn't about Fiona, it was about you."

"Me?"

"I gather that Eoin is smitten with you and plans to marry you. But he can't just yet, because you're known in all provinces as a righteous woman, and he isn't free in the eyes of the Church." He paused and added a bit of advice. "Lassie, life is too short to worry about such things. Marry the man if you love him."

"Go on." I'd heard the advice before. More than once in the last few weeks.

"Anyway, some of the local biddies were in here one evening, having a bit of craic. Let's just say it came out that Molly is worried that should Eoin marry you, he'll sell the farm, and they'll be displaced. Much harder these days than those years ago. I suspect that Molly doesn't fancy another go at a council flat."

I was taken aback. I'd never thought of myself as a threat to anyone. The last time I made that mistake, it almost cost my life. I wondered whether it would cost Eoin his this time. Not a comforting prospect, but I decided in for a nickel, in for a dime. Or was it penny and pound? "Anything else?"

Devon had gone from wiping the bar to polishing glasses. He smiled. "Well, now, there might be. A bit ago, another woman showed up here on the island. She popped in here because it was a foul day, rain almost sideways, and I'm just about the only thing open on the island in winter."

"An elegant redhead?" I remembered Charles' slip about Fiona and Ballycastle.

"Not at all, lassie. It wasn't Fiona. I've seen her pictures in the papers. It was a short woman, all right, plain as toast. She said her name was Dee Matthews and when the rain stopped, I saw her heading up the road in the direction of the East Light. English her name is, but she's as Irish as I am."

I mulled that bit of information over again in silence. Devon put the glass away and continued. "But sure, the East Light is something to see, and the Connor farm is right nearby. You can't miss it." He grinned. "I expect you'll want to head up there yourself, but don't expect Terry and Molly to greet you. They went into town on the first boat. Shopping day. I gave them a list for myself. No sense all of us going."

Devon lifted the gate on the bar and stepped out. "Let's see what I can find in the lost and found that might keep you a bit warmer on the walk."

***

Pilar finished washing the last of the cutlery and stacked it neatly in the drainer. She had never gotten the habit of using the machine for doing dishes. Taking care of them herself gave her a chance to relive the day, the plates and cups and pots serving as icons for the threads that all came together in the day's meals. As she washed, she thought and she gave thanks. For the family she shared, all those lives connected to hers. For Señora Doctora. For the food, of which, for once, there was an abundance. For the kitchen, large and warm and comfortable and the house it was in. For the time to cook for people she cared about and who cared about her. For those who had less. And for the small priest who had been with them the past few days.

Yesterday morning, when he sat at the counter, a raven had appeared at the window behind him, cocking his head this way and that. She had shooed him away. The big black birds were an omen of bad luck. One — perhaps the same one — had appeared on the sill the day that Señor Eoin returned, and that evil woman had arrived to unsettle everything. She crossed herself involuntarily at the thought of her and all that followed, especially Señor Eoin in jail and Señora Doctora who had gone after him. She despised the birds. The thought made her glance at the window again. No raven. Good.

The priest had laughed at her, teasing her good-naturedly about her superstition. They spoke, as always, in Spanish, hers the language of the Mexican streets, his of old Castile. And, as always, he moved easily between times and places, as though the borders of life did not exist anymore for him. Yesterday he mistook her for some young woman he knew long ago in Barcelona. Her name was Eva. It made Pilar smile. To be mistaken at her age for a young woman, obviously so important at one time to this odd man, was a pleasure. His world was confusing, but somehow it was still beautiful. The terrors had not set in, and she shuddered to think of what they might be like for him. Her own Pablo had descended into darkness all too soon. For him it was the terror of being chased and caught. Perhaps it was death that chased him. Perhaps this good man would not experience that. She smiled as she cleaned the counter and offered a prayer to St. Michael, protector of the innocent and escort of the faithful to heaven, that he intercede for it to be so.

The small priest was still asleep, unusual for him. Like so many old men, he nodded off during the day and could not sleep at night. He was almost always at the table before everyone else. Today, Lupe and Isa and the children rose, ate, and were off, and he was still abed.

Suddenly, the raven appeared again, this time in the window over the sink. A chill went down her spine. She dropped the sponge into the last of the soapy water, and, drying her hands on her apron, hurried up the stairs.

The small priest was still in bed, the light on the table still burning, a rosary of wooden beads tight in one hand, the sheets clutched in the other, his knees drawn, and one leg half out of the bed. She knew without touching that he had already gone cold. She made the Sign of the Cross, reached out with gentle hands to close his staring eyes, and arranged the bedclothes to cover his leg before calling Father Matt.

CHAPTER TWENTY-TWO

As a southerner, I always take directions that end with "you can't miss it" with a grain of salt. It generally means the place in question is so far off the beaten track that it requires a local guide and three mules to get you there. In this case, however, I was prepared to believe Devon Burke was right, in part because of the local geography. The top of the island, which I reached easily by a paved road, was rolling with green, low vegetation. Anything man-made, including the rock walls that divided the pastures and the skeletons of a couple of windmills, was easily visible. I took my time, enjoying the landscape and the views out over the ocean, now that I was bundled up in a warm, wool scarf and had Devon's own black watch cap on my head.

The Connor farm was at the end of the road, Devon said. I turned onto a gravel path that led through a well-kept stone wall to a small and traditional thatched cottage, whitewashed and sturdy. The yard around it was tidy with beds, now cleared, waiting for spring planting. The door to an outbuilding was open, and tire tracks confirmed that my bartending co-conspirator was right. There was no one about.

I decided to take a stroll around the premises. The location was breathtaking. The lighthouse was a formidable sight on one side, and on the other, the land simply dropped off in cliffs that ended in a spill of rocks at the sea below. I stood at the wall that would keep the unwary man or beast from falling into the surf below, watching the waves for a long time. No wonder Eoin liked this place. It was a wonder he didn't retreat here to write. Molly need not worry that I would inveigle Eoin to sell it, though I might have conned him into building a second little cottage, just for us.

I shook the thought from my mind. There was no "us." Not now, at least, and it was looking like not ever. I might prevent Eoin's being convicted by tossing out a few more equally likely suspects, but nothing I had found so far proved his innocence to me. I was willing to give him the benefit of the doubt, but not my heart. It surprised me.

The wind at my back tossed the end of the scarf back over my shoulder as I walked to a stone building built low into the ground, half-buried, with a rough, wooden door and no windows. As my eyes adjusted to the dank interior, I saw that it was divided into stalls on one side. The closest stall had been converted into shelves, covered with the sort of detritus that tends to accumulate on a farm. I stepped inside, switched on the flashlight on my smartphone, and inspected the place.

A variety of implements were stacked against the wall: a hoe, rakes, a spade; and a box of smaller tools: trowels, an adze, a mortar hawk, a couple of chisels, and a bolster. These were dusty and most of them rusted. By contrast, on the wall of the last stall hung an assortment of other tools, clean and well-polished: shears, clippers, hammers, two saws, and a level. It was easy to see what work was regular here. A snag of white wool bespoke sheep. I wondered where they were.

On the top shelf were bottles of liniment, linseed oil, two different pesticides, a bottle of fish emulsion, an assortment of paint, some whitewash, and some bushes, and like the hanging tools, all clean and tidy. And modern. The second shelf was another story. The boxes, jars, and cans were from another era, with faded, simple labels from time past. Something called wound powder. A jar of old nails. Something labeled 'black salve,' in a squat, round tin. They were covered with dust, and a few cobwebs were strung among them. I surveyed the shelf more closely, looking for something out of place. At one edge, I found it: the mark of something recently removed, the clear, rough wood surrounded by the same thick dust that covered the bottles and boxes. No doubt the prior home of the Black Leaf 40.

No surprise. I knew that the poison had its origin in the Connor farm. There was simply no other explanation for it, especially given that Eoin's fingerprints were on it. What I had proved was how easy it would be for someone to get to it, if he knew it was there. This little stone building was apart from the house, half-hidden by a swale and accessible by a path that went between the pastures, no doubt to give tourists access to the spectacular views of the coast without disturbing the residents or the sheep when they were in residence.

The question was, who and when and why? Dee Matthews loomed faceless in my mind. The name was familiar, but I was not sure why. I'd revisit the file and figure it out when I got back to Belfast. My fingers touched the ring where the bottle had been, and I drew a sticky glove. *Well now,* I thought. That bottle leaked.

That was interesting. The first reflex most people had

when handling a bottle like that would be to wipe it off. But that would not make sense if preserving fingerprints were foremost in your mind.

That gave me plenty of fodder for thought as I took the long way back to the pub.

***

Sadie dropped by Leona's for lunch, as had become her custom. Until the last two days, the old man dropped by, too, and they had lunch together. Some days she was Sadie, and some days she was Liana. It didn't matter. He was entertaining and charming, and it made lunch more pleasant. He even walked her out of the restaurant every day to whatever her next stop was. The last day she saw him, she was headed to the Proserpine office. It was one of the times he didn't recognize her, but he was agitated when he left her there. She wondered why.

She kept checking her watch, but he didn't come. She was beginning to worry about him. He was clearly in the throes of dementia but not so far gone as to be unpleasant to be around. She wondered what might be wrong.

When noon came and went without him, she sighed and shifted her seat so that her back was to the wall, and pulled out the growing sheaf of papers that constituted her file on the deaths of the Gleason kids. Toxicology confirmed that the stain on the bedclothes contained coniine. There was no being sure, but Sadie was pretty certain that it meant the poison came from a liquid. Not that that made it easier. Hemlock poisoning usually came from someone using the plant in a soup or a stew. Unless, of course, this was a murder and someone concocted an extract for purposes of killing off two perfectly healthy and innocent kids. And, for that matter, their sainted grandmother, who turned up with coniine in her blood, too. The more that she dug into the matter, the more complicated it got.

At her suggestion, Lucy went back to the Gleason house and inventoried the bedrooms. Nothing. Sadie really needed to talk to the mother again but hesitated. That was crossing a line. The consultant gig was tenuous enough by itself; its only hope of success was if she confined herself to paper. An in-person interview would for sure send Dr. Wallace into orbit when she found out.

Lucy won't do it, either, and she has fewer people skills than I do, she thought. She flipped through the papers one more time, hoping for inspiration, but found none. Unwilling to waste any more time, she began to straighten them when the words of the old fellow came back to her. Children live in a world of make-believe. Maybe the answer lies there.

Maybe it does, Sadie thought, *but you can't prove it by me.*

Leona herself took her check at the register. As she was waiting for change, a tall man in black came into the restaurant. Sadie recognized him as the priest who was always hanging around the Center. She regarded him with narrowed eyes, weighed the merits of asking him what had just popped into her mind, and decided to risk it. She collected her change and sidled up to his table.

"Father?" She hoped that sufficed. His name escaped her, though she was sure she had heard it before.

The priest looked up from the menu. "Sadie!" he said, his face lighting up. "Have a seat. How have you been? How are things at the Center?"

Was it possible he didn't know? Given that Dr. Wallace left right after firing her, she supposed it was, and it played into her hand. "Um, no thanks, I'm on my way out," she stalled, then added with a grin, "but there's always work to do." *Both true*, she thought. "I am having trouble with a case I was working on before Dr. Wallace left. Those kids."

The priest's eyes showed interest, so she continued. "Two kids. They were poisoned and so was their grandmother. The problem is that I can't find a source. I need to interview the mother again, but," she hesitated, "I'm not good at it." She paused for a moment, unsure how to proceed. Flirting clearly would not work; she didn't know this man at all, and there was no reason he should grant her a favor. She decided to jump in and see what happened. Nothing ventured, nothing gained.

"Priests are supposed to be good at talking to people at times like this. Could you? I mean, would you?"

"Go talk to her?" He smiled. "No, Sadie, I can't." His smile reassured her that he wasn't angry, just amused that she would ask. "I know nothing about this matter. The family is not part of my parish. I don't know them. There's no reason for me to call, and it would be way out of line. That is your job. You can do it. Otherwise, Dr. Wallace would not have trusted you with it."

If only you knew, thought Sadie. "Well, thanks, anyway." She turned away to regroup and then remembered the old man. He was a priest, too.

"I used to see an old fellow in here. We had lunch a couple of times until...oh, a few days ago. I think he's a priest. Monsig..." She stumbled on the honorific. "Jamais, anyway."

The man's eyes clouded. "I'm sorry, Sadie. He died last night in his sleep. I thought you would know. His body is down at the morgue right now." He patted her hand, and his face wrinkled a bit. "How on earth did you know him?"

Sadie's eyes rounded. She turned away before he could see her cry. She didn't answer.

***

It took about an hour for her to settle down.

She was surprised at how the news of the man's death affected her. She ought to be happy for him. After all, neither he nor his family and friends — she assumed he had some — would have to endure his slow descent into unknowing. Dying in bed — that was a good death, no suffering. Still, she would miss him. She already did. Her mind drifted back to that first day, and his advice still nagged at her.

At length, she hoisted herself out of her sadness, stood up from the bench, the one outside the Bean that she had been occupying, and walked with purpose down the street toward the Gleason house, oblivious to the people around her and framing first one, then another introduction. She wished she had paid more attention to Dr. Wallace's instructions on interviewing now.

Sally Gleason answered on the first knock.

Sadie took a deep breath. "Mrs. Gleason, we're — I'm — making some progress on finding out how your children got into that poison, but I...I need to ask a few more questions. I hate to bother you but..." She paused. "May I come in?"

The door opened to admit her. The living room was as dim as she remembered it from before.

"Please, have a seat." Sally Gleason's voice was soft and toneless.

Sadie took a seat and a deep breath, and remembering the face of Monsignor Jamais, started to talk.

Half-an-hour later, she left with excitement that she may have solved the puzzle, which competed with sadness at how unnecessary it all was. Both the grandmother and the children had been suffering from colds. Grandmother had a family cold remedy she used, homemade, and she came by with it the day she died. Hugs and kisses all around, and the children got sick a few days later, after Grandmother's death. She didn't use the remedy on her children, not trusting her mother-in-law's home concoctions. At best they were ineffective, at worst they were unpalatable, truly impossible to take. But instead of refusing it, in order to keep peace in the family, she accepted the offering and put it up on a shelf in the bathroom. She never opened it.

When Sadie asked to see it, Sally Gleason returned, white-faced, with the bottle. There was a smear of liquid on the outside. "Someone used it," she said in a whisper. "Oh my gosh, someone used it. Is this what killed my children?"

"I'm not sure," Sadie had told her. "We'll check." Odds were that it was, though, given it was the only thing the children and the grandmother had ingested in common. And the vanity label with Elsie Teague's name surrounded by pansies and hearts made her almost certain it was the culprit. In a delicate cursive, it read *Wild Carrot*

Wine for Cough and Fever.

When she connected with the babysitter, still out of town but reached with the new cell phone number Sally Gleason provided, she had it nailed down. The sitter hadn't given it, either. But she'd come in to find Summer clutching the bottle and a tiny paper cup from the bathroom. She remembered that this was medicine from Grandmother and decided to play doctor with her brother when his cough started up. Sadie shuddered at the words the sitter repeated. "I had to show him how to take it first, though. He was pretty sick, so I gave him two cups. It tastes nasty."

The sitter had forgotten the incident altogether by the time the parents came home less than an hour later. The children were asleep, and the vomiting had not started yet. But she remembered that the stuff had dripped from the cup and stained the bedclothes on Skye's bed. And she was pretty sure that when she compared this bottle to the one in the picture of the Elsie Teague's bedroom, they'd match.

CHAPTER TWENTY-THREE

January 24

It took a few minutes of skimming articles to find who was representing Eoin. Was he a lawyer? Barrister? Solicitor? Even years of reading Rumpole of the Bailey had not taught me the details of the British legal system. Not for the first time in this investigation did I bemoan the limits of the information I was working with. Mostly information that was gleaned from public sources. I managed to get a copy of the tox report only because someone inadvertently leaked it to the press, and Ben was able to sweet-talk the erstwhile defender of the fourth estate out of it. It was a lot easier working in an official capacity.

The firm was located not very far from the Malmaison. A quick assessment of the vagaries of trying to get through to a complete stranger with a wild tale convinced me that I'd have better luck in person than on the phone. I tidied myself up, dressed in the only decent clothes I brought along, ran a brush through my hair, and headed out.

The building was unimpressive from the outside, all gray stone with a small, nondescript plaque that simply announced 'Law Offices.' Inside was another story. The lobby was spacious and modern, with sleek red couches, oak tables, bright lighting, and a huge vase of fresh roses. Behind the glass table with a computer and another, smaller vase of roses sat a receptionist: young, blond, wearing a dress the color of the roses, topped with a lace bolero and set off by one long, gold chain. The whole effect was professional but stunning, and it made me feel mousy in my plain black dress and matching jacket. What I lacked in panache, I'd have to make up in presence.

"Dr. Jane Wallace here to see Mr. Suskind about Eoin Connor."

The receptionist — the nameplate on the table announced her as another Jane, Jane Reilly — made a few motions with her mouse, frowned at her computer screen and finally responded. "Do you have an appointment?"

"I do not. But I have some information that is important to his representation of Mr. Connor. He will wish to see me. It will not take long."

Jane scanned the computer again. "He has some time day after tomorrow."

"That will not do. This will take only a few moments."

"I'm afraid Mr. Suskind is booked solid for the day."

"I am happy to wait until he is free between appointments."

"I'm afraid…"

I may not have a law office of my own, but I know how they work, and it's universal. Scenes are never permitted. I turned away from the fetching Jane, took a seat on the couch, and opened one of the luxury travel magazines that was on the side table, a smaller version of Jane's own desk. It's difficult to argue with someone who isn't prepared to engage, and my strategic retreat sent her into a tizzy. She regarded me for a moment, buzzed through to someone.

Within minutes, a no-nonsense, older woman in a skirt and twinset appeared. They talked for a moment in hushed tones, and then the woman in the twinset came forward to address me.

"I am Mr. Suskind's assistant. May I help you?"

I continued to scan the article on the Azores for two heartbeats before I looked up. "You may tell Mr. Suskind that I have information that is important — no, essential — to his defense of Eoin Connor. That I am here to talk with him about it. And that I will be happy to wait until he has a moment to see me." I went back to the magazine and without looking up, added, "You might also tell him that Mr. Connor might take it amiss if he doesn't see me." I flipped the page to hide the fact that my hands were shaking and hoped the lower register of my voice hid my anxiety. Courtroom intimidation I could manage. Getting past the lions at the gate of an office was quite another matter, and it was out of my wheelhouse. I looked up again and smiled confidently. I hoped.

Her expression assured me that I had fooled her not in the least. "Dr. Wallace, you said. Jane Wallace?"

I nodded.

"Mr. Connor has mentioned you. He wondered why you haven't been in touch. He might not be so happy to hear from you as you think."

"If the concept of reasonable doubt is as applicable in Ireland as it is in the States, he will."

She smiled again. "I believe Mr. Suskind's meeting is just about to end. Please follow me."

I breathed a sigh of relief. The woman led me down a

hall unadorned, except for an occasional oversized photograph of Belfast on the wall and a rank of filing cabinets. I was glad to see the Information Age had not put the paper companies out of business. If this office was anything like mine, computers meant that we kept additional copies in cyberspace, not that it forwent the paper ones.

Peter Suskind's office was just like all the other attorney offices I had ever seen, though for a moment I wondered whether he was a barrister or solicitor and whether attorney covered both. The woman with the twinset motioned me to sit in a straight-back chair opposite her desk, which held several neat piles of papers and files. Her nameplate gave her name away: Evelyn Watts. Once I was seated, she returned to her desk and computer without a word.

About ten minutes later, the door to the adjacent office opened, and a tall, black-haired woman dressed in a powder blue suit emerged. She paused at the doorway, half-turned back, and said, "I'll be back this afternoon. I think I can get what you need by then."

"Wonderful, Roslyn. Thank you," a cultured voice from inside the office said. Roslyn waved a passing goodbye to Evelyn, cast a critical glance in my direction, and left. Evelyn rose, smoothed her sweater, and preceded me into the inner sanctum.

It was a well-appointed office that bespoke a successful and lucrative practice. Unlike the modern lobby, this was done in very traditional, masculine furniture, all wood and leather and brass, with a little discreet plaid thrown in for good measure and to break the monotony.

"Mrs. Wallace asked to see you. I told her that you might have a few moments between appointments. She has some information about Mr. Connor."

"Doctor Wallace," I corrected Evelyn, with a glance in her direction while I stepped forward to extend my hand to the man seated behind the desk. The corner of her mouth turned up. We both knew what she was doing. Point to me this time, game, set and match, and my undying gratitude to Evelyn Watts for getting me in.

Peter Suskind was dressed in a dark blue suit, all the better to set off his blue eyes. He shook my hand and motioned to the wing-back chair, one of a pair that shared between them an oak table with a coffee service on its inlaid top. "Please, Dr. Wallace, have a seat."

I did, and he joined me in the other. "What brings you here today? You know Mr. Connor has been disappointed that you have not been in touch. I must say I am surprised to see you here."

His words stung, and I wanted to get this interview over as quickly as I could. "Mr. Connor didn't ask you to contact me, did he? I thought not. No matter. I'll only take a little of your time. I've been doing a little research on this matter on my own. There are several other people who had reason to kill Fiona Idoni and also had access to the poison that could only have come from the family farm. One of them seems more likely than the others. Did you know that Fiona sent her assistant Dee Matthews to Rathlin Island just a day or two before she died? It would be a simple matter for her to take the Black Leaf 40. It was kept in an outbuilding at some distance from the main house and was in plain sight."

He leaned forward, interested. "Did you know that the police found a smear of Black Leaf 40 on Eoin Connor's coat?"

For a long moment I could not breathe. Then I remembered. Reasonable doubt. "All the more reason to investigate Dee Matthews. I know she was there, because the publican on the island remembers her. I know the poison was in plain sight, because I saw where it had been on the shelf by the dust that was on the shelf. And it might interest you to know that the bottle leaked. There was a smear of it on the shelf. Unless I missed my guess, if you check with the investigators, they will confirm that. Now, Mr. Suskind, what on earth do you think would keep someone from wiping off a sticky bottle?"

"How do you know she didn't — assuming it was Dee Matthews?"

"Because there were still Eoin's fingerprints on it."

"Point taken. Do I take it that you are implicating Mrs. Matthews in Fiona's murder?"

"Why not? From what I can tell, everyone who had anything to do with Fiona hated her."

"And why would Fiona send her to the island in the first place?"

He had me there. That particular missing piece bothered me, too. Might as well be honest. "Who knows? To curry favor with the family? And perhaps that backfired. Perhaps while she was there, they decided in concert to kill Fiona; none of Eoin's brothers and sisters liked her, either. She'd wreaked havoc with their lives. Perhaps they wanted revenge for her treatment of their brother, who is their benefactor, as much as the prosecution thinks Eoin wanted it."

Peter Suskind leaned back in his chair. "I must say that's interesting, Dr. Wallace. But it's hardly proof of Mr. Connor's innocence."

"I know. It disappoints me, too, but it's the best I have, and it might just do. You have the information. I suggest you pursue it. If nothing else, it leads to an excellent argument for reasonable doubt. I believe that is all that's required." I stood up to take my leave before being dismissed, but added, "I forgot to add: the ferryman remembers Mrs. Matthews. She came over with nothing but a coat and a purse — a brown coat and green leather purse. She came back the same way. That sticky bottle had to be in one or the other, don't you think? I don't have the ability to chase that to ground, but you do."

He brought his hands together in a slow clap. I couldn't decide whether it was admiration or cynicism until he spoke. "Well done, Dr. Jane Wallace. Well done, indeed. I shall have my staff look into it right away." He looked solemn for a moment. "You know I cannot tell you anything about the case, but I don't think it's a breach of confidentiality to remark that the evidence is substantial against your...friend. This gives a different perspective, indeed."

I saw the door open a crack. "I believe my next appointment is here. Please leave your information with Evelyn so that I may stay in touch. And may I pass anything along to Mr. Connor?"

I considered his offer for a moment. Anything I wanted to say was as confidential between Eoin and me as his case was for his lawyer. "No," I finally said. "But thank you."

***

Sadie sent off her report on the Gleason kids, short, sweet and to the point, a marvel of forensic brevity, to Lucy Cho. Tying up that loose end gave her a great deal of satisfaction. As she was closing out the file on her computer, she remembered the other case Lucy had sent along. Josie Beck. She knew Dr. Wallace was certain the child had been murdered, and she couldn't argue. But she also knew the nurse who took care of the little girl in the Center. She was a friend and a colleague.

Still, it was a loose end, and it bothered her. The only way to resolve it was just to ask outright what happened that day, and that's what Sadie decided to do. She found Mavis Butler sitting on the worn sofa of the Telluride Medical Center employee lounge, finishing the last of a container of yogurt.

"Hi, Mavis," she said, and took a seat in one of the chairs around the small table. They were alone.

The woman on the couch looked up and smiled. She scraped the last of some strawberry from the side of her container as she answered, "Good to see you, Sadie. What's up?"

"Not much. I'm just following up on the death of that kid, Josie Beck. Remember her?"

"How could I forget? It's not every day I get held hostage."

"You doing okay with that?"

Mavis crossed the room and tossed the empty container in the trash before answering. "As well as can be expected. A little PTSD. I'm seeing someone. I think it will get better. But I'll tell you, I'm ready to pack it in."

"I bet. Listen, can you tell me anything about that kid and her family? What made the dad go off like that?"

"I know the mom pretty well. She says her husband just couldn't deal with the kid's illness. Kept chasing after every possible treatment, looking for a miracle. It broke them up. Bankrupted them, too."

"That's a shame."

"I know. Can you imagine? The last time I talked to her, she was almost out of her mind from it all. What bothered her most was how that kid suffered, and her husband was just oblivious to it. Couldn't see anything but the next miracle cure. And all their religious friends — the ones who said Josie was a gift and that she would turn out to be a blessing? After the first few weeks, nobody came to help. In for the diagnosis, but not for the long haul. No wonder she snapped. I would, too; it's been a long four years." Mavis pulled a granola bar out of the polka-dotted lunch bag at her side. "Want some?" She proffered it to Sadie, who shook her head.

"No, thanks. Listen, Mavis, I've been looking at the case, and something doesn't fit. I've been over everything, all the reports, everything. I can't find a reason for that kid to have died, even as sick as she was."

"Sick? She was trying to die, and her father wouldn't let her."

"I suppose. That's pretty terrible. Too bad she was so young. If she had been older, maybe we could have helped her avoid all that suffering. I think Dr. Baladin is right about that. There's too much suffering, and medicine doesn't do much to alleviate it."

"Yeah, it's a shame, all right. No reason to let a kid hang on like that. Last time I saw her mom, all she could say was how it would be better if Josie died. She asked me if I could help, now that there's a right-to-die law in Colorado. I told her officially, no, because the law doesn't cover kids. But just between you and me, it's a good thing that potassium can't be traced." Mavis looked at her watch and rose. "Gotta get back to work," she said, as if it were the most normal conversation in the world.

CHAPTER TWENTY-FOUR

January 25

After a long night of dreamless sleep, I awoke to light flooding into my room and my cell phone ringing insistently. I fumbled for the phone and caught it just as the last ring faded away. I squinted at the number. *The Center.* I punched redial and felt around for my glasses. Don't ask me why, but I can't really hold a conversation until I get my specs on. Can't see, can't talk.

Tim answered on the first ring, bless him.

"Someone called me, Tim. Not sure who. Can you find out?"

Just about that time, a voicemail notice flashed on my screen. "Wait a sec," I told him and pulled it up. Thankful for the translation feature the newest iteration of the smartphone software included, I added, "It was Lucy. Can you put me through?"

"Sure thing." There was a moment of silence — I abhor hold music — and Lucy answered.

"Cho here."

"Hi, Lucy. Sorry I missed you. What's up?"

"We found the hemlock."

Good news for once. At least someone was making headway in the realm of forensic mysteries. "What was it?"

"Turns out Grandma Elsie made wild carrot wine for coughs and colds. She delivered a bottle to the Gleason family, and she'd used some herself for her own cold. Only it wasn't wild carrot. It was hemlock."

My turn to be silent. Wine from hemlock. I could only imagine how much of the coniine would leach out into the wine during the fermentation process.

"Good work. How'd you figure it out?"

"I didn't. Sadie did."

"Sadie wasn't supposed to be working on the case. I fired her." I was trying hard to hold my anger in check. I thought the staff knew better than to countermand my orders.

"I know. I hired her back as a consultant. We weren't making any progress. I figured I would rather you be mad at me for using her as a consultant than have you be mad at all of us for not solving this."

My staff knew me too well.

"How did she figure it out?"

"She says that some old priest told her the answer was in the kid's world of make-believe."

I wasn't following this at all, and I told Lucy just that.

"Some old guy she had lunch with. Told her that kids go from make-believe to reality all the time, and maybe the answer was in make-believe, not the real world. He was right. The mom didn't want to use the concoction, because all the homemade stuff the grandmother brought was too nasty to take. But the older kid heard Grandma telling Mom that this was good for colds. When the little boy got sick, big sister decided to play doctor and treat him. And she took some herself to show him that it was all right to take. It was enough. The babysitter confirmed it."

I had to admit, I was impressed, especially because it meant that Sadie had done some one-on-one research. Good for her, even if she and Lucy had circumvented my very explicit wishes. Sometimes all it took was a different perspective to see the way clear to an answer. For now, I would take it.

"So can I tell her she has her job back?" Lucy could never be accused of beating around the bush.

"No."

"Aw, c'mon, Boss. She does great work. I mean, look at this. Even *you* didn't figure this out."

"Lucy, this is not a subject for discussion." I had no intention of explaining that Sadie's good work was not the issue; it was the quality of some of her other works that worried me.

Lucy knew when she was at least temporarily bested. "Anyway, that's one thing off your mind," she finished.

"Yes it is, Lucy. Thanks." I punched end and looked at the clock. Nearly ten. If I didn't hurry, I wouldn't get breakfast, and I was suddenly ravenous.

I was about to step into the shower when my phone rang again. Father Matt.

"Good morning, Jane," he said.

"Hi, Father. What's up?" I weighed the merits of heading to breakfast unwashed, and started pulling on my jeans, my phone wedged between my shoulder and my ear.

"Jane, I have some bad news I need to share."

I hated those words. I sat down on the side of the tub and braced myself.

"Monsignor Jamais died unexpectedly, just after you left."

Some things just have to be said straight out. My response was a reflection of my daily bread and cheese as a medical examiner. "Please tell me it wasn't foul play. And it wasn't suicide. Or some terrible accident."

I thought I heard something like a smile in his voice. "No. Not at all. A ruptured aortic aneurysm, at least that is what your friend Mike Delatorre told us. Quick and relatively painless and in his own bed, rosary beads in hand." There was a small silence. "Thanks for giving him a place to die among friends." Another silence, and when Father Matt broke it, his voice was small and sad. "I just wish I had been nicer to him when he arrived."

I knew all too well how the last days before a sudden death play over and over in the minds of the survivors. After John was murdered, I recalled every slight, every sharp word, every moment of impatience or irritation I had visited on him, and the more I remembered them, the worse they became. "Father, you took him in. You shared your home. You took care of him when he overdosed. You found him a better place to live, and I know you visited him and said Mass with him and prayed with him. That's as much as any man could do. Nowhere is it written that you get to be perfect or that he does, either, for that matter. He was a sometimes difficult man, and you befriended him, anyway. That's a lot. He forgave you; that is one of the blessings of dementia, at least in the early phases: no grudges. Forgive yourself."

"I suppose. Anyway, I thought you should know."

I smiled to myself. He thought I needed to know and more than that, he needed to share. Works for me. "I appreciate it. I'll light a candle for him after Mass." Then, as an afterthought, "Keep well, Father."

***

I opted for salmon and eggs for breakfast; to my surprise, I found soft Irish scrambled eggs to my liking. That and good Irish tea. I wondered if I would keep up my habit of tea at all hours once I got home. I sat alone with my thoughts, the last person in the brasserie, and dawdled over my food, enjoying a second pot of tea and eating every crumb of the sweet breads that were in the metal basket.

The mystery of the children was solved; Josie's death was no mystery and would never be remedied, and I still wasn't sure about Eoin. I had some circumstantial evidence to suggest reasonable doubt, including at least a plausible explanation for the Black Leaf 40 in Fiona's rooms. Her minion's — Dee Matthews' — visit to Rathlin Island made it at least possible for someone else to have brought the stuff. I had high hopes that, with that in mind, the investigators would find a way to connect her more concretely to the poison and thus let Eoin off the hook. But who knew for sure that would happen? The medical examiner in me wanted something more.

By now it was after eleven. I poured the last of my tea into my cup and headed back upstairs. I suspected that the staff was used to finding odd bits of hotel china when they cleaned, as I was always bringing a cup of tea or my dessert from the table to my room. The bits magically disappeared every day, and I was reasonably certain they were not being added to my bill as recompense for lost items.

The day was bright and clear. I showered and changed into a new pair of jeans and a sweater before sitting at the desk overlooking Victoria Street, finishing my now-cold tea and reviewing the information in my file for the umpteenth time. So much of it was agonizingly familiar and tantalizingly unsatisfying. I reviewed the toxicology report again, hoping that perhaps it magically had morphed into demonstrating some other poison, but no; it was still nicotine.

Giving that up for the present, I flipped through the newspaper clippings; another batch had arrived from Ben last night, and the hotel had printed them out for me. They were all society articles about Fiona, except for one: a lurid tabloid article filed in the aftermath of her death, front page news. There was a huge photo of the "death suite." Fiona, of course, was gone, but her rumpled bed was there, pillow on the floor, clothes strewn about — standard stuff in my line of work. There wouldn't be much of real interest in the image; anything critical to the investigation would've been censored (at least at home it would've been) by the officer in charge of the scene. And this looked like a stringer's photo taken long after the fact, probably as the result of a bribe to be admitted to the rooms before they were cleaned for the next visitor.

I had no sooner wondered whether there might be more images than my phone pinged me a notification that I had new email. From Ben. This might be interesting.

Mom. Attached are the rest of the photos that tabloid

photographer took of Fiona's suite. Thought you might want them, so I contacted the guy who made them. It didn't cost too much. And I haven't found a single thing more on Deirdre Connor. Not a thing. Let me know if you need anything else.

Bless Ben's heart, he read my mind. Or anticipated it. I flipped open my laptop to take a closer look at the images he had sent along. More of the same. Close-ups of the sheets, the pillows, the bathroom counter (messy even by my lax standards), and the bedside table, on which lay a book, a small, overturned dropper bottle, and an odd, rectangular gizmo encrusted with what had to be rhinestones, with what looked like a pipe stem protruding from it.

Nothing there. Demoralized, I needed a walk to clear my head. St. Malachy's Parish was around the corner, just a few minutes' walk away. I checked the website; Mass was at one. As good a place and time as any to light a candle for Monsignor Jamais, and I had time to make it.

The interior of the church was cold, something I found common to most Irish churches. But it was beautiful, lots of white marble that made the space light and welcoming. It had clearly been renovated, but whoever did it had managed to retain all the beauty of the old church while renovating it for modern practices. The old altar still stood against the wall behind the new one, and the old, ornate reredos was still in place. Above it all were huge paintings, the central one of Christ falling under the weight of the Cross. That made particular sense to me just now. I stood a long time looking at it in silence and in wordless thought.

The renovation had even preserved a portion of the old

altar rail on both sides. I stepped as quietly as I could across the mosaic floor to light a candle in one of the blue votive holders by the Mary chapel and recollect myself before Mass began.

It hit me just as the priest elevated the Sacrament before the Our Father.

I tend to get lost in Mass, and my mind wanders, often far afield. It's not unusual for me to get some long-elusive insight in the course of my wool gathering, and this was no exception. It bothers me; I'm supposed to be attentive. Father Matt says it's the only time the Holy Spirit can get a word in edgewise, so let it happen. In any case, I wasn't prepared to argue today, because what dawned on me was that I needed to look for another source, just like for the hemlock. We'd thought it was food. It was drink. Everyone jumped to the conclusion that the nicotine in Fiona's drink was from the Black Leaf 40 because it was there. Maybe there was another source. If I could prove that, then it might clear Eoin altogether. I couldn't wait to get back to the hotel and check the tox report.

Back at the hotel I thumbed through the file again until I came to it. There it was, in the graph of the gas chromatograph-mass spectrometry of the residue in the glass, not in the report of the findings. There, apart from the peak that was nicotine was another cluster, not nicotine, and I knew not what. I looked for a control GC/MS of the Black Leaf 40, and there wasn't one. From what I knew of it, it was pure nicotine sulfate. Whatever killed Fiona wasn't pure nicotine; there were those other peaks. I was not entirely certain it wasn't something from the Campari, but I didn't think so. There was more to the tox report, too, a drugs-of-abuse screen. It showed a low level of barbiturate, nothing exciting and certainly not fatal. The GC/MS was where the money was in this case: a highly accurate way of separating out the very molecules, almost like a fingerprint, specific to each compound and mixture. Someone dropped the ball by not running a control to make sure the preparation they suspected was the one that actually killed the victim, though it proved nicotine was the culprit. My question was: just nicotine, or nicotine and...? I kicked myself for not seeing it sooner.

My mind went back to that bejeweled rectangle and the bottle with the dropper. Old photos showed Fiona smoking. With all the anti-smoking emphasis these days, had she switched to vaping, using those mechanized electronic cigarettes that were nothing more than a glorified device for delivering nicotine to the habituated? I couldn't be sure.

I considered calling Charles, but he'd never tell me even if he knew. But the voluble Paul might. I called the front desk and asked him to come up. I cast about for some plausible reason and settled on another bottle of Mal Plonk.

It worked. He arrived with the requisite bottle of wine and put it alongside the one I had not opened, yet without so much as a raised eyebrow.

I pulled out all my Southern Belle stops, charm and helplessness oozing from every pore. "While you're here, Paul, can I ask you something? I found this." I pulled up the photo of Fiona's bedroom and put my cursor on the mysterious object. "I wonder, do you know what that is?"

Paul didn't even inquire why I wanted to know.

"That's the Countess' e-ciggie. Quite the elegant one, isn't it? And she had quite the habit. I delivered a half a dozen refills for it the day she arrived. Along with her prescriptions."

"Prescriptions?"

"Two of them, both from the States. A Dr. Brownmiller. One of them a sleeping pill, one she used a lot. We'd picked it up for her before. And something else. The apothecary told me it was a pain pill."

God bless him, he'd never make concierge; the man was a sieve. But I swore to myself that if he ever needed a job, I'd move him to Telluride myself. Vaping fluid was a combination of nicotine and various fragrances and flavors to make it more palatable to the smoker, something that would give precisely the same sort of profile I saw once I finally registered all the details of the tox report instead of just the bottom line. And it was just as lethal as Black Leaf 40. The literature documented deaths of children and adults alike from ingestion. I'd be willing to bet that Eoin's fingerprints weren't on the dropper bottle, and I'd stake my life on its being the source of the nicotine. For the moment I forgot the Black Leaf 40; it wasn't important anymore. And it explained that low level of barbiturate in her blood; I'd be willing to bet Fiona was addicted, unable to sleep without her drowsy pill. Schnockered with drink and barbs, Fiona might not notice that her drink was laced with something. Only the something was not Black Leaf 40.

Reasonable doubt in spades. First, I would make another call to Suskind and then a call to arrange a return charter. I wanted to go home.

***

It was time to go clean Señora Fiona's room. Isa Robles, one of the three women who shared the big house with Dr. Wallace, gathered her supplies. It was nice to be distracted from the worries about the lady doctor, Señora Doctora to them, Lady Doc to the Anglos in town, who seemed to like her one moment and did not quite know what to do with her the next.

Señor Patterson called her to do the cleaning of Señora Fiona's residence. The room was not part of a crime scene, he said, but the police in Colorado were asked to take a walk through it for the police in Ireland and found nothing there. Everything had been packed up, and the place was empty of personal belongings. Even so, the regular cleaning staff refused to go in, because the woman had died so publicly, and her rental of the room did not include cleaning services in the first place. The condo management was making a fuss. No matter that she died somewhere else, they would not go in, and the place needed to be cleaned. It was easier just to take care of it himself. Would Isa help? He would be glad to pay her; he was sure he could get reimbursed. Father Matt said she did good work.

Por supuesto, of course, of course. Right away. But Dios mio! First Señor Eoin left and Señora Doctora was in a terrible mood, then word came that he was in jail, then Señora Doctora left, then the small priest came to live with them, and then he died. Somehow cleaning the house of an absent woman seemed unimportant, and she let it go for a day. But now she would scour from top to bottom. It was a good way to think, and thinking was all she could do. Isa Robles pulled a coat on over her tidy black uniform, the one she bought herself when she got regular jobs in the good part of town. Her black hair was pulled back in a ponytail; her coat was new and warm, and her sneakers were the best, bright red, a gift from Señor Ben, the redheaded son of Señora Doctora, the one who worked magic with computers.

No one told her very much about all that was happening with Señora Doctora because of Señor Eoin, except for Padre Matt. She knew that Señor Eoin was in jail for murder, for killing the woman who claimed to be his wife even though she had left him long ago. Isa held no illusions about the ability of a passionate man to do violence, but for Señora Doctora's sake, she hoped that was not the case this time. She thought it might not be. But then, Señor Eoin had broken the door at the Center; that she overheard from the man at the morgue when she delivered some papers to Señora Doctora before she left. He could be a violent man, as well as a passionate one. She worried about that.

The day was bright and sunny. She opened the curtains over the window that overlooked the ski slopes to let in the light — the better to see, the better to think. There were a few dishes in the sink, crusted and hard with some sort of red sauce and cheese, a glass with pale, brown water in the bottom, and a coffee cup with a skim of mold on top of the black coffee remains. Isa wrinkled her nose as she disposed of it in the sink. They should have called sooner. Then she drew some water in the sink for the dishes to soak and went to the bedroom to strip the bed.

She pulled back the bedclothes, made short work of the sheets, and then grabbed the few clothes that were in the hamper and the towels from the bathroom, and set them washing. The architect designed the bedroom with a washer and dryer in the huge closet. She liked that. If she ever had a house of her own, she'd do that, too. She didn't think she would need such a big closet, though, and this one was empty, with only a few hangers and the plastic from some dry cleaning scattered on the floor. The closet was almost as big as her bedroom in the old gray house in Montrose.

Señora Fiona was not a tidy woman. Her bathroom was filled with scattered tissues and towels smeared with makeup. The sink was scummed with soap and a few red hairs clung to the sides. The counter had spills of toothpaste and something sweet-smelling on it. And there were burned matches in the wastebasket, as well as a small bottle with a dropper top and a bit of yellowish liquid still in it. She smiled at the paper towels on the counter, untouched, not a one in the wastebasket. Señor Eoin's rooms were much different: barely touched, always clean, even down to the sink, with a pile of paper towels in the trash to attest to his fastidiousness. Men — women for that matter — who wiped out their sinks after they used them were rare indeed, and this one was not that kind. Nor did she expect her to be. She hummed as she cleaned.

On the wall under the window in the bedroom was a desk with papers scattered over the wooden top. She collected them as she had been instructed and put them neatly into the cardboard box that the sheriff had provided. Someone else could decide what to do with them. She sealed the box and put her initials over the tape, just as he told her to.

Isa dusted the top of the desk and reached to the side to empty the shredder, then frowned and inspected the teeth that showed through the black opening. It was a fancy one, like the one Señora Doctora had, with a deep, narrow slot for things to be put in. She saw a long, rectangular notecard stuck in the mechanism. She started to push the button to continue the shredding but hesitated. This was not the sort of thing she usually found in these machines. It was mostly bills and important papers. This was different. From the part of the envelope that still stuck out of the shredder, she could see that it was a letter that had not been sent. She started to pull out the paper as gently as she could but stopped, remembering the bullet in the wall she had found when cleaning the house of another dead person.

The paper was thick, scented with perfume and so studded with seeds and flowers that it had gotten stuck in the blades. She had seen similar paper in some of the fancy stores in town, shocked at the expense of it. The paper was covered in fancy writing with purple ink. It was hard to read because of the way the letters were made and because the very bottom part hung in strips beneath the mouth of the shredder, but she was able to figure it out with enough concentration and a few prayers. It was a letter to Señor Eoin, that was obvious. But the return, in the top corner, the one she could see best, had a name, the name of the woman who claimed to be his wife — this one she was cleaning up after.

It was all she needed. She stopped cleaning, stepped back out of the room, and called Padre Matt, explaining what she had found. Then she sat on the sofa, carefully in the middle, her hands in her lap, until she heard a knock on the door.

She opened it to admit both the priest and the sheriff.

The sheriff greeted her by name, and the priest gave her a quick hug.

"This way," she said. She showed them the shredder. Padre Matt watched silently as the sheriff put on gloves and backed the envelope out of the metal teeth, and then he photographed it front and back. Isa peered over his shoulder. It had not been opened. She was right.

When that was done, the sheriff took his knife out of his pocket and carefully slit the top of the envelope to read the contents. He gave out a low whistle and smoothed the paper carefully. The purple ink and the flowery letters made it hard reading, Isa suspected, but somehow he managed. When he read it aloud, it took her breath away.

"All I wanted from you was for you to love me again, and you don't. I can't live knowing how I'm going to die from this brain cancer I have. I don't want to die, and I can't live. With you, I might have been able to do it, but without you, I won't. If you'd just loved me, you could have had your Jane in a few months. But you didn't, and now you'll never have her, either. She'll never marry you now. She doubts you too much, and she'll always be just a little afraid of you and that temper of yours. I've seen to that. You never could resist rising to the bait. Goodbye, Eoin. I am going back to Ireland, and I'm going to make an end of it — to me and to us — once and for all."

The sheriff slid the note back into its envelope, shreds and all, tucked it in a plastic bag, which he then put in his pocket, and looked up at her. More to herself than anyone else, Isa said, "It is important, like the bullet was," she said, remembering finding something important to Señora Doctora once before. "Only," she paused, "I was very careful this time. I think it means Señor Eoin did not kill that woman."

The sheriff smiled at her. "There's more to it than this, but yes, I think that's exactly what it means, Isa."

"Good," she sighed, smiling. Then, taking a long look around her, she asked, "Then may I finish cleaning? Señor Eoin should be back soon, yes?"

CHAPTER TWENTY-FIVE
January 29

Back home in Telluride, coffee seemed the right choice for morning. I supposed I left my taste for tea behind me in Ireland. I had decompressed with a few days visiting my pregnant daughter, Zoe, at her Park Slope walk-up. We took long walks in the neighborhood, dreaming of the not-too-distant day when she'd be another Brooklyn mommy pushing a stroller along the sidewalks. I helped with preparing the nursery; we explored local restaurants and spent hours in the botanical gardens. And I regained my taste for coffee at her breakfast table, where the events of recent days and Eoin were never mentioned. Zoe, my oldest, knows me well. She was content to let me stew in my own thoughts for a while. But fish and visitors (even moms) start to smell after three days or so, and I left New York for Telluride, mended at least a bit in spirit, with a promise to return as her delivery date approached.

The front door squeaked a bit as I tiptoed onto the porch; so much for trying to sneak out into the early morning light. I hoped the sound was not loud enough to wake anyone, but figured the doyenne of the house had not only heard me, but she very likely was on her way to find out where I was going. Pilar would fuss at me, but I needed more peace and quiet than the breakfast table in the big, green Victorian would provide.

The Bean was just opening when I arrived. I ordered a cup of American and one of their muffins and took my customary spot on the green bus bench in the window, the better to watch Telluride go by.

Sadie Jackson, on her way down the street, passed by, looked up, caught my eye, and came in. Without preamble or ordering coffee, she sat opposite me. I nodded a greeting.

"I have something to tell you."

"I know about the Gleason kids. Good job, though Lucy had no right to hire you to do that."

"No, it's about the other case. Josie Beck. She was murdered."

"Old news. I know that. I can't prove it."

"I can. I don't think it matters, because there's nothing except my say-so, but I can prove it to you."

She had my attention. "Say more."

"I talked with the nurse, Mavis. We're friends; we both volunteer at Proserpine. She all but admitted to me that she gave her a dose of potassium chloride. She knows the mom. She's a mess because of the kid. She couldn't handle it anymore, just waiting for her to die. And the dad wouldn't listen to her, shut her out. All he could see was Josie, and all he wanted to do was everything he could do to save her when we all know he couldn't."

I tried to remain impassive. I managed, but it was hard.

"It's not right, you know, to let that kid suffer so much. If the Dad hadn't insisted on trying every last treatment option, none of which was going to help her, she would have died long ago. All that treatment did was prolong her suffering. That kid has been dying from the day she was diagnosed, before that even. All that happened was that medicine made the dying longer and worse."

I hated to admit it, but she had a point. Maybe there is a point at which it's best to step aside. Maybe my noble lawsuit on behalf of Josie wasn't the best idea after all. Maybe it was ill-advised lawyerly jousting at windmills, and the wrong ones at that.

As if reading my mind, she continued, "Her dad was treating himself, not Josie. He couldn't let go, and he tortured that kid and his wife because of it."

"And..."

"But. It's a but. The but is that Mavis had no business taking that decision into her own hands. That's not what Proserpine is about. It's about helping people manage their own care, not taking it out of their hands. And the law doesn't provide for ending the suffering of children. At least not yet. Maybe it should." She looked me square in the eyes. "But it seems to me that we have to play by the rules, whatever they are. The rules say Mavis couldn't do that."

She surprised me.

"Anyway, I wanted you to know."

I considered her astonishing revelation for a moment. "What made you try to find out?"

Sadie looked genuinely confused and took some time to gather her thoughts. I had my coffee and a muffin and let her think. "I think it was that old priest. Nothing he said. More like who he was. I can't really put my finger on it." Her face grew thoughtful. "He's the one who gave me the key to figuring out the poisoning deaths."

To me, too, I thought. Sadie's breakthrough had fostered my own. Funny how that works.

Sadie continued, "Once I had that out of the way, I couldn't stop thinking about Josie. Something about it bothered me. Mostly, I guess, that you were so sure it was a murder, and I had to agree when I looked at it that I thought so, too. Letting someone die is one thing. Murder is another. So I thought I'd at least try to find out, for my own sake, if not for you. It seemed right."

"Would you be willing to testify to what she said to you in court, if it came to that?" I wasn't sure what we could do with it, but I'd be willing to try. Sadie would be an unlikely ally if I did.

Sadie looked puzzled. "Sure, but why would anyone take my word for it?"

I refrained from an explanation of the rules of evidence and exceptions to hearsay and statements against interest. I just told her, "You'd be surprised. They might. But I doubt it will come to that. But I would like to take this to the state's attorney and to the Board of Nursing. Regardless of our differences, can we agree Mavis isn't fit to care for patients?"

Sadie nodded. "Sure. I guess I can help." She took a deep breath and drew herself up and looked me in the eye. "I'd like my job back."

I smiled. The ulterior motive revealed. And here I was thinking that Sadie had had some sort of epiphany. I told her no, but it took me a bit of reflection to make the decision.

On the way back to the house after my meeting with

Sadie, I had a lot to think about. On the one hand, I didn't want to risk having someone with Sadie's views on death in my office; that's my prerogative. On the other hand, she was good at what she did, the risk for the office was small given the current social climate in Colorado, and she'd demonstrated her desire to adhere strictly to the letter of the law in regard to assisted suicide, which was something. My better self rose to challenge me: if those of us with different ideas on the topic never talk to each other, how would we ever come to deal with the problems such topics raise? I suppose it would ultimately boil down to how much I wanted to risk myself in the process, and right now, for my lesser self, that wasn't much. I stood by my refusal, but felt the better for hashing it out in my head.

I had no sooner walked into the kitchen than Pilar told me that I was needed at Tom Patterson's office immediately. Given my state of mind regarding Sadie and the fact that I have a streak of paranoia a mile wide and just as deep, all I could imagine was some disaster involving the Center, so I headed off without so much as a nibble at the breakfast Pilar was loading onto the kitchen counter for the rest of the tribe.

I found the sheriff, boots up on the desk and on the phone. I expected a tongue lashing for barging in but instead, he just hung up his phone, dropped his dusty size-elevens to the floor, and rocked back in his chair, hands behind his head in an attitude of complete comfort, an enigmatic look on his face. It unsettled me. Father Matt was in the chair opposite the desk. He looked like the Cheshire cat. Something was up.

"Well, well, the wanderer has returned. How was

Ireland? I see by the papers that your Irishman was released." Tom half-stood and shook my hand.

"He was? I expected he would be, but I haven't seen the papers. I figured after I convinced the powers that be that Fiona didn't die from Black Leaf 40, it was only a matter of time."

"What?" Tom seemed surprised. "I thought it was because we convinced them she committed suicide with it."

Now it was my turn. "Suicide?" It made sense. Completely. It even explained that prescription from Jennie Brownmiller and the barbiturates that were found. Not enough to kill her, but there. Had Fiona hoped to be asleep when the nicotine did its job?

How could I have been so blind? Working alone, I supposed, with no one to bounce things off of. Life, even forensic life, is better in community than it is lived in isolation.

"Yup." Tom shoved a piece of paper across the desk to me. I read it, and I felt my eyes grow wide. There it was: the final piece. The doubt I created was reasonable, after all. I wanted to cry. I was relieved. I was ashamed. I'd sort out the other emotions later.

"What's this about not dying from the insecticide?" Father Matt asked. "We had it figured — and so did Peter Suskind — that Fiona was looking around for a way to kill herself that would implicate Eoin. Black Leaf 40 certainly did that."

"That it does, but there's a problem with the tox. When I finally got to looking at the printout of the toxicology on the glass, I realized the profile didn't fit. Black Leaf 40 is nearly pure nicotine, but there was another cluster of peaks, something other than nicotine, and it was pretty large. Long story short, it was the volatiles that are in those fancy e-cigarette concoctions. More palatable, I suppose, than decades-old Black Leaf 40, which gets thick and dark and smells awful. So the Black Leaf 40 was a red herring, designed to point towards Eoin as the murderer."

I left it at that. Reasonable doubt. I paused a moment, wondering how much more to say. "There were a lot of other suspects once that was discovered. Ultimately, the investigators found smears of Black Leaf 40 on the inside of Dee Matthews' purse." I conveniently ignored the smear on Eoin's jacket. It didn't matter now. That wasn't the poison that killed Fiona. But in the back of my mind rested the question: Did Eoin provide the Black Leaf 40 to Dee Matthews, or did she get it herself? Was it there to frame Eoin, or were the two of them in cahoots to kill Fiona? And Dee just decided to use vaping fluid but planted the insecticide to divert the investigation and frame Eoin — which still made him an accomplice in the eyes of God and man? Did Dee just decide to use something more convenient and palatable and forget about the insecticide? Was it possible — still — that Eoin was, if not a successful murderer, a putative one?

"You mean Deirdre Connor," Tom Patterson said.

"What?" Now I sat down in the vacant chair. There was too much to process standing up. I hadn't seen that coming, and even Ben had not figured out that connection. "Eoin's long-lost and not terribly lamented sister, the one who went off with Fiona and never benefitted from Eoin's largesse," I said.

Some of the doubts disappeared. "No wonder she knew where to find the stuff, and small wonder that she would cooperate with Fiona. I wonder if Fiona promised to write her into the will?"

"No, at least that is what Deirdre says; the better to be seen as the faithful minion who helped her dying boss commit suicide and punish her ex-husband. Suskind tells us that the porter told Deirdre that Fiona changed her mind about revising her will the same night Fiona died, and that might make a pretty good motive for murder." Tom Patterson's expression made it clear he was chewing on my news as much as I was struggling to wrap my mind around his.

"That and the fact that Deirdre spent two years in jail because of Fiona." I quickly explained the history of the jewels, which sounded more and more to me like Deirdre was the patsy in a plan to defraud the insurance company. And a more and more likely suspect in the death of Fiona.

"Truth be told, I am not sure we'll ever be completely certain who put that nicotine in Fiona's drink. Could be she did, and washed down her sleeping pills with it. Could be Deirdre gave her the sleeping pills, and then, when she was drowsy, finished the job with the nicotine." Tom Patterson suddenly grinned. "I am so glad whoever did it did it in Ireland and not here. That's a mess to unravel. Nothing worse than having a murder and knowing you can't prove it."

That I knew, and for a moment, my mind went back to Sadie and her request for employment; perhaps I needed to think about that a little more. Then I took back up the thread of thought at hand. I was still castigating myself for such utter blindness. Perhaps I had been blind to the possibility of suicide, because I really did think Eoin might be responsible. The thought did not please me. The fact that the information I had at hand did not dispel those doubts completely pleased me even less.

"Did you know she was dying?" This time Father Matt tossed the curve. "Makes suicide a little more probable."

Another bombshell. "No. How?"

"Brain tumor. You didn't see the autopsy?"

"No. I just saw the tox. I didn't have access to the investigative file." Out of stubbornness, I realized. I'd never contacted Eoin's lawyer until I had some proof he didn't do it. Afraid of what I might find? Again, the thought did not please me. My postmortem on my own actions was not turning out to my liking. "Tunnel vision, I suppose." Maybe it was time I reread my own procedure manual. *Unless you have all the facts, you can't have the whole story*, I reminded myself. And with the whole story, it was clear: Eoin Connor was not just not guilty. He was innocent. I breathed a sigh of relief just an instant before shame washed over me. I knew the man. And I still suspected him. I would never have suspected John. My pleasure at solving the puzzle was short-lived, but at that moment it all dropped into place for me: Fiona, Eoin, everything.

"She came back to Eoin because she didn't want to be alone," I said. The same pride that made her color her hair and tuck her face made her want to be desired, not pitied — to have Eoin come back to her because of her, not because of a mass in her brain. And that made me sorry for her all the more, all of a sudden, and greatly. It also made sense of her connection to Joseph Baladin, too. What might have happened if, instead of encouraging her death, Baladin had counseled her to be honest with Eoin about her fears and about her needs?

Suppose he had told her that we are all a package of hopes, fears, body, soul — desirable parts and ones not so desirable, and ultimately, we choose to be with the whole person, all parts included, or we don't. That dividing ourselves up and parsing out our motivations doesn't always help. Relationship commences at a level far deeper than the intellect, and too often, when we start thinking about it to try to control it and figure it out, we mess it up. Suppose he had said that it's better to risk the chance of refusal in honesty than it is to gain the agreement by deceit. But that, I suspected, wasn't part of Proserpine's routine. It might have ended in life rather than death, and death is what Proserpine sells.

I reread the note. "I guess she decided not to send it when she decided to frame Eoin for her own death to punish him, as well as me."

"Looks like it. That's my best guess, anyway. It certainly wasn't your Irishman, anyway." Tom's voice was quiet. He knew me well enough to know that there was a lot going on inside my head, though I suspected he wasn't sure what it was.

"I suppose. How did you find it?"

"Isa. She was cleaning Fiona's room when she found it in the shredder."

I laughed out loud. *Good for Isa!*

"That's twice now," Tom continued. "I'm thinking maybe we ought to send her in to the crime scene when we are finished. She's pretty good at unearthing things. My guys missed it when they made a pass through the room for the guys in Ireland."

I raised an eyebrow.

Father Matt broke in. "Eoin's lawyer was happy for it, as it turns out."

I laughed again, the best laugh I had laughed in two long weeks, and it felt good. Refreshing. Cleansing. As though the world were set right again. Here we were, on opposite sides of the world, both of us trying our best to get Eoin out of jail. Tom Patterson ended up working with the lawyers he so disliked — no doubt a result of Father Matt's benign influence. I, on the other hand, was busy trying to throw a spanner in the works of the conventional mills of justice that I customarily worked to serve. Go figure.

"Spiteful bitch." Tom's voice interrupted my train of thought. "She was too afraid of dying to live. That's a shame. Worse yet that she would ruin a man's life because he'd found another woman to love. I'll never understand jealous women."

"Or men." I'd seen my share of if-I-can't-have-her-no-one-can murders in my career. I reflected for a moment. I had been too hurt by my own pain to see any in Fiona, but there it was. I wished I had realized it earlier. Once her life wasn't the perfect façade she had so carefully engineered over all these years, she didn't want it anymore. Her life just wasn't worth living. Not to her. I found it unbearably sad. And I wondered what facades I was trying to keep in place myself.

"Poor woman," I said, more to myself than to Tom. "If

she had just told Eoin outright that she was dying, he'd have stayed by her side to the end. She would have passed on holding the hand of a man who cared for her and cared about her. Instead, she died alone and in terrible pain, all of it of her own making. Nicotine poisoning is just not a nice way to go."

Father Matt looked at me and crossed himself, no doubt offering a prayer for Fiona's poor soul. "True enough."

A pause, a heartbeat too long to be spontaneous, and it came with the silent sound of shifting mental gears on the good Father's part. It made me wonder what was coming next. He was measuring his words.

"Eoin's on his way here now. He shouldn't be long. We thought we'd take him out for a celebratory lunch. Join us?"

For a moment, I anticipated Eoin's face, until I realized I wasn't a part of his life anymore by my own stupid choice. I hadn't loved him enough to make the choice to stand with him, because I was afraid of what I might find out about him. I was afraid that the Eoin wasn't the Eoin I wanted, and I was not able to risk the difference. Not unlike Fiona, in my own way. That realization hurt with a pain that was almost physical. "No, Father. I'd best go. I doubt he wants to see me. He certainly doesn't need me."

Tom stared at me. "What? You don't think that brawling Irishman needs you? Who's going to keep him out of jail?" He smiled at his own poor joke.

I shook my head, hoping that my expression didn't betray the sadness I felt, smiling a smile I did not mean. "He'll not have me now. I know that much about him. I flinched, Tom, when he needed me most. It's over and done with, and it's my fault that it is. I abandoned him. I ran away." It took a moment to compose myself enough to continue. "It's probably time I moved on, anyway. He helped me get over John. Maybe that's all he was supposed to do." I'd keep telling myself until the ache in my heart stopped. This time I was the one who had deprived a good man of a life with wife and family. And it was worse this time, because I knew full well what that was like. This, I reflected, would be a great time for the earth to open up and swallow me. It didn't. It never does when I want it to.

Patterson snorted. "For a smart woman you sure are dumber than a fencepost sometimes. A broken fencepost at that. If this," he waved the file under my nose, "is your flinching, you can flinch in my defense any time. Damn fool." I wasn't sure whether he was talking to me or not. He and Eoin had a strong man's respect for each other. They'd end up real friends if they stayed around each other long enough.

I stood up, looking at Tom until I could look no more, and avoiding Father Matt, then examining the toes of my boots. I was caught between and betwixt, not knowing what to say, wanting to leave and not knowing how to go. Finally, I just shrugged. "I'll see you later, Father; Tom. Thanks for everything. I'm tired, and I still haven't unpacked."

"Don't you want to stay?" It was more a statement than a question, and it was from Father Matt.

I shook my head. "No." I made sure the words carried more conviction than I felt. "Thanks, though. Tell Eoin..." Tell him what? The interchange was beginning to play out in my head like a third rate soap opera. I backtracked to the last point of composure and dignity. "No, thanks." It was an awkward end to the conversation but the best I could manage. I turned, listening to the sounds of my distinctive, heel-striking walk on the linoleum floor as I walked away. I'd never been good at taking my leave.

I paused outside the door long enough to hear two deep male voices in conversation behind the door. I turned away with a half-smile and was almost to the stairs when I heard Eoin's voice, bellowing down the hall. "Woman! Where the hell do you think you're going?"

I hesitated, and then turned around. Eoin, in a faded denim shirt and jeans, his shearling jacket open, stood at the door of Tom Patterson's office, Tom and Father Matt right behind. He looked thinner. He hadn't shaved since I saw him last, and a full, gray beard framed his face. His wiry hair was in need of cutting. Altogether he looked rather wild.

Wild, but not threatening. Temper or not, I knew Father Matt was right. I had nothing to fear from Eoin. "Woman," he intoned again, slowly, raising his voice on the last syllable and stating the next sentence firmly and clearly. "Where do you think you are going?"

I shrugged, but I couldn't move. I raised my hand in a helpless little gesture and shook my head. My eyes stung, but I was determined not to cry. I just stood at the end of the hall, biting the inside of my lip and looking at Eoin Connor.

He ran a hand through his unkempt hair and debated with himself about I knew not what. He looked past me and then at me. He closed the distance between us, and took my hands in his, regarded them and kissed them, as he had not so long ago. I was growing to like that gesture.

"Jane Wallace, darling girl," he finally said. "I'm a free man, once and for all. Marry me." Then he took me in his arms and kissed me, as he'd later describe it, strong and proper.

I suppose he read the answer in my eyes. I kissed him back.

Acknowledgments

As always, many people helped bring this very different book to life.

Thanks as ever to Doreen Thistle, literary midwife extraordinaire, Ellen and James Hrkach of Full Quiver Publishing, and Marisa Corvisiero for continuing to believe in Jane and me. Thanks to James Hrkach for his artistry in creating two beautiful covers.

Thanks to everyone who enjoyed *Dying for Revenge* and told me so. Having a cheering section is so important to keeping going. I hope that you enjoy this part of Jane's story as much as you enjoyed the first installment.

My bioethics writing group (Ann Marie, Wes, Ashley and Fr. John) have talked me through many a discussion on physician-assisted suicide from all the possible angles. I hope the fruits show up here.

Trying to portray how others see the world is always a challenge for a writer. Thanks to Bertin Glennon for his continuing assistance on the journey.

Rathlin Island is a magical place and the perfect spot for the Connor farm. My thanks to Alan and Hilary Curry for hosting my visit there, for introducing me to some of the local folks, and for answering questions as they came up. Any errors about Rathlin or UK police procedure are mine alone.

Msgr. George Schmidt (may G-d be good to him) lost his struggle with dementia as I was polishing this manuscript. His loving presence accompanied me as I came down to deadline. Msgr. Jamais shares an illness and a charm with Msgr. George, though they are not otherwise much alike. I was privileged to know Msgr. George and I miss him.

Msgr. Tomas Halik's writings have influenced how Jane and I look at the world of faith. Although others have noted the wonderful way in which children move from fantasy to reality the way he presented his thoughts on the subject in *The Night of the Confessor* provided the key to solving one of the mysteries in the book. I've never met him, but I am grateful to his literary presence in my life.

And, of course, thanks always to my husband — who is still not Dead John — and my daughter and son, for living with a crazy woman and writer. But perhaps I repeat myself. I love you; thank you all for putting up with me.

Last and certainly not least, Our Lady under the title Undoer of Knots and Our Lady of Guadalupe, St. Luke, and St. Martha walked every step of the way with me.

About the Author

Dr. Barbara Golder is a late literary bloomer. Although she's always loved books (and rivals Jane in the 3-deep-on-the-shelf sweepstakes), her paying career gravitated to medicine and law. She has served as a hospital pathologist, forensic pathologist, and laboratory director. Her work in forensic pathology prompted her to get a law degree, which she put to good use as a malpractice attorney and in a boutique practice of medical law, which allowed her to be a stay-at-home mom when her children were young. She has also tried her hand at medical politics, serving as an officer in her state medical association, lobbying at a state and national level on medical issues, writing and lecturing for hire, including a memorable gig teaching nutritionists about the joys of chocolate for eight straight hours, teaching middle and high school science, and, most recently, working for a large disability insurance company from which she is now retired

Her writing career began when she authored a handbook of forensic medicine for the local medical examiner office in 1984. Over the years she wrote extensively on law and medicine and lectured on medicolegal topics. On a lark, she entered a contest sponsored by the Telluride Times Journal and ended up with a regular humor column that memorialized the vagaries of second-home living on the Western Slope. She now is a full-time writer and speaker, concentrating on how storytelling helps illuminate the issues of the day. She has been active studying and writing on the topic of end of life care from both medical and legal perspectives since the mid 1970s.

She currently lives on Lookout Mountain, Tennessee with two dogs, two cats and her husband of 42 years and a regular stream of visitors.

Full Quiver Publishing

PO Box 244

Pakenham, ON K0A2X0

www.fullquiverpublishing.com

Bookstores: For bulk orders and reduced rates, please contact us at: fullquiverpublishing@gmail.com

To contact the author: ladydocmurders@gmail.com

Author website: http://ladydocmurders.weebly.com/

69075057R00192

FEB 1 2 2022

Made in the USA
Lexington, KY
24 October 2017